THE DARK WATER

PAUL O'CONNOR

Published in Australia by Silverbird Publishing Pty Ltd.

First published in Australia 2024
This edition published 2025
Copyright © Paul O'Connor 2024
Cover design, typesetting: WorkingType (www.workingtype.com.au)

ISBN: 978-1-922958-80-8

ABOUT THE AUTHOR

Paul O'Connor was born in Frankston, Victoria. He has a Diploma in Computer Science and an Advanced Diploma in Computer Systems Engineering. He is well-travelled, both in Australia and overseas. He wrote several class-leading stories in high school. He lives on the Mornington Peninsula. *The Dark Water* is his first book.

*To Fiona, who provided the much-needed
encouragement to finish the book and
launch myself into the literary world.*

CONTENTS

CHAPTER 1

Jeremy Williams made his way as quickly as he could through the pre-lunch crowd, milling into the canteen and diverted to the senior common room, where he knew there would be relative peace and quiet. Most of the senior students were out watching the inter-school basketball game. He was also keen to avoid the canteen matron, known to the students as Mrs Voorhees, a woman with a striking resemblance to the *Friday the 13th* movie character, over a minor debt. He planned to meet three friends there, have a much-needed energy drink, and show them some drawings he had worked on before all four boys traipsed off to their indoor cricket game.

He arrived in the spacious room with its easy chairs and sofas a few minutes early and headed for the drink machine. A minute later, with a Monster energy drink in hand, Jeremy settled down in a corner booth with a table, waiting for the other boys to arrive. He reached into his backpack and produced a manila folder. Some girls wandered in and sauntered over to the kitchenette. Jeremy heard coins rattling in the drink dispenser. He placed the folder on the table, opened it, and flipped through the A4 sheets inside, reassuring himself they were all there.

Jeremy was a self-confessed nerd. At six-foot-two and of slim build, he looked the part. However, he backed up his Professor Nimbus aura with a sharp-thinking brain, superior memory, and a great capacity for work, which some students described as machine-like. He wasn't the most handsome guy at the school, but if this bothered him, he hid it well.

The three boys he arranged to meet up with he had known since kindergarten. As Jeremy settled into the sofa and took a gulp of his drink, he cast his mind back to some of the activities the four boys had gotten up to over the years. They had diverse interests, and some of their peers said the four had nothing in common. But it was what they *did* have in common that bonded them together. All four were above average intellect, and two could have done well in a modelling competition. It was never a good idea for any of the four to leave the group for any reason. Good-natured backstabbing would start almost immediately.

Another student wandered in and meandered to the opposite corner without noticing Jeremy. Jeremy spread the folder contents on the tabletop and appeared to study them, though he knew them by heart. In recent weeks, each boy had suggested ways to spend the holidays and see out 2018. He was pleased they had finalised their decision the day before. Now, it was time for the actual planning.

They discussed their plan at school and in their homes, with the pros and cons thrashed out over Super Mario Brothers games, indoor cricket, and here in that most sacred of places, the senior common room. After much deliberation, they decided upon a raft trip to an unnamed lake. The raft idea had been Jeremy's baby, and he wasn't sure how the other boys would take it.

It wasn't exactly a new idea. When the boys were eight, they had gone camping at Lake Nagambie in the state's north. At that time, there were adults present as well. Before they went, the boys had built a simple raft from two wooden pallets with a tarp, forming a simple shelter. Paddle power had been the order of the day, and the four youngsters had trekked all over the lake.

Jeremy was comfortable that they were accustomed to his ideas, but he knew he would be up against trips to the Gold Coast and Bali this time. Over a few beers, Harry Turner pointed out that a trip to the sunshine could always occur at the end of their *final* year.

Jeremy heard a commotion in the hallway and turned to see two of the three boys enter the room and stop to talk to the girls before making a beeline for his table. Daniel Graham and Harry Turner were the newcomers. Daniel was the same height as Jeremy, just over six feet tall, with an athletic build. On the other hand, Harry topped out at five foot three but made up for it with model good looks, no doubt due to his Asian parentage.

The two boys settled at the table and produced smartphones from their backpacks. While his friends were seemingly engrossed in their devices, Jeremy said, significantly, 'Well, I've got it all here', patting the papers on the table. 'This is a hard copy of the drawings I sent you earlier.'

Daniel and Harry picked up random pieces of paper and studied them with a mix of bemusement and wonder. They looked at the construction plans and supply lists for what appeared to be a timber raft complete with a deckhouse. Daniel spoke first: 'We weren't expecting the *Ronald Reagan*, but this is ridiculous.' Harry said, 'Yeah, I envisioned a simple timber deck with drums underneath, like our original raft, maybe a bit more sophisticated.'

'There's more to it than that, but this isn't much more. It's just that I've gone slightly overboard with certain features,' Jeremy defended himself. 'The whole thing has to be sturdy and fulfil other criteria.'

'Other criteria,' Harry exclaimed. 'Like what?'

'Transportability and reusability. We can take the raft to other lakes and rivers if this trip goes well. Plus, it must be strong enough to support camping equipment like fridges and gas cylinders.'

Harry and Daniel picked up other sheets of paper and studied them. Daniel paid more attention to dimensions and figures due to *his* engineering pedigree. His father was an engineer at a newly built local steel works. In his mind's eye, he saw the approximate length and width of the raft and tried to fit four teenage boys into that space.

Jeremy said: 'Don't pay too much attention to minor details. I was getting a bit carried away.'

'No kidding,' muttered Harry.

'The main thing', Jeremy continued, ignoring Harry's remark, 'is the four of us on a raft with sufficient space without giving each other the shits. We'll have to have shelter on board as we will probably use the raft as a mobile campsite. Then we can stay wherever we want without tents to hassle with.'

Harry was just about to reply when his attention moved to the main door of the common room. The fourth group member, Sam Dillon, strolled into the room and made straight for the kitchenette with a cheery wave to the other boys. He procured an energy drink and walked over to the table. He greeted each of his friends, deposited his can on Jeremy's plans and drawings and flopped down into a chair.

Sam was a few inches taller than Harry but was still short of Daniel and Jeremy. He was blessed with Italian good looks and quick wit, which made him very popular with the girls at school.

'Sam, glad you could make it,' said Jeremy, noticing the green stain at the base of Sam's can and on his drawings. 'We've just started going over the raft plans, and I decided that a temporary or permanent cabin on the raft is the way to go. There are rough sketches of both.'

'If we've got a raft with a half-decent cabin, that's all we need,' Sam said, picking one of Jeremy's drawings and studying it while sipping his drink. 'No tents.'

'Just what I was telling these two. Harry, you were about to disagree.'

Harry cleared his throat and picked up a random piece

of paper, and flipping this over, he began to make a rough sketch on the back. 'I thought we could use the old tarp with a few pegs and guy ropes for shelter.

'That would be okay, but I've decided that the raft can also be used for shelter. You'll appreciate some shelter when we're out on the lake, and the wind gets up. Plus, we will need a sheltered area to cook in.'

'And room to stock beer,' added Sam.

Harry wasn't finished. 'We're going to cook on this tub?'

'Cook, eat and sleep. It should all be possible, not to mention fishing, which brings me to the next point. I will appoint people for various tasks based on your capabilities. It's easier that way and fairer. I want you to collect junk mail and go through it for items such as LED lighting, hardware, etc.'

Sam spoke up: 'Can we get off the raft at any point for some onshore activities?'

Jeremy looked offended. 'Obviously. We'll study my area maps and note suggestions for places to go.

Daniel said: 'I hope they're OS (Ordinance Survey) maps. Dad swears by them. We've been camping heaps and always take OS maps of our area.'

'Is there anything worth looking at in the area?' Sam asked, tipping the last dregs of his drink into his mouth.

'Yeah, an abandoned mining area to the North and there's some kind of ruin about two kilometres from the shore, up in the hills'. But the big one isn't on any maps at all. It's under the lake, the old town of Rupertsvale.'

'How are we going to explore *that*,' asked Harry, sarcasm heavy in his voice. 'With aqualungs? Or are we going to build a bathyscaphe as well?'

'No, with an underwater camera.'

'That you have, presumably?' Daniel half asked.

'Dan, I do, and all will be revealed on the weekend. One final thing for today: we need a place to build the raft.'

'I can't help noticing that you're looking at me, Jeremy,' Daniel exclaimed. 'But I'm sure it'll be okay. I'll get Dad on the blower.'

Daniel picked up his smartphone and dialled away. Jeremy began clearing the papers, examining the green ring on some of the sheets. Harry gathered the empty cans and took them over to the recycle bin. Sam joined him and grabbed a glass of water just before Daniel announced: 'You can turn Dad's workshop into Harland & Wolff. Just be sure to clean up afterwards. Dad can spot fly shit in pepper from fifty paces.'

CHAPTER 2

Sam Dillon looked around the familiar workshop, which was attached to the rear of Daniel's home's double garage. Not for the first time, he thought Daniel's dad had a great setup here, and he felt reassured that he and his friends would be able to construct a sturdy raft and have a great time on whatever lake they chose. Unlike most backyard workshops, this one was the epitome of neatness. There was an accumulation of power tools and every piece of equipment to make the average backyarder green with envy, yet everything had its place. Sam instinctively recognised the power tools and other gadgets the boys would use most, having completed some minor woodworking projects himself.

Sam had cycled to Daniel's house after breakfast that Saturday morning, planning to meet the other boys there. Daniel and Harry were inside the house when he arrived. Jeremy had said he would be a bit late, doing some chores around his house. Harry stepped into the garage with a mug of coffee in each hand and strode into the workshop, offering one of the mugs to Sam while sipping from the other. 'So, this is where the *Empress of Ireland* is being constructed', Sam said, referring to his favourite shipwreck.

'Yep, we're going to be as busy as Beirut bricklayers if this thing is to be built to Jeremy's specs', Harry replied, sipping his coffee. Getting it organised this early should give us the time we need'.

Their discussion was interrupted by the timely arrival of Jeremy on his bike, somewhat out of breath, with a small backpack over his shoulder. 'The plans of the stealth battleship, I see', remarked Sam, eyeing the backpack. 'You got that right', answered Jeremy, parking the bike to the side of the garage. Removing his backpack, Jeremy opened it, slid out his Hewlett-Packard tablet and set the device down on a nearby workbench.

'Hi, Jeremy, can I talk you into a drink?' Daniel said aloud, appearing from inside the house.

'Yeah, a cuppa would hit the spot,' Jeremy replied, 'then we can get down to the nitty-gritty'.

Daniel disappeared into the house while Jeremy flicked through various drawings on his tablet. The three boys studied them, Harry and Sam pointing out various details that Jeremy reassured them were okay. The side door into the house opened, and Daniel reappeared with a steaming mug of coffee. He handed it to Jeremy and announced: 'Well, Dad said we can use anything in this workshop, so it's up to us to organise materials.'

'Speaking of materials, what are we going to use,' asked Harry. 'Remember, according to your plans, we're on a limited budget.'

'The raft itself will be subdivided into two parts', explained

Jeremy. 'One will be the frame, floats and the deck. The other will be the cabin. The budget was only a guide to prevent cost blowouts. I've decided that planning for this holiday will fall into two separate categories: the raft itself and the destination. As you've all seen, there are various options when it comes to construction, both for design and materials. The first on the list is the rather traditional approach, where a simple deck is fitted to some drums. We'll call this design the 'Harry Special'.'

'Thanks, Jeremy, I appreciate that'.

'The next idea is the use of PVC pipes for floats and possibly the deck as well. Then there's the idea of a flat box type of raft. This could also take the form of - don't laugh - one of those slimline PVC water tanks, albeit with a sturdy deck on top.'

Jeremy paused, then said, 'That's all for the hull. The next thing is the deckhouse or cabin. We should have one for general shelter, not to mention cooking and sleeping. A few ideas there.' Jeremy went on to detail different construction methods and materials.

'And now for the destination.' He put away the raft plans and produced a general road map of Victoria. The boys leaned forward. 'I know we came up with several options and even 'agreed' on one, but let's look at our options. Access and nearness to Melbourne were the *main* but not the only criteria. Additional geological features, ruins, fishing, and man-made structures are also to be considered.'

Sam said: 'We haven't had as much access to those

Ordnance Survey (OS) maps in the library at school as we would have liked.'

'Well, your worries are over,' Jeremy said calmly. 'I have the best OS maps of the areas in question right here. Anyway, the *other* purpose of today is to finalise the *destination*. We've mainly talked about the raft itself. So, now, I say speak or forever hold your peace.'

The other boys looked at each other, and three pairs of eyes met Jeremy's. Harry spoke: 'For the maiden voyage, Lake Eildon is the top place. It's not like we can't go to those places some other time.'

'Exactly what I was thinking,' said Jeremy. 'Eildon has everything going for it. Just think rafting, camping, bushwalking, to name a few, all in one area. Plus, *not too far from help if something does go wrong.*'

Sam couldn't help noticing that Jeremy's voice was almost pregnant with foreboding, but he let it pass. He said: 'So Eildon's the place, now what? How long are you thinking of going for?'

'We will *all* have to come to some agreement about the length of our stay, but once we arrive at a figure, then the list of to-dos will be something like this: the raft itself, food, clothing, cooking gear, food/ gear-storage and transport for the raft. I've probably left things out, but it's a start. The fact that we have somewhere to build the raft is a great start, and I know there's an assortment of coolers and mini refrigerators lying about, so that's another list item we don't have to worry about.'

'Dad might be able to assist with the sixth item on the list,' Daniel said, draining his coffee cup. 'His work has a trailer, one of them tandem types that he can use when he needs to. Who's for another cuppa?'

That Jeremy looked relieved at that bit of news was an understatement. Daniel collected coffee mugs and went into the house. Harry stated: 'We can start planning the layout of the raft on the workshop floor with chalk or string lines.'

'And we can place things like coolers, the fridge and camp mattresses within the raft outline to make the best use of space,' suggested Sam.

'Well, the first thing we've got to do is decide what type of raft we're going to build,' Jeremy reminded them. 'Harry, you mentioned a simple design with an attached deck and barrels. Could you draw what you were thinking of?'

'How much detail do you want?'

'Don't try to be Frank Lloyd Wright, just the basic idea.'

Harry sketched on a pad offered by Jeremy. When he finished, he and Jeremy studied the drawing and a list of things the raft would require. The two boys mentally tried to marry the plan and the list to devise the final design. Sam interrupted their thoughts: 'I have an idea for mounting the drums if we're using them.'

'I'm all ears, Sam,' Jeremy replied. 'You can use the pad when we've finished with it.'

Daniel reappeared at that moment, bearing mugs of coffee and some good news. 'Dad says we can use his old generator, and I've thought of a way to mount it on the raft so that it won't stick out like dog nuts at a cat party.'

'I should have brought another pad,' exclaimed Jeremy. He was relieved when Harry tore off the page he had been scribbling on, plus one page for Sam's groundbreaking idea, and handed the pad to Daniel. Daniel deposited the mugs on the workbench and walked, pad in hand, over to a cupboard, opened the door, reached in, and produced a compact generator. 'It's Dad's old eleven hundred-watt four-stroke. We took it camping a few times until he saw one of the other campers with a generator (geni) that looked like the power unit from a B-class locomotive. So, of course, instantly jealous, Dad vows to get one similar. And the rest is history.'

The other boys laughed in remembrance of the five-thousand-watt Ryobi generator tucked away under wraps in the workshop. Sam finished his sketch and showed it to Jeremy while Harry wandered over to look at the small generator with Daniel. As the boys studied the unit, Harry read off the DC output and suddenly looked concerned.

'I think we might have a problem, chaps. The DC power from this thing wouldn't boil the car kettle, let alone run two trolling motors.'

'Well, we must modify the power supply configuration,' Jeremy countered. 'We can use that high current power supply unit at my place. Dad won't mind. There'll be enough AC power from that little geni for that purpose.'

'Okay, so that's propulsion power sorted. Now we have to

decide on motors', said Harry. 'I know Dad will lend us the one he has. But Jeremy wants two.

'What thrust rating is that motor?' Jeremy asked.

'Fifty-something, I think,' Harry replied.

'Pounds,' said Jeremy. 'That will be heaps of thrust. I only suggested two motors because I had only seen about eighteen pounds thrust.'

'Okay,' Harry continued, 'that's that taken care of. 'Okay, Sam, what was your idea for mounting the drums'.

Sam picked up his rough sketch and held it up in his left hand so the other boys could see it. 'My plan is designed to allow the raft to be transported in different types of trailers by mounting the drums on separate frames so that they can be easily moved sideways to allow for different trailer widths.' The boys absorbed the information in the sketch.

Sam continued pointing out details of his idea and could see that his friends were suitably impressed. When he had finished, Jeremy spoke: 'Brilliant. That has got a major stumbling block out of the way. *But*, we may not have to use it if the trailer Daniel's dad can get hold of is wide enough. I think we have achieved what we set out to do today. There is one more important issue: bedding. Dad and I recently saw some camping bunks in Fletcher's Camping Supplies. These were made of light tubular steel with one bunk above the other. They seemed to fit the bill, but I thought of a major stumbling block with the basic design.'

Daniel gave Harry a knowing look. Jeremy seemed to find fault with most things. Their friend continued. 'The main problem was that they didn't fold away easily. On our raft, this would leave very little floor space. However, Dad and I thought of a simple way to overcome this. I'll show you the plans during the week. That, I think, is the last of the main items.'

'I must leave soon because I'm going out for dinner with the family, so next weekend, we've only got the deck house to think about and design, and naturally, that includes the galley, which will probably be some modular entity. Of course, we must be able to source the materials as well. During the week, we should all make lists of construction materials and any other items that will make up the raft. Email these to each other or show them at school.'

Harry said: 'To add some comfort items to our workspace, I'll bring in a ghetto-blaster next week, and Sam can bring his Jackeroo 3-way fridge, so we'll have somewhere to keep refreshments. As for tools, Dan, what's off limits?'

'Dad has made it clear that we can use anything we like,' Daniel said, 'but if in doubt, he'll show us how to use anything we're unsure of.'

Jeremy rose from his chair and stretched. 'Well, that clears up another point. I'm going to have to head off now, but I'll see you guys at school.

The other boys got up and all four ambled through the garage towards the open roller door. They said their goodbyes on the driveway and either walked or cycled home. Daniel returned to the workshop and collected the coffee mugs and went inside the house. His sister was in the kitchen and quizzed him when he entered: 'Who is the dark-haired boy, the short one?

Daniel smiled when he remembered that Harry *was* rather pint-sized. 'His name is Harry.' He placed the mugs in the dishwasher and retreated to his room with the thought that the raft idea was going well, and his sister was trying to hit on one of his friends.

CHAPTER 3

The noise and clatter of the school cafeteria penetrated Sam Dillon's thoughts as he sat alone at the plastic table and idly flipped through some chemistry study papers. Sam heard Ed Sheeran's *Shape Of You* softly playing in the background and hummed the tune when Harry Turner dragged the chair next to him away from the table, sat down, and dumped his backpack on the table with a loud 'plop'.

'I think I'll go to sleep,' Harry said, closing his eyes and trying to assume an ad hoc sleeping position. Sam interjected: 'Trust me: you can't sleep on these chairs. I've tried many times.'

Harry gave up and joined the world of the living. 'I think I'll get a V. Want one?'

'Yeah, why not.'

His friend wandered to the vending machine, leaving Sam with his chemistry papers. The two boys had a free lesson and waited for their friends instead of going home. Sam gathered the sheets, deposited them into his bag on the floor, and produced a manila folder with the words 'Study Notes' on the front cover. Placing this on the table before him, Sam opened it and flicked through some A4 sheets until he found what he was looking for. It was a photocopy of part of an Ordnance Survey (OS) map. Notes in Sam's handwriting were visible in the margin of the page.

Harry returned with two tall cans and placed these on the table. 'Thank God it's Friday,' he muttered to nobody. He turned his attention to the map fragment Sam was reading. 'That where we're going?'

'Yeah. Right here,' Sam replied, using the tip of a pen to indicate a small 'bay', just a re-entrant on the map. 'But here, about two kilometres away, there is a ruin of some kind. So, one of the treks I plan to make is to this place. Find out what it is. Then I reckon we all should go and check out that old mine here.'

Harry was just about to reply when the end-of-day bell sounded. Suddenly, a mass exodus came from the canteen as students said their goodbyes and made plans for the weekend. Sam said, 'We'll wait for Danny and Jeremy. I want to show them these ruins while I think of it. Tomorrow we'll meet at Dan's place. Jeremy has more plans to show us, just the final dimensions.

Harry perused the map, familiarising himself with the lake and surrounding country. 'I think you and Dan will be doing most of the trekking; that country looks very steep.'

This time, Harry was interrupted by the arrival of Jeremy and Daniel, who burst into the cafeteria and made their way over to Sam's table. After procuring chairs from another table, the boys sat noisily down. Without asking, Daniel grabbed the map from Harry and immediately began giving Sam the third degree about all the handwritten markings. Sam defended himself by saying he was looking for additional activities in the area.

Jeremy reached into his backpack and produced a bundle of papers joined with a large bulldog clip. He laid them on the table and flipped through the pages until he found what he was after. 'This chap is the deckhouse ideas and plans.'

The boys bent over the table to better view the papers. They comprised a collection of Jeremy's CAD drawings that he was fond of, with dimensions everywhere and various parts circled with a highlighter pen.

'I only suggested we meet here after school because all of us are busy tonight and won't be able to catch up until tomorrow. Also, Dad suggests that we at least buy the timber for the frame tomorrow and get that part completed.'

'I'm for that,' Sam cut in and looked at Daniel and Harry for support. They nodded in agreement. Sam glanced at Jeremy as if to say, 'That's settled'.

'Fair enough,' Jeremy said. 'Okay, the plan for tomorrow is this.' He took the sheaf of paper and thumbed through it until he found what he was looking for. 'The first thing we must do is figure out the dimensions of the raft, and once we've agreed upon a size, we can write down the dimensions of all framing timber and deck panels. I've thought of another idea for the cabin. In a nutshell, the cabin could have four walls and a roof. For transportation, we could merely disassemble it into its parts and stack them on the deck, lashing them down securely.'

Sam was curious: 'How would we assemble the panels, Jeremy?'

'With lengths of plastic angle and plastic nuts and bolts. It'll be quite strong enough.'

'Dad can get plastic forty-four-gallon drums from his work,' Daniel offered. 'How many will we need?'

'Either six or eight,' Jeremy replied without looking up from his notes. 'Six should give enough stability, but eight would be better. We can fit the additional drums without affecting the design radically.' He paused. 'Well, I think that about covers it for now. We'll meet at Daniel's place tomorrow at about nine-thirty. I know you'll be a bit late, Sam, because you're going into Dandenong first thing. I'll bring these notes, and I think that's all we'll need for now. We'll have to work out Sam's drum attachment method. I believe it's a great idea and should we prioritise it.

The boys gathered personal belongings from the table and packed them into bags. Jeremy and Daniel returned their borrowed chairs to the correct table while the other two slid their chairs under their table, and the group of four boys headed for the canteen door. Once outside in the afternoon sunshine, Daniel and Jeremy said goodbye to Harry and Sam and shuffled off to indoor cricket.

As the boys walked to the local sports centre for their afternoon game, Daniel had no illusion that the following day would be busy. Jeremy seemed to have worked things out thoroughly. He planned to spend the evening getting his father's workshop ready for the next day, knowing he would have to be up early to get the raft project underway.

CHAPTER 4

Daniel woke early on Saturday, intending to get his breakfast out of the way before his friends arrived. The previous evening, he had helped his father prepare the workshop for today, but this had taken longer than he planned because his dad had been using some of the equipment. He made toast in the kitchen and focused on the needed materials. Jeremy had planned the raft to minimise material costs. This process had involved some scrounging here and there, but now, at least on paper, the boys had everything they needed for their raft.

Daniel was brought out of his reverie by his sister's muttering about four teenage boys together on a raft for a week. He ignored her and continued spreading peanut butter on his toast. Megan persisted, 'How are you going to build this raft?' she asked.

For an answer, Daniel produced several folded A4 sheets from his pocket and slid them across the table to Megan. 'Here are the blueprints,' he joked. To his surprise, she studied them intently and was reluctant to return them when Daniel reached for them. 'You're interested, aren't you?' he said.

Megan remarked, 'Jeremy loves going into detail, doesn't he.'

'Annoyingly, yes,' Daniel answered. 'But then he says you can ignore half of it. The trouble is, you don't know which half to ignore. Still, we can't complain. He includes everything. We have the base and deck sorted, but the jury's still out on the deckhouse.'

Megan was just about to reply when her attention was distracted by something out the window. 'Speak of the devil.'

Daniel looked up and saw Jeremy and Harry approaching the front door. He rose and, wiping crumbs from his mouth, strolled out of the room and down to the front door. He opened it and greeted the boys warmly, getting Harry in a friendly headlock. Jeremy was laden with rolls of paper, which Daniel guessed would be more plans for their future raft.

Jeremy patted the rolls as if reading his friend's mind, saying, 'It's not as bad as you think.'

'I would fucking hope not,' Daniel said with a laugh.

'These drawings are large and clear, without my crappy handwriting all over them. I've even included a meals menu, which Harry has been sweating over.'

Harry beamed. 'Yeah, Dad and I put some work into this. He said it was essential to have meals organised properly to make food go as far as possible. It will also keep our cold storage to a minimum.'

The boys drifted into the kitchen, chattering nineteen to the dozen about various aspects of the forthcoming vessel. Listening to them, one would think it would be the *SS Great Eastern*. Megan made room at the table for the new arrivals. 'Do you want me to go?' she asked her brother. Harry answered for him, 'No, Meg, we may need a woman's intuition on this project.'

Megan blushed and said, 'It's nice to be appreciated, Harry. I'll get our guest some coffee.' She gave Daniel the evil eye for forgetting his guests and busied herself at the kettle. Daniel shrugged off the remark and pored over the A4 drawing sheets on the table. He stabbed his finger at various points that caught his eye. Jeremy didn't bother going into explanations and merely mentioned aspects that Daniel's critical eye had missed. Harry had the rough drafts of his menu in his hand and went through them with Megan as soon as she had set two steaming mugs on the table.

The reverie was interrupted by the sound of a car in the driveway. 'That'd be Samuel,' Daniel said, more to himself than anyone. Eager not to cop another rebuke from Megan, he leaped up from the table and strode out of the room. He wasn't quick enough because his father, clad in his dressing gown, had the front door open, was saying good morning to Sam, and was ushering him into the house. Sam uttered his usual pleasantries to Mr Graham and greeted Daniel with the typical shenanigans of teenage boys. They entered the kitchen, and Sam jostled with Harry and Jeremy, seemingly not noticing Megan.

'Good Morning, Sam. Would you like a cup of coffee?' Megan asked.

'No thanks, Meg,' Sam replied. 'Just returned from Dandenong with Dad, and we stopped at Rotten Ronnie's.' Sam produced McDonald's napkins from a pocket as if wishing to present evidence of his breakfast. 'Gave me enough of these to mop up after the *Exxon Valdez*. So, what's the Nerd been boring you with?'

Accepting a glass of orange juice from Daniel, Sam spied the plans and drawings on the table. 'Oh, look, everyone, just what we need – more intricate plans for our new ship.'

Jeremy was ready for the sarcasm and replied: 'Eat shit, you dago prick'.

Daniel and his friends went outside, through the garage, to the workshop. Jeremy unrolled the drawings and laid them on a side workbench, using heavy stainless steel bolts as paperweights to hold the corners down. The boys gathered around and waited for Jeremy to give his instructions. Jeremy turned and surveyed the workshop, particularly the floor.

Harry and Daniel, at Jeremy's directions and armed with coloured chalk and a tape measure, began to make markings on the floor and write figures next to the marks. Then Harry joined the marks using a long, thin strip of timber as a straight edge. Ten minutes later, they had a large rectangle drawn on the concrete floor, twenty-two-hundred by forty-four-hundred millimetres. Jeremy told the boys to position the folding chairs within the rectangle to give an idea of spacing. Having done this, Jeremy divided the rectangle in half transversely and told the boys to re-position the chairs in one half.

'Okay,' he announced. 'One half is the open deck, and most of the other half will be the cabin. Regarding this structure, there are various options. We can go completely rigid, a box, or we can have a flexible structure that can be reduced in size to create more deck space. The beds are going to be the biggest items. These are going to be the camping bunk type. This will make the best use of space in the cabin, whatever we choose.'

'Each type of structure has its pros and cons', Sam chipped in. 'I can whip up a sturdy cabin, no probs. It'll even look good, too! As for making extra deck space, why don't we make the raft a bit longer?'

'That's a great idea. It solves a few issues without causing too many concerns. I *was* worried about the overall length, but Daniel's dad assures me that the trailer he's procuring will meet these requirements. The deck itself is going to be made from sheets of marine-grade plywood. Not very original, I know, but it is the best. I realise that other materials are available but at a greater cost. The deck will be mounted on a sturdy timber frame, which Sammy will build. We will get the wood for that and the deck today.'

Sam asked, 'What kind of nails are we going to use? Stainless or galvanised?'

Jeremy replied, 'We are using wood*screws* for everything. They're much easier and stronger. These will be stainless. We must also call the marine store and get some plastic cleats. I think about five will do. Drums. We will use the forty-four-gallon chemical type that is square in profile. It's much easier to mount. That will involve a modification to the frame, Sam.'

'Got that, Nerd. It's in here,' Sam said, waving his tablet.

'Well, I think that does the raft itself. Now for food and storage. Harry, what have you got?'

Harry picked up several foolscap pages from the workbench and organised them briefly before speaking. 'I will be the cook on the trip. I've prepared menus, which might seem overkill, but it makes things easier in the field. I will decide what cooking utensils and gear need to be taken in addition to cold storage items. You have all made great meal suggestions, and I'll try to accommodate you as much as possible. Speaking of food and cooking, I was thinking of a simple kitchen module in the cabin, just something to support a Coleman three burner and some bench space. Keep everything together.'

'I think the fridge should also fit into that module, Harry,' Sam said. 'Just give me the specs, and I'll get right on it.'

For an answer, Harry produced a notebook out of thin air and handed it to Sam, who began studying Harry's drawings closely. 'You know what else this module should contain?' Sam asked Jeremy. Before his friend could answer, Sam said: 'A sink, water supply, and waste containers. Being modular will make it easy to shift out of the way when we want to re-organise the deck.'

Now for propulsion and electrical. As I said earlier, the raft is being propelled by two trolling motors, which will run from a generator via a high current power supply. The advantage of this system is that the motor itself is virtually silent, and the generator can be explained by saying it is being used to charge batteries. I have chosen interior lighting for the cabin and external deck floodlighting. Harry's galley module will also benefit.'

'You forgot to mention that we already have all the components for the propulsion system,' Daniel reminded him. 'I think that's its biggest advantage. So now all we must do is wait for Dad to have his breakfast, and we can buy the materials. We've done well on cost so far. Dad getting that packing crate was a bonus. The warehouse agreed to keep it in their yard until we picked it up.

'Who would have thought it would become our future home in a sense?' Jeremy wondered aloud.

Megan appeared in the doorway from the house and announced that Mr Graham was ready to go if the boys were.

Mr Graham's work vehicle was well equipped to fetch the building materials, with roof racks and other supports for carrying lengths of timber. The boys piled in and chatted excitedly about their project. Daniel held onto the cash that the boys had saved over the previous year and to the list of materials and fixings that Jeremy and Sam had meticulously prepared. Due to its size and dimensions, the crate- future cabin- was first stop on the ride. It would have to be collected and driven back to the Graham residence. The other materials were to be purchased on a separate trip.

* * *

Armed with a tape measure and a pencil, Harry Turner joined Daniel Graham in sorting the lengths of treated pine into longerons and transverse members. These were then marked at the cut-off point and labelled as to their position within the frame. Once this had been done to all frame components, Sam readied the drop saw and with Jeremy's help, positioned each timber length onto the workbench. Meanwhile, Harry and Daniel started on the sheets of plywood, using the tape measure, pencil and a speed square to mark out the deck panels.

Sam cut all the main members and started on the corner bracing pieces. As each piece was cut to length, Jeremy removed it from the workbench, applied anti-weathering compound to the cut surfaces and laid it on the floor, corresponding with the chalk marks. Ten minutes later, the raft's complete frame lay on the concrete, and the boys stood back and admired its size. 'Now to screw it all together,' Sam said, taking a handful of stainless steel wood screws from a packet on the bench. 'Dan, get the corner brace,'

Daniel was one step ahead of his friend and already had the heavy metal framing jig in his hand. He passed it to Sam and the two boys fitted it to one corner of the raft's frame. Harry positioned spacers under parts of the frame as directed by Sam. Jeremy passed Sam the cordless drill and the first screws were driven home. The thing to do, according to Sam, was to complete one corner and then move on. This would help to ensure that the frame was square, he said.

Sam seemed to be in his element fitting all the pieces

together and running a trained eye along corners, constantly checking for errors. The other boys simply did whatever he told them and just over an hour after the first woodscrews went in, the frame was almost complete. It was time for the modification Sam had suggested. This involved placing pieces of plywood horizontally between the frames where the drums were to be fitted. This, Sam explained, was to create more contact area for the adhesive. Once this task was complete, Sam directed that the frame be lifted and fully suspended on sawhorses. When this was done, he had the other boys lay the pieces of marine ply on top of the frame, one at a time, and these were marked for size and cut using a circular saw.

Megan appeared and asked the group if they would like a hot drink. Harry replied yes for them and volunteered to help, much to the bemusement of the other boys, who downed tools and took stock. They tried to visualise the deckhouse and drums in position. The deck was the next cab off the rank and Jeremy scrutinised the plywood panels. 'You've cut these well, Sam,' he remarked. 'We should be able to get the deck done in no time. I think we'll seal it with tung oil. Give it about four coats. Be generous with the stuff.'

'Dad was asking me if next weekend would be okay for a test sail,' Daniel changed the subject. 'There are a couple of options here. We know someone down at Warneet, and they said that access to the local boat ramp is easy, plus we can park the car and trailer on his lawn after we launch. The alternative is our next door neighbour said we can use their pool. That will suffice for the basic flotation test.'

Jeremy reflected. 'Good. That's another thing crossed off the list. With the electrical system, everything will be modular, that is, plastic boxes connected by flexible plastic tubing with wires inside. Switches and warning lights are mounted in the boxes. We'll take measurements when we mount the deckhouse, and I can make the wiring loom at home.'

The three friends made small talk until Harry appeared with a tray of mugs and biscuits. He placed the tray on the workbench and said, 'Dig in.' Harry grabbed a mug but ignored the plate of biscuits.

'Not hungry?' Sam enquired.

'I've had one. How long will the deck take?'

'Twenty minutes or so. Everything's cut to size. Why? Have you got a date?

Harry laughed. 'No, I just want to see the cab on the deck. The raft will almost be complete then.'

'Yeah, we'll get the cab on, and we can fit the drums as well, but it'll be tomorrow before we can mount the drums permanently.'

However, Jeremy put paid to that idea. 'The construction order from now on is Frame (complete), drums, deck, cab, electrical loom and lighting,' he announced. 'That's how it has to be to stop one process from getting in the way of another. Now, I suggest we get on with the drums. These will be glued but strapped initially until the glue sets.'

The boys finished their drinks and wandered outside into the backyard, where eight black forty-four-gallon chemical drums were lined up neatly against the brick wall of the workshop. The drums weren't cylindrical but had flat sides, giving them a boxy profile. A faded label on one of the drums indicated it had once contained fertiliser. Just beyond them lay the timber crate that was to become the cabin of the raft. Jeremy announced, 'The drums aren't heavy, just awkward. They should fit through the doorway. Two to a drum.'

Sam and Jeremy grabbed the first drum and Daniel and Harry the second. Daniel exclaimed, 'I thought you said two per drum; we've only got one-and-a-half'.

Harry, about whom the comment had been made, replied, 'Gee, that was so funny, I forgot to laugh.' Once inside the workshop, the drums were positioned, standing on end, next to the area of the frame where they were to go. Sam went over to a cupboard and, opening it, produced the biggest caulking gun the other boys had ever seen. 'We'll start here,' he announced, patting the frame next to him. 'This stuff will stick to anything.'

Instinctively knowing what to do, three boys lifted that corner of the heavy frame sufficiently to allow the sawhorse to be removed and the drum to be positioned under the frame. Before lowering the frame, Sam went crazy with the glue gun, applying seemingly tons of the thick grey substance on the drum's flat surface where the plywood panel would contact the drum before giving the word to lower the frame. Once lowered, Harry produced two adjustable straps and began to loop them through the frame and around the drum before tightening each using a small ratchet mechanism.

This process was repeated for the remaining three corners and intermediate drums, and soon, all were mounted solidly. Harry suggested another short break and went inside to try to rustle up coffee. Daniel and Jeremy began to place the pre-cut deck panels on the frame while Sam put the caulking gun away and helped his friends position the plywood sections.

Sam was eager to get the deck on, so he grabbed a few wood clamps and began distributing them around the edges of the frame. Daniel went to the cupboard and grabbed the smaller caulking gun. Jeremy lifted the rearmost deck panel sufficiently for Daniel to apply waterproof wood glue to the frame, then lowered it back into position. Sam applied the wood clamps and wiped off the extra glue with an old rag. In the centre of the raft, Jeremy and Daniel placed concrete blocks on the deck panels, where clamps could not reach.

The deck was complete when Harry appeared with a tray containing four large mugs. 'You took your time,' Daniel said accusingly.

'I was showing Megan the plans for the raft, telling her how we would fit the barrels,' Harry defended himself.

'The deck is done, but we'll need you when we bring the crate in.'

'Do we have to wait until the glue is dry?' Harry enquired, helping himself to one of the steaming mugs.

'No, we can do that now,' Jeremy explained. 'I want to finish it today so we can design the wiring loom and plan where lights will be mounted. I can finish the wiring loom tomorrow and bring it over. I've already done a lot of work on it but need actual dimensions.'

The four friends reflected on their work so far and finished their drinks. Then, it was all systems go as they prepared to retrieve the crate. Daniel opened the rear roller door to the workshop and joined his friends in the yard by the crate. With each boy to a corner, they moved the crate from the yard through the roller door and placed it onto the raft's smooth deck. The much-stencilled crate fitted on the deck with room to spare on each side. It had one open end, which faced forwards.

Glancing at his watch, Sam said that he had to make tracks. The other boys agreed it was getting late, so they began cleaning the workshop and traipsed inside to leave their coffee mugs in the kitchen and say goodbye to Daniel's parents. Jeremy said he would be there to do the wiring loom, but Sam and Harry would be no-shows due to study commitments. They parted, and Daniel returned to the workshop to remove any loose items and shut the roller door. He returned through the garage and took a final glance at the raft for the day. The deckhouse, with its missing front wall, stared back emptily.

CHAPTER 5

In a less salubrious part of town, John Allen stood in the kitchen of the weatherboard house he had been staying in for the past few days and, leaning on the stained Laminex benchtop, peered for the hundredth time through the filth-encrusted window out over the untidy front garden towards the street. Today, hopefully, the sooner, the better, someone would arrive and relieve him of having to live in this hovel. The phone call that signalled the end of his purgatory had come late the night before as he was getting ready for bed.

It wasn't that the house was terrible. It was just that John was known to be a bit of a snob, and he naturally compared this place with his neat townhouse. Thinking of this helped him pass the time until the call came. His bags were packed and resting on the table. Not that they'd been fully unpacked. He couldn't find a clean surface anywhere, so he lived out of his two duffel bags for the duration.

Turning away from the window, Allen surveyed the kitchen and adjoining dining room with a tinge resembling sadness. He was the type of guy who, with his own hands, could have transformed this small bungalow into a place somebody would be proud to call home. He was fifty-seven, just over six feet tall, going grey with dignity, as women liked to say, and was still conspicuously handsome.

He was idly thinking these thoughts when a car horn bleeped briefly. He turned to the window again and saw a beige Ford drive slowly into the driveway. At first, he didn't recognise the driver through the window, but anxious not to keep the driver waiting, he grabbed both duffel bags by their rope cords, hoisting them over his shoulder, and stepped into the small entrance hall. He fumbled for the single key he had been given, opened the deadlock with his free hand and swung the door open. After stepping out onto the weathered concrete porch, he closed the door, stomping down the few steps and across the weed-infested front yard to the waiting car.

The driver leaned across and opened the door from the inside. John opened the rear door, deposited his duffel bags on the back seat, and climbed into the front beside the driver. He realised now that he knew the driver well. It was Dennis Hayne.

Like Allen, Hayne was an original member of the firm that had pulled The Big Job, which was five, no, six years ago now. He was not renowned for intellect; Allen was surprised Hayne had gotten the address right. But he had his uses. Strength and fearlessness were two attributes that went well with the activities these two men and others called work. Hayne was slightly shorter than Allen but built like a pocket battleship. Fear wasn't in his limited vocabulary. But loyalty was, which was okay with Allen.

The two men hadn't seen each other since The Big Job, but that was how Charlie Munro had wanted it. Charlie had organised the job, a bank robbery on a First District Bank branch in Bayswater. The firm had to split, and Charlie would handle any communication between the members. This arrangement suited John Allen fine. It had allowed him to get on with life. The only concern after the job from Allen's point of view was when Charlie Munro passed away from cancer. He felt that the firm would have to come together again too soon. It was known well before the job, that Charlie was sick but not to the extent that he was. The real problem, from the viewpoint of the firm members, was that Charlie was a well-known criminal. Therefore, his funeral would attract attention. Not good for a bunch of unknowns who had recently pulled off a big heist.

Had he not played his cards as well as he did, Allen and Hayne may well have been cellmates. Allen did what most criminals don't. He kept his nose clean; so much so in fact, that he was well respected in the small community where he lived on the New South Wales coast. Hayne wasn't as careful and went to prison on an unrelated matter a year later.

Dennis Hayne had received his phone call the previous evening as well. He had one additional instruction; to pick up John Allen and another man. One of these tasks accomplished, the pair now headed to what would be their home for the next two weeks. Hayne wasn't much of a talker, so Allen broke the ice:

'Haven't seen you since the big one. Charlie told us to keep busy and I guess I did that all right'

Hayne seemed to relax and finally spoke.

'Yeah, you could say that I've been busy too. Just not the way I'd planned. I don't think it was all bad luck though.'

'Oh. You think someone lagged?

'I know someone lagged. A prick by the name of Shane Hill. Know him?'

'I heard he came to a sticky end,' Allen said, trying to remember the gist of a news report of a badly decomposed body found on waste ground north of Melbourne.

'Yeah, sticky alright. Serves him right too. He upset a lot of people; cops included. I wouldn't like to have been selling hot dogs at his funeral. Anyway, we've got one more stop to make. Got to collect Bob Pitman.'

'How is Bobby these days? Still got that little business over in Doveton?

What passed for a smile crossed Hayne's face. 'Oh, yeah, he's been quite busy. Strange thing is, he was always a busy mechanic, so it beats me why he got into crime in such a big way.'

'Like the rest of us; greed,' said Allen.

They drove in silence for a while, as the car meandered through the back streets of Dandenong. Hayne seemed to know where he was going. John Allen didn't know this part of the world well so he couldn't even guess at their destination. He decided to remain silent reasoning he had no control over where they stayed; only hoping it was an improvement over the place he had just left.

'Here we are,' Hayne said suddenly, and the car slowed to a crawl outside a two-storey, brown brick block of flats. A figure emerged from the side of the driveway next to the garbage enclosure. Allen recognised him straight away -- the weathered face, and the shock of untidy hair. The man carried a duffel bag like Allen's and as he approached the car, he went to the back and knocked on the boot. Hayne pressed the boot release, and the man deposited his bag in the rear and shut the boot lid with a thud.

Bob Pitman climbed into the back seat of the car and smiled warmly at his two former partners in crime. He shook hands with Hayne and Allen and settled back into the seat and put the safety harness on as the car drove slowly down the street. John Allen leaned back in his seat and spoke to Pitman. 'Well Bobby, how's it been? Dennis tells me you've been working hard and keeping out of mischief.'

'I *have* been busy and with that new regulation about catalyst converters, the garage has been busier than Bob Trimbole's travel agent. But I'm not complaining.'

Hayne's eyes swept the street, every vehicle, footpath and alley came under his scrutiny, but he saw nothing to give him the slightest twinge of concern. He relaxed once more and cut into the conversation. 'Robert, it's great to see you again. Tell you what, we've got some catching up to do.'

'I'll second that,' said Allen. 'And speaking of this place, what's it like and where is it?'

'Another five minutes and we're there,' Hayne offered. 'The house is alright, 'bout the same as the one you just left.'

'Oh, so were not going to the Ramada,' Allen joked.

'Not if Charlie had anything to do with it,' Pitman remarked. 'By the way, who actually attended his funeral?'

'Frank and Les,' said Hayne 'so they tell me.'

'I wonder who else was there,' Allen said to no one in particular. 'It was bloody frustrating not being able to go'

'The powers that be supposedly wanted minimal exposure at the funeral, so just a few got to go. I'm sure the attendees were chosen randomly.'

'The fact that they were local boys probably had as much to do with it as anything,' mused Pitman. 'The rest of us would have needed to travel quite a way.'

Silence descended on the vehicle again and presently Hayne turned into a street off the main bypass road and after travelling some hundred yards or so he slowed, flicked his right turn signal on and turned into the driveway of a dilapidated bungalow, somewhat beneath the house John Allen had just left.

'We're sure not going to the Ramada,' Allen muttered under his breath.

'Look on the bright side, there's a load of beers in the fridge,' Hayne offered helpfully.

'I don't care if there's a bull that pisses Jack Daniels.'

The three men got out of the car and fetched their bags from the back seat and boot. Pitman started to say something, but the words were drowned out by a large truck that roared past carrying steel lengths and belching black smoke. When it had gone, Pitman spoke again. 'I was just saying, there's a shop down the street where we can get fags and other niceties.'

'I might go and live there,' Allen replied, unable to keep the sarcasm out of his voice.

'It's better inside,' Hayne said, reading his thoughts.

'It would want to be.'

The three men strolled along the paved path and trudged up the front steps to the porch. Before Dennis Hayne could knock on the door, it swung open, and a smallish man in his mid-fifties stood there, beer can in hand, with a welcoming smile. Stan Reed, better known as 'Stan the Man' and an original member of the firm, stood aside and let the three arrivals ease past into the entrance hall. They took in their surroundings with varying levels of expectation. To Dennis Hayne and Bob Pitman, it was dingy but livable, as expected. But John Allen had seen abandoned houses better than this, and he knew then that the next two weeks would be more complicated than he had prepared for.

Reed opened a door off the hall, which led into a spacious living room equipped with modern, comfortable-looking easy chairs and sofas, two occupied by men who appeared to be in their mid-fifties. Stan Reed closed the hall door and introduced Frank Taylor and Les Truscott, although this was a mere formality.

'Well, the next item on the agenda is drinks. Les, you know where they are. And the good stuff for our friends. In the meantime, we will show our new guests to their quarters.' With that, Reed strolled over to a second door, which John

Allen hadn't noticed, opened it and stepped out into the hall again. Turning left, he led the three newcomers through another door into a short hallway extension. Two doors punctuated the right side of this. 'Take your pick: Superior is the first, and Deluxe is the second.'

While the men sorted out their rooms, Les Truscott got up from his easy chair and wandered into the kitchen through an arched doorway at the back of the room. He went to the corner, opened the car fridge on the floor, and produced two small bottles of Tennent's beer. He placed these on the benchtop, grabbed the bottle opener, and removed the caps of each one before heading back into the living room.

Frank Taylor sipped a beer quietly in his easy chair and reflected that it was good to have the old gang back again. Like Hayne, Frank couldn't stay clear of the law. In his case, he had recently been discharged from prison for receiving stolen goods. It wasn't a long stretch, but annoying, nonetheless. The one thing he'd been able to salvage from the wreckage was that the crime was unrelated to the big job.

Stan Reed returned to the living room, rubbing his hands together. 'Well, that's got the boys sorted. Now to have a drink and a chat, then lunch. At about five this arvo, we will get down to business.'

'This place has been swept?' asked Frank Taylor. 'I would sleep better at night if I knew it had.'

'Several times,' answered Reed. The remainder of the men wandered into the living room, chatting about life since they had last seen each other. Stan Reed and Les Truscott rearranged some of the furniture so that everyone could talk comfortably. Les took a drinks order and re-entered the kitchen to replenish empty glasses and bottles.

Five of the six men drank and talked about life, except for John Allen. He remained strangely quiet, not fitting in with this group. Of all the men here, only Allen had led anything resembling an everyday life, only getting involved in The Big Job because of an overwhelming urge to purchase a flash cabin cruiser. Not having the ready cash and not wanting to take out a reverse mortgage on his home, which he owned outright, he was persuaded to take part in a job with some other guys. In the meantime, as luck would have it, a relative had passed away and left him enough money to buy his dream boat.

Now, he sat in this old house sharing a beer with men whose company he enjoyed but had surprisingly little in common with. His tongue loosened after a few beers, and he began to enjoy himself. Stan Reed played the perfect host and kept disappearing into the kitchen to check on the lunch he was preparing. When it was ready, the men consumed it hungrily. They played cards or talked more throughout the afternoon until about the appointed hour of five, when Stan, wearing a different hat now, got everyone's attention and announced that it was time to get down to business.

CHAPTER 6

Stan Reed directed that the curtains were to be closed and additional lighting turned on. Les Truscott strolled over to the window and, finding the cord, closed the faded floral drapes. The light level in the room hardly changed, for Frank Taylor found the light switch panel and flipped two of them down. The room was bathed suddenly in bright white light from LED downlights recessed into the ceiling. The rest of the group, Reed included, arranged the seating to face the back of the room. Reed opened some cardboard boxes stacked in the corner and produced a laptop computer, a projector and other peripherals. An extension cord also appeared, and he disappeared into the kitchen, returning with the ubiquitous card table. After some minor rearranging of the seating, he positioned the table in the centre of the room and placed the project on it.

After connecting the extension cord, Reed, positioned to the right side of the group at the front, pressed some keys on the laptop and cleared his throat. At the same time, the back wall lit up with an image of a '70s-style building with what appeared to be police cars parked haphazardly in front. The scene was very familiar to the group, marking a beginning.

Tonight's meeting was to signify an end, so the men gathered here hoped.

At a hand signal from Stan Reed, Frank Taylor dimmed the downlights from the wall panel. The room grew strangely quiet. Reed spoke: 'I think you all recognise this building. This picture was taken on that day all those years ago by a Herald-Sun photographer whom Charlie knew. He was our contact in the media, chosen because of *his* list of useful contacts. He informed Charlie of the police's progress in the investigation after the robbery. Frank and Les might remember him from Charlie's funeral.'

Frank and Les looked at each other, clearly not remembering such a man. 'Never mind. He was there. He probably didn't approach you for obvious reasons. Anyway, after the job, we went, via a very roundabout route, to the factory where Charlie was waiting. As per the agreed plan, that was the last any of us saw of the money. The money was taken from that place and hidden, and I'm sure you've all been wondering about your little nest egg from that place to this day.

A murmur went through the group, especially those who weren't financially well off. 'Well,' Stan continued, 'today is your lucky day. Today, you find out the general area where the money is hidden. We will stay here for a while, make plans for distribution, and then head off to the destination in a few days. You find out exactly where the loot is when we get there.'

Les Truscott was curious: 'What vehicles are we using, Stan?'

'We leave from here in the Ford and go to a yard a few miles from here where we get into two other cars, one of which will have a tinny attached.'

'Woa,' said John Allen. 'Is that clue number one, Stan?'

'It sure was, John. As Mr Allen has just pointed out, the first clue to our destination has been mentioned. It is the town of Rupertsvale, by Lake Eildon. When we get there, which is a caravan park, by the way, we make camp, and just play cards and drink coffee and look respectable until it's time to go and retrieve the loot. At some stage, not long after we make camp, I'll send two of us to the hiding spot just to check. I normally don't like doing this because of the additional exposure.'

'In the tinny?' asked Bob Pitman

'Possibly, or on foot. It's an hour or so of walking, but that's okay because you won't be carrying anything. When we go to retrieve the money, we'll use the tinny. We can also use it to fish. We must keep up appearances. So, the way I foresee this is that we go out fishing every day and on one of those days, we collect the loot. This will have to be done at night for obvious reasons, so there will be evening fishing trips to cover this trip.'

Reed started a slide show of the photos and diagrams that had been used in the planning of the robbery. The pictures brought back vivid memories for the men, taking them back to a time when the Big Job was still to be pulled off and nerves and tempers were getting frayed. John Allen clearly remembered trying to juggle his blue-collar job and what some of the other guys called 'crime practice', likening rehearsing for the job to footy training.

Charlie had made them all take everything very seriously. He seemed to have contacts everywhere, including, but not limited to, the police. He knew, for instance, when Dennis Hayne had received a speeding infringement. 'I have to know these things, Dennis,' he would say. 'It's all about unwanted attention.' Charlie had given the five men a list of places to stay away from, including pubs, gambling establishments, racetracks and other areas where they might get the wrong kind of attention if something should go wrong. And it went without saying that they had to keep well away from the suburb of Bayswater, where the job was going to be pulled.

'When was the money last checked up on?' John Allen piped up. He was more concerned about its physical condition than whether it was there or not.

'I personally did so six months ago,' Reed said, popping an after-dinner mint into his mouth. 'It was an interesting trip because I had to do it virtually hiking to the spot to avoid any caravan parks or motels. I had to leave the car hidden and hike the rest of the way and ended up camping at the location. This brings me to the next point. Once the loot is collected, which will be by all of us, we take it to the tinny, which will be tied up to the shore as near as possible to the location. From there, two of us sail back to the caravan park and wait.'

'Wouldn't it be better to circle the lake and kill time until it gets properly dark?' put in Frank Taylor. 'We still have to wait for the others to return from the hiding spot.'

'Yeah, that's a good point, Frank. Okay, describe a few circles on the lake and try some lure fishing. Hell, you might even catch something. Meanwhile, the rest of us can return to the camping ground, where we can arrive at certain intervals. The boaters can contact us by radio, and we will wander down to the jetty with two or three coolers and collect the catch.'

Only Hayne laughed at the word 'catch' sounding so much like 'cash'.

'One problem I *can* foresee is other anglers on or near the jetty when our tinny pulls in. The boaters must ensure that the jetty and surroundings are vacant before they dock. They can do this with a small pair of binoculars I will provide. Then, they will inform the other members of what's happening. The guys walking back may arrive well before the tinny, so they will hang around the caravan until we get the word.'

Stan Reed decided it was time for a brew and asked Les Truscott to do the honours. Les strolled into the kitchen, and while he was there, Reed said: 'When Les has gotten everyone a cuppa, I'll talk about the cash distribution. As you were all made aware at the time of the robbery, the total amount was twenty million dollars to the cent. Our contact was reliable and kept *her* nose to the grindstone throughout the planning process, even before it, because *she* was the one who told Charlie that this amount would be there, all in one-hundred-dollar bills.'

Truscott entered the room again with a tray bearing

six steaming mugs and a small plate of biscuits, walking in the projector's beam and making a shadow on the wall. He placed the tray on the table behind the projector. Various hands grabbed mugs and a biscuit before settling back into their chairs. Reed returned to business: 'Twenty million dollars in one-hundred-dollar denominations. That's two-hundred-thousand notes. In bundles of one-hundred notes, that's two-thousand bundles. From memory, there were twenty bags. One hundred per bag.'

'Now you remember the big canvas bags that the loot was in. They are cumbersome and stick out like a beer mat on a billiard table. You can't exactly walk down the street with one of these and not get unwanted attention. Our problem is this: at what point in the process do we get rid of these bloody things? I am open to suggestions. I want to burn them, but that can only happen when we have some cash storage alternative. '

Reed sipped his coffee and continued: 'We must get the loot into one of the vehicles as quickly as possible without anyone watching. The main problem is that the jetty is about one hundred yards from the caravan, and that's as the crow flies. You must duck and dive down narrow paths; you know what these trailer parks are like. So, you see, we need some type of receptacle big enough to hide the money and look inconspicuous at the same time.

John Allen spoke: 'What about taking the boat to the main launching ramp at night and meeting up there with the car? Do the money transfer there? That way, we can use the original money bags to transfer the money and dispose of them back in Melbourne when we do the distribution. This way, when we bring the tinny back to the jetty, she'll be as clean as wind-driven snow.'

Reed was silent momentarily, then he spoke: 'I think you might just have it, John. It would look natural for one of the vehicles to leave the campground for a while and then return. The only restriction is that we will have to ensure that the ramp and surrounds are completely clear.'

'Yeah, and when the car does come back', said Frank, 'we could grab a slab of cans out of the back as if we had just bought them. You know, keeping up appearances.'

Red spoke firmly: 'Okay then, it's final. John's idea does tick all the boxes. We must ensure the tinny has additional fuel for the longer journey. Personnel-wise, there'll be two boaters and two in the car. That leaves two back at the campsite. We can sail the boat back to the jetty without arousing suspicion.'

'Now for the distribution. That will take place here. Twenty million divided six ways is roughly three point three million each. That still allows for smaller distributions here and there. I'll give you the main list when we get to Rupertsvale and the actual amounts we each receive.'

Reed began a slide show of Lake Eildon itself and Rupertsvale. There were shots of the much-talked about jetty and the caravan that Reed had booked for the men. The men thought he had chosen the place well, and to a man, they were looking forward to the trip, notwithstanding the lure of a vast amount of cash.

CHAPTER 7

Jeremy Williams cycled through the early morning gloom to Daniel Graham's house. He had set off somewhat earlier than planned. He had promised to help his father on a drainage project in the back yard. To fit in helping his father, he took the components of the wiring loom and detailed instructions to Daniel and tasked him with assembling the loom and control boxes.

Jeremy got to Daniel's home at 7:30 am and was about to park his bike near the front door, when he noticed lights in the garage. A radio could just be heard. Leaning the bike against the wall of the house, he walked softly over to the open roller door and peered in. He could see through into the workshop where a tripod-mounted LED work-light brightly illuminated the raft. Daniel was there, standing beside the raft with his back to the garage door, cordless drill in hand, studying a sheet of paper which was resting on the deck, doubtless one of Jeremy's plans. Daniel's radio was on the edge of the deck, so Jeremy stole over to the raft and switched off the radio, cutting the Foo Fighters off mid-song.

Daniel turned around, woodscrews protruding from his mouth. Placing the drill on the deck, he gestured to Jeremy and mumbled hello with several woodscrews between his teeth. Jeremy held up the plastic bag containing the wiring loom components and set it down on the raft.

'We're both early birds this morning,' Daniel said, removing the screws from his mouth. 'Good thing too. Got some good news last night. The Tomlinsons said we can do the flotation test in their pool and use their trailer to get it in there. That'll save us frigging about towing the thing somewhere and back. So, I'm going to get the deck screwed down and we should be right to take the raft over. Dad and Mr. T have organised quite a gang to help lift it onto the trailer and take it around via the road and back it down their driveway.'

'Pity I can't be there, but my dad really needs help with this drain project; that I mostly designed I might add. You could try ringing the other two slackers, but I think you'd be as popular as a cigarette lighter on the Hindenburg. They'll be studying like crazy today. They've both got exams early next week. Incidentally,' Jeremy said indicating the bag, 'this is the wiring harness. The drawings are quite straight forward.'

'Your drawings are never straight forward, but I'll give it a shot. I'll finish the deck off first then float it and after that I'll do the harness. That might be tomorrow though.'

'That's fine,' Jeremy said, glancing at the yellow dial of his Doxa dive watch. 'I'd better make tracks or Dad will have hired some illegal alien workers to help him. See you tomorrow. Text me with the big float test details.' With that, Jeremy walked to his bike and pedalled back to his home.

It didn't take Daniel long to complete getting the plywood

panels screwed down and by the time he had finished, a small group had begun to gather around the raft, his father and sister being among them.

Each member of the group grabbed the raft by the edge of the deck and lifted the craft out through the garage and onto the Tomlinson's eight by five trailer. Lengths of framing timber had been placed across the trailer's top edges to accommodate the raft's width.

Steve Graham backed the trailer expertly down the Tomlinson's driveway and into the back yard. He positioned the trailer adjacent to the pool. The raft was lifted sideways off the trailer and slowly made its way to the hardstand surrounding the pool. The lifting party lowered the raft and took a breather, then resumed their task. The floats on one side of the raft were lowered into the water followed shortly by the other set.

The raft bobbed on the water, riding higher than Daniel expected. He decided it was safe enough to climb aboard. He organised ropes to attach to the only two cleats yet installed and had these run out to various heavy pieces of pool furniture. Once steady, Daniel climbed up onto the deck and walked around, pressing his weight here and there, not omitting to go inside the cabin. Even when standing on one side, the raft hardly seemed to notice the weight. Satisfied, he hopped off and walked around the pool paved area, surveying the raft from every angle.

Daniel felt that it was time for the final and most important test. He called for volunteers. His dad and sister were conscripted. Mr Tomlinson put his hand up and Daniel gratefully accepted. He double checked the mooring lines and the four climbed aboard. The vessel didn't protest, and Daniel asked the group to stand in all four corners. This achieved satisfactory results and Daniel was quick to phone the other three boys to tell them the news.

Over the telephone, Jeremy arranged for the four to meet the next afternoon to install the propulsion system and lighting. Now the group of testers lifted the raft out of the pool and onto the trailer. Thanking his neighbour profusely, Daniel walked back to his house and helped release the trailer from the car. The trailer was then wheeled through the garage and into the workshop. After a quick tidy up, Daniel retreated into the house to hit the books for the rest of the evening. On the way, he strolled into the kitchen and thanked Megan for helping. The two siblings chatted for a while, before Daniel went off to study and Megan to help get dinner ready. The television blared in the background. What Daniel missed, however, was a news anchor's voice saying something about a light plane having collided with a microwave coms tower in the state's North-East, knocking out all mobile phone services between Melbourne and Eildon and surrounding areas. The anchor also mentioned that land lines in the North were unaffected.

CHAPTER 8

Harry Turner strolled into the senior common room earlier than expected on Friday morning, the last day before the summer break began. He briefly chatted to two girls who quizzed him about his earliness and then made his way to the kitchenette for his morning coffee. He wasn't required to be in class for another hour and a half, due to a free lesson, but he wanted to catch up with his friends, all of whom had classes first up. He made his drink and glided over to a curved sofa, dumped his backpack down on the floor and produced a tablet from his bag.

Despite the exams of the last week, Harry was relaxed. He could afford to relax because he had two exams behind him, and he knew he had done well in both. Now, the trip to Lake Eildon lay ahead and he knew it was going to be difficult to keep his mind on the few remaining classes for the day. An announcement over the Tannoy brought him out of his daydream. He looked up to see Jeremy and Sam bound into the room and make straight for his location.

The two boys were a bit rushed, as they both had morning classes. They didn't even accept a cup of coffee or Monster when Harry offered to get it. They sat down next to Harry and made brief plans for the afternoon, the gist of which was that there would be beers at Harry's house after school. They made small talk until Sam got up and pointed to his watch, at which time Jeremy also rose, jostled with Harry and the two boys left the room.

Harry didn't have long to wait on his own. Daniel made his way to the common room laden with rolled-up maps. He plonked these down on the table and settling into a chair, accepted the offer of coffee from Harry. Harry returned to the table with a steaming Styrofoam cup, and setting it down on the table, grilled Daniel about his wares.

'Okay, the maps are likely Lake Eildon but what scale are they? Harry inquired.

Daniel took a long sip from his coffee and both boys absorbed themselves in the roll of survey maps.

A bell sounded somewhere, and the boys resignedly packed up their bags, got up from their seats and headed off to their first class.

The end of the day came soon enough, and the boys found themselves out in the bright sunshine, chatting to friends and loosening school uniforms. Daniel had a squash game after school, so he told Harry to keep a beer cold for him. Jeremy and Sam joined Harry and after dragging him away from a group of girls, the three pals sauntered out of the yard.

The boys walked along glad that they would soon be out of the dry afternoon heat. 'Did you invite any girls over this arvo', Sam suddenly asked.

'Yes, including the two you and your partner in crime

hauled me away from. At least I managed to give them the address. Why? Do you plan to smuggle one on the raft trip?'

'I might just do that. How far is it to your house, Harry', Sam complained, knowing the distance perfectly well. 'I can smell beer from here. What brands are on offer?'

'I told Dad to choose from Heineken, Guinness, Carlsberg, Tennent's, Grolsch, plus some of those German beers we had at Daniel's place a few months back.'

Sam seemed satisfied at this. Jeremy interrupted his thoughts: 'I might go home first and change, Harry. I'll bring sleeping gear and toiletries in my camping backpack. I'll only be about five minutes later.'

'Yeah, okay, see you there. There'll be an ice cold four-forty mil can waiting for you.'

Jeremy surged ahead and turned left into the street that led to his house. The other two proceeded straight ahead and soon reached the Turner residence. Upon arrival, they made straight for the path that led around to the back of the house and entering by a French door, stepped into the cool embrace of the rumpus room. A noisy air conditioner rattled somewhere, but the boys ignored it and strode over to the bar. Harry produced two tall cans of Tennent's from the mini fridge and the pair cracked them open gleefully, finally putting the school year behind them.

Harry's mother breezed into the room from the front of the house with two girls in tow. 'Harry, you have some guests. Hello Sam, how are you?'

'Well thanks, Mrs Turner,' Sam replied and simultaneously

acknowledged the girls. The four teens mingled, with Harry organising drinks for the new arrivals. Sam put on a CD and rummaged through the others in the rack, choosing some to play later.

True to his word, Jeremy strolled in through the French window, dressed casually, taking advantage of the hot day. He greeted the two girls and jostled with Sam and Harry, accepting a beer from the latter. He deposited his pack in an alcove and joined the group at the bar, chatting about the school year just passed and the one to come.

More teenagers arrived bearing insulated bags containing bottles or cans. Harry had deliberately kept numbers to a manageable level, partly so he could keep a mental note of who should be there. Daniel was about the last to arrive. He wasn't as happy as the boys expected, having lost his squash match, but he soon cheered up after taking Sam's advice to drink beer and forget it.

The last guest to arrive was Megan Graham, partly invited by her brother and partly by Harry. Harry practically ignored the other teenagers for much of the evening after Megan's arrival, with Jeremy and Daniel taking over host duties. That said, the gathering went well, with Mr and Mrs Turner only making the occasional appearance.

By the time Harry got into bed that night, he was worn out, and the thought of going on any trip, let alone a rafting one, was almost too much to bear.

CHAPTER 9

Sleep did not come easily for John Allen. He and his friends were one step closer to that pot of gold that they had dreamed about for the past six years. He studied the room he was bunked in with Dennis Hayne. He was an observant man and he had noticed a series of small details that would have seemed unconnected to a lesser man. One such thing was high on the wall of the room he now occupied. An unobtrusive, gunmetal grey plastic box, two opposite sides of which contained LED strip lights, now off. The front side had a switch and a small red LED light, which glowed brightly.

Allen had seen these boxes in every room in this house. Not surprisingly, Hayne had wondered what they were, but Allen knew an automatic emergency light when he saw one. With these units in mind, he had kept his eyes open for other security features, and soon started finding them. Door locks and hinges on all external doors had been replaced with massive heavy-duty types. There were small wires on every window he'd had the chance to study closely. These must be for alarms, Allen mused.

John Allen wondered what other security measures Charlie Munro had installed in this place. External cameras were a certainty, but Allen had failed to spot them. Knowing Charlie however, the cameras would be there, hidden but there. The house itself was an anomaly. From the outside, it looked like it was abandoned. Inside, it was as if somebody's grandmother lived there, the only thing missing were china wall ducks. The place hadn't been modified internally in its history, except for the recent security and lighting measures taken by Charlie and his henchmen. But that was how it was meant to be. It was to look unobtrusive. Charlie would have said: 'Crap on the outside, livable on the inside.'

Allen reflected. Stan had said the previous day that they would be leaving for Rupertsvale in the next few days. That meant tomorrow might be the final preparation day. There wouldn't be much for the men to do. Stan and perhaps one other would see to it that the vehicles and the small boat were ready to go. The caravan park would be contacted using his habitual false name (under which the caravan was being rented) to let them know that the holiday-makers were soon on their way. Then there was the question of firearms. Which to take? Allen himself hadn't much experience with them, even in his private civilian life. Stan had hinted that some 'shooters' would be going along but a few of the guys had wondered why.

Finally, was the men's own personal kit. John Allen finally went off to sleep thinking about that. He intended to keep this part as simple as possible. If Lake Eildon lived up to its reputation as a holiday recreation area, then he might consider going there again. Who knows; he may even buy a cabin or a caravan there. After this final part of the job was over.

He was awoken out of a deep sleep sometime later by the light in the room being switched on. He lifted his head off the pillow and realised that the light source wasn't the main light fitting but the box on the wall. The two side strip lights shone brightly, bathing the entire room in white light. Allen noticed that the small red light on the front panel of the box was extinguished now. Allen mused that there must have been a power failure.

He climbed out of bed and walked softly to the door. Opening it a crack, he peered out into the hallway. This area was also illuminated in the same white light. Somewhere he heard a door close softly. Not seeing anybody out there, Allen opened the door and strode out of the room, turning towards the living room and kitchen. He almost collided with Stan Reed who had been in the kitchen. Reed spoke first: 'I've just been outside, you know, having a look around. Appears that the whole area is out. Full blackout too.'

Allen knew what his friend meant by 'full blackout'. He had wired a few houses in his time and realised that all three phases were out. He also understood that Reed was just being cautious. 'Car's probably hit a pole,' Reed said. 'Well, at least these work' Allen said, indicating the small grey box on the kitchen wall. 'That they do. Charlie had them installed about a month before he died. Said it was in case anyone cut power to the house, we'd still have light.'

Satisfied that all was well, the two men went back to bed.

Allen was about to get back into his bed, when he noticed that Hayne had not stirred, despite the room still bathed in light. That light would prevent him getting back to sleep, so he draped a T-shirt over the emergency light unit, reducing the bright shine to a dull glow. Satisfied, he crawled into his bed once more. This time he was asleep in no time.

It was bright sunlight that awoke John Allen the next morning. He didn't get up immediately but lay in bed listening to the sounds of the neighbourhood as it greeted the new day. His roommate was up, however, so Allen reached to the bedside table for his wristwatch. He studied the digital display. Nine-thirty. He heard sounds coming from the kitchen, so with thoughts of a hot cup of coffee in mind, he roused himself and grabbing a dressing gown, made his way there.

Dennis Hayne was enjoying a cup of coffee at the table, an empty plate with knife and fork, pushed away in front of him. Les Truscott stood at the stove frying eggs and bacon. He turned when he heard Allen enter the kitchen. 'John, how about some breakfast?'

Allen accepted and sat down at the table with Hayne, who was flicking through a day-old newspaper. 'Stan's just gone out to get the papers,' Hayne said helpfully, figuring Allen was about to ask. Allen accepted a cup of coffee from Les and gazed idly out the window, then turned to address Hayne: 'You slept through the blackout last night, Dennis. Missed all the excitement.'

'Les told me all about it, whole area was out. Those bloody little light boxes on the walls woke everyone up. Except me, that is. Big Charles says that they're necessary.' He had removed some advertising literature from the newspaper and jabbed a finger onto an open page. He said: 'I'm gonna get one of them soon,' to nobody in particular.

Somewhere at the back of the house, a door opened, and footsteps were heard in the hall. Presently, Bob Pitman put his head around the kitchen door. 'I thought I could smell something good,' he said joining Dennis and John at the table. 'Maître d', I'll have black pudding, eggs and bacon. '

'Don't serve riffraff here,' Truscott replied without turning around. He was putting the finishing touches to John's breakfast. He served it and spoke to Bob: 'May I take your order now, Sir.'

'I'll have one of your specials, with tomato sauce.' Turning to Hayne, he continued: 'What have you found yourself there, Dennis?'

'A pressure washer.' Hayne showed him the picture of a shiny new machine. 'Petrol model. Great for cleaning out my garage.'

'Cell, more like,' Allen thought. Changing tack, he asked Bob: 'Today's the big day. Who is checking to see if the cars and the boat are ready?'

'Frank has been allotted that task. Stan is going to touch base with the caravan park himself, so they'll recognise his voice. The only other thing to do is organise someone to stay here while we're away.'

'Where *is* Frank?' enquired Allen, between mouthfuls of his breakfast.

'Out for his morning walk,' Les answered, scooping bacon and eggs onto a plate. 'He'll be in soon. I'd better get some of this going for him.' Les handed Pitman his breakfast and immediately began to make a fresh round for himself and the absent Frank. 'I wouldn't go for a walk any time of the day around here unless I had a mean dog in one hand and a .45 in the other.'

When Les had his own breakfast on a plate, he sat down at the table and consumed it while chatting to the other men. A disturbance at the front door indicated the arrival of Frank Taylor, who walked briskly into the kitchen, rubbing his hands together. 'Hope there's some of that for me, Leslie,' he announced in a cheerful voice.

Without looking up, Les indicated a plate with a cover on it. 'All yours, just the way you like it.' Frank took the cover off the plate and savoured the delicious aroma before walking around the table to a vacant chair next to John Allen. 'You look like you're enjoying that, John.' Allen nodded in agreement but continued eating. The five men worked on their breakfast or drank coffee without further small talk. Stan was still to appear with the newspapers and would probably start issuing orders as soon as he got in.

Stan appeared in due course carrying two folded newspapers and a plastic bag with some grocery items in it. He deposited the bag on the kitchen counter and placed the papers on the table. 'I would like to get started as soon as possible this morning,' he announced to the five men and glancing at his watch. 'Quarter after ten. I'll allot some tasks for everyone now. The sooner we get them done, the sooner we can relax. There's not much to do, so here's the list. Bob, do the clean-up inside. Frank, ring the yard and check if the two cars and the tinny are ready. Even if they say yes, I suggest you take one of the cars here and go over there and have a quick gander. Les and John, get the toys out and give 'em the once-over. We've got plenty of ammo but were only taking a small amount. Dennis, ring Roger and confirm tomorrow. Tell him that there's enough food here for the week. I'll ring Rupertsvale Caravan Park and confirm our booking. Then I'll get stuck into the lawn and just tidy up outside. And I think that's that.'

One by one, the men picked up their empty plates and cups and got up from the table and deposited them at the side of the sink. They went about their various tasks in an unhurried manner. Allen had to get a list of firearms that would accompany the men and the keys to the gun locker from Stan and having procured them, went with Les to the front bedroom and over to the wardrobe, inside which was the gun safe. Allen unlocked the heavy door and the smaller ammunition compartment as well.

Les sat on the single bed closest to the wardrobe. 'Pass 'em out Johnny and we'll see what we've got.' The first weapon Allen grabbed in the near darkness was a pump shotgun. He passed it to Truscott, who took the weapon in hand and worked the action and studied the breech. Satisfied, he placed the shotgun on the bed. Allen, meanwhile, had found the light, a small LED unit inside the safe itself. Now able to see properly, he picked guns at random and toyed with them before handing them to Truscott. The next to come out was a .45 pistol and then a .357 Magnum revolver. Another shotgun, an automatic this time, then a military rifle. John Allen could hear the actions being worked by Les and the sound of each weapon being dumped on the bed.

Somewhere, the sound of a lawn mower carried through the partly open window, and presently, the smell of damp cut grass and two-stroke fuel. A car being started told the men in the room that Frank was on his way to the industrial yard a few kilometres away to properly check on the Mazda van and the Commodore utility that were the modes of transport to Rupertsvale.

Les and John finished checking the firearms and Allen placed them back in the safe, switched off the light and swung the steel door back until it clanged shut. Locking it and pocketing the key, the men left the room and returned to the kitchen. From the back of the house, the sound of a vacuum cleaner could be heard. Spying the breakfast dishes and pans, Les said: 'Let's get these cleaned up and give Bobby a hand.'

The two men cleaned up the kitchen and John Allen made a round of coffee for everyone. The screaming throttle of a weed trimmer could now be heard from outside. Allen took his own mug plus a mug for Stan Reed outside, while Les distributed the two remaining mugs to Bob and Dennis. Stan finished the trimming and switched off the machine. 'Well, that does it. We go inside now and put our feet up and wait for Frank.'

John Allen and Stan Reed put the gardening equipment away in the small tool-shed and returned to the house. Everyone gathered in the lounge room and settled into chairs and sofas. Dennis Hayne switched the television on and Les got a round of drinks going. Bob rearranged some of the furniture and set up the card table. The sound of an approaching vehicle heralded the arrival of Frank Taylor. His footsteps were heard a few minutes later traipsing in through the front door. He stood in the door to the lounge holding an enormous carton of grog. 'Just got some refreshments,' he said unnecessarily.

'Whack 'em in the Westinghouse,' Bob suggested helpfully.

Stan said: 'Frankie, what's the situation with the jalopies?'

'There's a Mazda E2200 and a Holden Commodore double cab ute. Plenty of room there for all of us. I gave 'em the once-over and they're fine. Full of fuel too.

'Good,' Reed said. 'Very good. Okay, listen up. We leave tomorrow. For the rest of today, pack anything you're not using and just relax. But I want everyone ready to go at about nine tomorrow.'

Frank Taylor marched through to the kitchen and began depositing the cans he bought in to anything that had room in it, including the thermoelectric fridge and some coolers. Then he went back out to the lounge room armed with several cans of beer. 'Who wants one of these?'

'What brand are they?' asked Hayne.

'I got Victoria Bitter for the masses and Carlsberg for Johnnie.'

'That's very decent of you, Frank,' Allen replied.

The men settled into a relaxed routine, playing cards, watching television and enjoying a beer or two. Only Stan made a few phone calls throughout the rest of the day but otherwise was as composed as the others. The men had dinner in the lounge room and by nine-thirty they had retired for the night. This time, John Allen slept like a top.

For a wake-up alarm the next morning, the men were treated to 'Jackie Wilson Said' playing very loudly on a portable radio in the kitchen, with Bob Pitman singing along. He was generally forgiven when the men discovered he also had breakfast well underway. The men ate hungrily and made small talk about the day ahead. Those who finished early went off to their rooms to pack the last of their gear. Bob and Les cleaned up in the kitchen. At nine o'clock, Stan Reed made the announcement that they'd better make tracks.

Each man carried his own bag out to one of the cars in the driveway before returning to the house for coolers, portable fridges and the firearms. These had been packed together in a box that once contained an imitation Christmas tree. Stan had been assured by the proprietors of the Rupertsvale Caravan Park that they need bring only the basics. By nine-thirty, they were done, and Bob locked up the house. He gave the keys to Stan and climbed into the rearmost car with Les and John. John, behind the wheel, reversed out and started off for the industrial estate where the vehicles that would take them on their journey, awaited.

The second car, a non-descript Toyota Crown, followed a discreet distance behind. Les gave some directions to John but beyond that there was no idle talk. The cars made the short journey through sparse traffic and arrived at the yard by ten minutes to ten. Stan leaped out of the Ford and tapped on the window of the Crown. He directed that the vehicles be parked beside a portable building visible now on the right side if the yard. Once parked, the men clambered out of their respective cars and five of the six stood in a group near the portable building. Stan dashed into the demountable and reappeared with two sets of car keys.

'The cars are over there,' he announced to the group. 'Dennis, you take the Mazda, I'll drive the dunny door. My vehicle will also tow the tinny. No other reason than I think it looks more normal that way. Both vehicles have been given the once-over. They're mechanically perfect. You all know the way to the town so we won't need to play follow the leader'

The men looked in the direction Reed had pointed. Almost hidden behind a large trailer loaded high with wooden pallets, were the van and the utility. 'Okay, let's load up and go. There'll be two in the van and four in the ute. Most, if not all the gear can go in the van.'

Making the transfer between vehicles took minutes. Stan made sure the Ford and the Toyota were locked and took the keys into the demountable. Re appearing, he said, 'Let's go,' and climbed behind the wheel of the Holden. He checked to see that he had all his passengers and eased the car with the trailer behind, out of the yard. Hayne, in the Mazda van slid the automatic gearshift into 'D' and made for the big double gates. He had to wait for some trucks on the street but was soon clear to drive out onto the road and in the direction of Rupertsvale and hopefully twenty million dollars.

CHAPTER 10

The Commodore utility containing Frank Taylor, Bob Pitman and Stan Reed rolled easily into Rupertsvale at a little after one in the afternoon. The tinny on the small trailer had behaved itself on the journey from Melbourne and the men were in a relaxed mood. Pitman drove at or below any speed limits they encountered, anxious to avoid any needless contact with hayseed cops along the way. Rupertsvale presented itself the way most small towns do - the odd small farmhouse here and there, then more prosperous places until they were in the town itself.

There was the usual assortment of country town establishments; a bait and tackle shop, a bakery, a farm supply business and a faux 1920's bank, which Bob thought looked rather tacky. He thought that the buildings were in surprisingly good condition, but then he remembered that this was the *new* town, the old town being not far from here. But *where*, he mused. He was jolted out of his daydream by Stan, who said simply, 'This is the place.'

The car had almost passed through the town. The road bent sharply to the right and continued into the hills. Straight ahead in front of the car the road became a wide gravel driveway and passed between large while latticed gate posts. A sign mounted on a timber frame over the drive announced 'Rupertsvale Holiday Village'. The car crunched on the gravel as it passed through the gateway and down the drive between tall eucalypt trees which provided welcome respite from the noon heat.

The main office was located to the left side of the driveway, in a neat log cabin building. Bob stopped directly outside. Stan alighted and strolled up the front steps and disappeared through the front door. Bob killed the engine and stepped out of the car. He was joined by Frank Taylor and the two men stood near the car, enjoying the fresh air. Stan appeared from the office armed with keys and beckoned to them.

The trio drove slowly through the caravan park watching families set up camp and mothers try unsuccessfully to control yelling children. The drive meandered around trailers of every size and description and made its way along the lake front. The lake stretched away to the west, dotted with small craft towing skiers or fishing. Stan pointed out the jetty, saying that the launching ramp was on the other side, out of view. Bob manoeuvred the car so the trailer could be reversed down the ramp. He backed down the ramp until the tinny was part submerged, then stopped. The men alighted, helping to unstrap the boat and push it into the water. Frank tied it to a mooring bollard on the jetty and the men climbed back into the car. Frank was cautious, 'She be alright there?'

'Safe as houses,' replied Stan.

Turning away from the water now, the car made its

way between caravans and a small park with swings. Stan soon indicated a site containing a large Millard caravan complete with annexe. Bob pulled up off the drive onto the grass verge in front of the caravan. Frank was out first and began unloading the bags and sleeping gear. Bob pocketed the car keys and grabbed the two coolers. Stan called for a volunteer to assist with the box with the firearms. He and Frank made their way casually into the annexe with the Christmas tree box.

The annexe was spacious, the front half furnished with comfortable-looking sofas and occasional chairs, the rear with sturdy looking camp beds. Bob placed the coolers against the canvas wall and flopped into an easy chair. Stan unlocked the caravan itself and stepped up inside. The interior was cooler than he expected, owing to curtains being drawn, but dark. He quickly found the light switch and flipped it on. The interior was bathed in bright white light, clearly the result of the lighting upgrade the park owner had mentioned. He walked into the kitchen area and opened the fridge, making sure it was stocked as he had requested. Satisfied, he began opening the curtains to let natural light in. Peering out, he saw the Mazda van pull up outside. Dennis Hayne climbed out the driver's door and, beer can in hand, strolled into the annexe.

Stan exited the caravan and did a quick recon of the outside. The van to the right side, next to the annexe, was unoccupied now, he knew. Over the other side, the lot was occupied by a large modern mobile home trailer. Stan walked casually around the circumference of his gang's van and pretended to study the plumbing connections, while trying to get a glimpse of the occupiers of the big trailer. Whoever they were, they were neat. What *was* visible was in its place. There was even a neatly kept garden. Stan was no detective, but these small points told him that whoever they were, they must be either permanent residents or come here very often. He guessed that they would be grey nomads.

Stan finished his examination of the surrounds and began to help John and Les with the supplies. He checked his watch. 'Time for a drink before dinner. Les, what have you got planned…for dinner, that is?

'Rack of Lamb with roast vegies. How does that grab you?

'Let's skip the drinks and have dinner now', suggested John Allen, but changed his tune when a can of Carlsberg was thrust into his hand. Presently, Frank Taylor entered the annexe with the bags and began to distribute them among the beds. 'Luggage has been delivered. Don't blame the porter if you don't like your roommate'.

The television set was turned on and soon four of the group could be found relaxing on the comfortable furniture. Les and John were in the kitchen of the caravan, preparing the dinner Les had promised. John enjoyed being in an environment where he could show off his culinary skills but was nonetheless surprised those displayed by Les Truscott. The man seemed to have a natural love of food which went down okay with John Allen.

Les put the roast in a slow oven, while John finished

preparing the condiments. The two men then joined their comrades in the annexe. The group of diehard gamblers spent the next few hours watching a race meeting at Warwick Farm.

As the sun set behind the hills and bathed the holiday park in an orange light, Les checked his watch and decided it was time to check the roast. Stepping up into the caravan, he was overwhelmed by the delicious aroma of roast lamb. After removing the meat from the oven and slicing it with a carving knife to confirm that it was ready, he was joined by John Allen. The two men prepared plates and set the dinette table

'Tell the hounds it's ready, John,' Les said, adding gravy to one of the plates. Allen poked his head through the door into the annexe and said above the din of the television: 'Grub's up.' The four men suddenly forgot the horses, stubbed out cigarettes, and headed for the door into the caravan. Dennis Hayne went via the fridge and grabbed a six-pack of Carlsberg.

Hayne was the last to sit down at the U-shaped dinette and plonked the beers down in the middle of the table. 'There's one each,' he muttered unnecessarily, wrenching one out of the pack for himself. John Allen thought 'I wonder where he learned to count'. The six men tucked in and soon talk was forgotten as the meal was consumed hungrily. The men even displayed reasonably good manners except Dennis Hayne, who might as well have used a bucket wheel dredge to get the food off his plate.

'Hungry, Dennis?' Bob Pitman enquired.

Hayne grunted something unintelligible and continued eating. Les looked around the table and smiled. Like all chefs, he was pleased that his cooking was appreciated. The men ate on in silence. The headlights of a passing car danced on the walls. Presently, Stan, who had finished first, got up and strolled into the kitchen. He deposited his empty plate in the sink, turned and spoke to the gathering. 'I have a small announcement to make.'

Stan Reed stood in the kitchen and tapped his beer bottle with a fork he picked up from the cutlery strainer. The murmur of voices around the table died down. He cleared his throat. 'I'm going to talk about the schedule for the next week. Most of it will consist of keeping out of mischief. However, there are two important missions to go on. The first is to verify that the loot is where it was six months ago. The second will be, obviously, to retrieve it. The reason I want it done in two stages is so we can set things up to give an appearance of normality.'

Allen thought, that would be Big Charlie's idea.

Reed went on, 'I've decided that two of us will go up to the location and check the loot. Then at the right time, we will use the tinny to collect it. Somebody will be back at base camp to keep up appearances. The day after tomorrow, Wednesday 19 December, Dennis and I will check the loot. Now I will tell you where it is.

If Reed didn't have everyone's attention before, he did now. There was a stony silence around the table. Reed spoke slowly 'The hiding place for the last six years is a disused motel about two and a half miles from here. Up in the hills, so it will be a bit of a hike. The loot is in one of the rooms. In the bathroom. Under the bath to be exact. When I was there last, I placed everything back normally. I also checked around the buildings for signs of anyone having been there, like tramps or urban explorers, but found nothing. The place has been cut off by road and it would seem all but completely forgotten about.'

Stan took a pull of his beer and continued. 'So, it should be a simple matter to collect the stuff and take it down to the tinny. This will involve five of us, although I would still like to have two here. The loot will be hidden in the boat under fishing nets and tarps. Remember, we're *not* going straight back to the jetty. We will be using John's idea and taking the loot over to the launching ramp and doing the transfer to the vehicle there. I think we'll use the Mazda for that. So, once the money is in the boat, the boat heads over to the launching ramp, the rest of us get back to the caravan park and two head of in the van to meet the tinny.'

Frank Taylor spoke: 'What about leaving someone back at base?'

Reed said: 'I've thought of that. We'll leave the telly on, and I've got a recording of you guys taken at the house in Dandenong. I'll play that loudly and it will sound like there's still a few of us here. When the Mazda gets back, we produce a couple of slabs as if we've just bought them in Eildon. The boaters should be back by then with the coolers, which will be empty.

'What then? enquired Les.

'Simple. We get pissed. Who's for a game of cards?

Frank Taylor and Dennis Hayne collected the plates and cutlery and cleared everything off the table not related to cards. Bob Pitman produced an ashtray and placed it in the center of the table. John Allen raided the fridge for more Carlsberg and soon the first hand was underway. The men chatted as the sorted through their cards, pausing only to watch the reactions of the other card players.

John Allen thought Dennis Hayne wasn't the most intelligent character God ever shovelled guts into, but boy could he play cards. They played several rounds, with Hayne winning small amounts. He seemed to have no reactions for the other players to read. Almost. Allen was an observant man. He would bet his share of the money that on the current game, Hayne had at best a mediocre hand. Hayne was acting otherwise. Allen had a full house, with high-ranking cards to boot. He doubted whether Dennis Hayne had a low pair, so he decided to play him at his own game and acted as if he had no cards of any value. The stakes went up until John Allen and Dennis Hayne were the only two left in the game. Hayne's façade was crumbling, and Allen moved in for the kill, calling Dennis's bluff and winning four hundred and fifty dollars.

The card game went on and the stakes got higher. It seemed that everyone had at least one win, with John Allen the clear leader, much to Dennis Hayne's annoyance. The men only paused playing for beer or coffee. Stan got up to open windows and the ceiling vent and kept the door to the annexe open to ventilate the cigarette smoke.

Allen was getting bored with the card game, despite having won several hundred dollars. He had brought a couple of paperbacks with him and only got involved so the others wouldn't think he was a party pooper. As another hand was just about to get underway, Allen announced he was going to bow out and go for a walk. Stan stalled him as he was ducking his head to go through the door. 'Johnny, keep your meat pies open. Have a gander around the jetty and the office area.'

'What am I supposed to be looking for?'

Stan was thoughtful. 'I don't know. Maybe I'm being over cautious.'

'That's understandable. Wish me luck, I'll write.' With that, John Allen departed on his evening walk. He intended to be out for at least an hour. He was getting tired, even at this early stage, of the constant 'crim' talk. It was as if the other men didn't have lives outside low level crime, yet he knew most of them did. Stan had said to check the jetty. Well, he would do just that. He decided to make the jetty the first stop on his stroll.

He stepped out into the cool embrace of the night air and pretended to adjust one of the fishing rods that had been placed in a small temporary rack at the side of the site, and apparently satisfied, strolled along the narrow tarmacadam road past the modern house trailer, which now seemed to be occupied. In the gloom, John realised that there was a woman standing in the front garden, tending to some roses.

He bade a cheerful 'evening' and walked on. Allen wondered if Stan was aware the big trailer was now inhabited. He decided to call and let him know. Rounding a corner, where the path became fine gravel, and out of sight, he produced his cell phone and dialled Stan.

Stan came on the line, answering with a false name, which he did if within earshot of anyone he didn't trust. Allen reflected that it was probably the same name he used to hire the caravan. He assumed Stan was now outside, probably enjoying a quiet cigarette. Allen explained that the next-door caravan now had people in it. Stan responded in the affirmative about some fishing tackle to disguise his meaning and hung up. Allen reflected that he'd done his first task for the night. That should keep 'em quiet.

He strolled along the narrow road, leather-soled shoes scuffing the gravel, taking in large lungful's of the cool air, more relieved now that he got away from the cigarette smoke and mindless drivel of the card table. Around a bend in the road and between some caravans, Allen caught a glimpse of the lake, glistening in the moonlight. As he got closer to the jetty, voices rose up from the water, boaters who had been out on the lake, now making their boats fast to the pier and stowing their fishing gear.

Allen kept out of the bright moonlight and observed the goings-on at the jetty from a dark corner of the park, next to a maintenance shed. It occurred to him that it would be about this time of night that they would be returning from their expedition. Stan would be interested to find out just who was about at this time. Sitting there in the shadows, Allen half-wished he still smoked. It would look more 'normal' to sit there, having a quiet cigarette. He checked his watch. Ten-thirty. He watched the boaters for a few more minutes. Then he stiffly stood up and continued his nightly stroll along the waterfront path in the direction of the main office.

Crunching the fine white gravel underfoot as he approached the log cabin that served as an office and reception, Allen observed nothing unusual in the area. He stopped for a breather, out of the glare of a floodlight that illuminated the forecourt area. Only one person seemed to be out and about, an older man making a call at one of the two public phones. The line must have been poor, for the man's voice was raised and Allen could hear parts of the conversation from where he stood. The man was talking about his neighbours in the caravan park, thought he recognised one of them.

Soon enough, the man rang off and exited the booth. Making his way along the road, John Allen followed; glad now that he was on tarmacadam instead of noisy gravel. A small alarm was ringing in his head. The man had been making enquiries about other campers, from a call box and late at night. It just didn't sit well with him. He was about to get one more surprise. Allen trailed the man down a familiar road, past vans and playgrounds he had seen on his way in that afternoon. Their caravan loomed up on the right side ahead. Allen dropped back further and in the glare of one of the LED streetlights, was able to see which van the man entered.

'Well bugger me,' Allen muttered. He glanced around and seeing nobody about, he rang Stan, who answered with his own name. John Allen described briefly what he had seen. Stan, who must have been in the caravan or the annexe by now, gave a couple of clipped commands and rang off. Allen retraced his steps until he came to a side road. He turned left, walking briskly now. He knew that this narrow road, winding between caravans of various sizes, would eventually bring him out behind the gang's trailer. He also remembered that the van behind them was not occupied. He reached the empty trailer and stole down beside it, keeping the modern mobile home trailer in view.

The lights were out in the big caravan except for some blue night lights and Allen could barely see the man he had seen at the phone booth walking towards one end. A light came on briefly, in what Allen assumed was the bedroom. Without any surveillance devices with them, Stan wanted him to get as close as he could and try to pick up snippets of conversation. Allen had seen no evidence of dogs in or around the big trailer, so he moved in as close as he dared. He was at the back wall of the mobile home now, protected by some low shrubs and in shadow. There was a window three feet above his head and it was at this that he listened intently.

The only voices he could hear were muffled and after a few more minutes, he gave up. Keeping low, he retraced his steps to the unoccupied van and made his way to the annexe of the gang's caravan. He could hear Stan in the caravan just about to clean up after a winning hand. Allen entered and made for the kitchen, where he made himself a cup of coffee. He strolled over to the U-shaped dinette where the card game was winding down.

'So, someone's interested in us,' said Stan. 'Well, it proves we were right about one thing. Your idea, Johnny. In the meantime, we play it extra cool. More emphasis on fishing and just relaxing. To keep up the pretence is going to be tough but very important. On Wednesday or Thursday, I'll give detailed instructions on the getting of the money. Until then, we just chill out.'

As he got into his camp cot later that night, John Allen reflected that under normal circumstances, Stan would have Dennis Hayne go and deal with anyone who was showing too much interest in the group. But now that would be a complication that the group didn't need. He fell asleep dreaming about rods, lures, and, above all, catching a rainbow trout the size of a marlin.

CHAPTER 11

Later, while the delicious feast was being consumed and washed down by bottles of Carlsberg, a car drew up outside the mobile home next door. In the dying glow of the evening sun, one of the occupants, a man, muttered something about the new neighbours to the passenger and unlocked the door to the trailer. His hand swept up and found the switch panel that controlled the lights, pressing one. The modern spacious interior yawned back at him as he stood aside to allow the other person to enter the trailer.

Raymond White's large frame moved quickly around the trailer that was almost his and his wife's permanent home. Even his six-foot two-inch tower was accommodated by the generous ceilings. His wife, on the other hand, was the opposite. Petite in every way, Beatrice's friends often said what an odd couple they made. But they knew better.

Ray was only half listening to his wife talking about the day trip they'd just returned from. In addition to fiddling with the mobile phone that refused to obtain a signal, something was bugging the former Detective Chief Inspector. He was trying to establish *when* the sensor in his brain had gone into overdrive. It wasn't on the outing itself, so it must have been since they arrived at the caravan park.

Beatrice pottered about in the kitchen, making coffee for them both. She recognised the signs of tension and alertness that she knew so well. Ray had sensed something, and it would be a while before he would translate it into 'normal speak' and explain it to his wife. Beatrice knew better than to question her husband's instinct. It had been the stuff of legend in the force, often outguessing even more qualified colleagues. She made two steaming mugs of coffee, set them both down on the living area's side table, and rummaged through a stack of glossy magazines, even though she had read them all.

Ray knew the missing fragment would appear in its own time, and there was no point trying to force it. He sat in one of the deep padded chairs and picked up one of the steaming mugs. They chatted for a time, mainly small talk, with Ray's filing cabinet brain working in the background.

Ray had seen tenants come and go in the van next door, everyone there for the fishing or hiking in the hills north of the lake. But this lot seemed different. While other groups had talked incessantly about whatever activity had brought them to this quiet holiday park, the men next door hardly seemed to speak outside the van or annexe. In previous years, he and Beatrice even had neighbours come to *their* door, asking about the fishing or the lake.

Later, as Beatrice got ready for bed and Ray brushed his teeth, she said: 'They can't be all bad. They've got a

Christmas tree with them, though I must say they were being cautious with it. They had two men carrying it in its box'.

For Ray, that was the clincher. He thought he had recognised one of the men, but where from had yet to materialise in his brain. Now, his wife, who was as observant as himself, had noticed something odd. An old saying came to mind from his favourite James Bond 007 book, *Goldfinger*: *First time happenstance, second time coincidence, third time enemy action*. From now on, he would watch the neighbours closely and make a few enquiries with his many contacts in the force.

He had a sudden brainwave. He wasn't sleepy yet anyway, and not wanting to try his mobile again, he donned a tracksuit and joggers, slipped out the front door, and walked down the road to the log cabin. On his way past the caravan next door, he could hear the television and the occasional chink of bottles being thrown in the trash.

The reception area was deserted except for a cat, which darted in front of Ray and disappeared behind the building. The public phone booths were empty; he stepped into one and dialled a number in Melbourne.

On his return, the former detective wasn't aware that his every move was being watched. He crossed the patch of front lawn, noting it was wet now. He removed the joggers and let himself in by the front door. He stole along to the bedroom, his fingers playing a drumming sound on the convector heater in the hallway. Beatrice was engrossed in a thick hardback and did not notice his return.

'Just nipped out to get The Slipper on the blower. Shocking line. I had to yell almost. He couldn't help me, as it turns out. I wondered if I would sneak some pictures and send them to him. Said I'd try over the next few days.'

'I couldn't sleep either. One of our neighbours walked past as I was watering the roses out front. He seemed quite pleasant. Rather handsome, too.'

'Don't get any ideas, Beatrice,' Ray said gruffly. Beatrice ignored this and returned to her Michael Creighton novel. Ray settled into bed and dozed off, thinking that maybe it wouldn't be so quiet this summer.

CHAPTER 12

Les Truscott awoke early on the third day, surprisingly refreshed after the late-night fishing expedition. Going out on the lake in two shifts, the gang caught eight massive Murray cod. Stan had told them the night before that today was to be an easy day. This meant all six men would be scaling and filleting the fish caught the previous night. He strode into the kitchen and put the kettle on.

Les heard someone muttering in the annexe, and moments later, an early morning cigarette was lit. He didn't need to head out the door and ask who was having coffee. While the kettle boiled, Les got six mugs from the draining board and put coffee and sugar into each one. He decided it was time to get breakfast going and rustled about for pans and ingredients.

Bob Pitman was the first customer of the day. He stepped into the caravan, a bundle of folded newspapers under one arm and greeted Les in his usual cheerful manner. 'Mornin' Les. I've just been down to get these,' he said, patting the papers with his free hand. He strode to the window, parted the Venetian blinds and peered out. 'Going to be another scorcher.'

'Anything in the papers?' Les asked, stirring a mug and ignoring the weather prediction.

Bob sat down at the U-shaped dinette and, placing two of the papers on the table, consulted the third. 'Bob Hawke's not to well. Surprise, surprise. Morrison's at a summit of some kind. The usual.'

Les reflected. 'Yeah, the usual, all right. No surprises about Hawke. Bloody bottle-baby. If he hadn't pickled his brains with booze in his younger years, he wouldn't be in the current predicament.'

A voice came from the door. 'Somebody speaking ill of my mate Bobby Hawke?'

The men turned to see John Allen poke his head through the doorway.

'Les was just giving some belated health advice for our former Prime Minister. How are you this morning, John?'

'Fighting Fit, Bobby. Does anyone know what's on the cards today besides scaling fish?'

'Stan is going to lay out the plan for retrieving the loot. Then we all play a gigantic waiting game. That's going to be the hardest part.'

The kettle boiled, and Les made three mugs of coffee. He distributed them to each man and then started getting breakfast proper going. Minutes later, the aroma of frying eggs and bacon wafted out into the annexe. The three remaining occupants decided it was time to greet the new day, aroused themselves from their slumber, and made their way into the caravan. Les made coffee for the late risers. After exchanging pleasantries, five men sat at the dinette chatting and looking through the newspapers.

John Allen took a bag of garbage out to the bin. Casually glancing around, he saw nobody about in the vicinity of the van. He wandered back inside and joined the others.

Stan cleared his throat and glanced at a notepad in his hand. 'Okay, I'll be brief. There's not much to say, but what there is is important. It suffices to say that having a wait period before grabbing the money was Charlie's idea. He was fond of his 'wait and be sure time'. So, here's how we'll do it. On the big day, the thirtieth of this month, one stays here and keeps the fort. One takes the Mazda over to the launching ramp and waits. One goes out in the tinny to that nameless bay. He moors just outside the inlet and wets a line until he hears the radio message or sees a colour light signal. Then he moves into the bay.

Meanwhile, the remaining three hike up to the abandoned motel. They retrieve the cash and take it down to the lake. We load it onto the boat, and two accompany it over to the launching ramp where the van is waiting. When or if the coast is clear, the money is transferred, and the Mazda gets driven back here, where we make a big thing of unloading the slabs of beer purportedly purchased on that trip.'

Stan took a long drink from his mug and continued. 'That is *what* we are all doing in a nutshell. It will be a matter of timing. The Mazda should leave early to drive into town, pick up some slabs from the bottle shop, and then make its way to the launching ramp. Later, the rest of us do our parts in the big scheme. No undue attention should come our way if we act like normal blokes and do it like Charlie said.'

'So we're only using one car on this part of the job?,' Frank Taylor enquired.

'Yes, Frank. There is no point using two when one will do. Anyway, the van will be better for the job, loading bags of money and slabs of beer.'

Stan went on, 'Getting the loot from the motel to the boat will require the use of the GPS unit that Mr Allen has. We sure don't want to get lost with all that dough. It might be embarrassing asking directions with bags of money in our possession.'

A snicker went around the table as each man imagined being caught in such a predicament. Les collected empty mugs and carried them to the kitchen. He filled the kettle and pressed the switch. Stan resumed, 'With the money back here, and we continue our holiday for a day or so, then pack up and head home. The main distribution will be done at Dandenong. The place is being watched and kept looking as normal as possible for our arrival. I think the Mazda should leave first, possibly early in the morning, and the Commodore can go later.

I think that wraps up this end of things. If anyone's got anything to add, let's hear it so we can adjust the big plan.'

'Have you decided who is doing what on the day?' asked Dennis Hayne, accepting Les's fresh mug of coffee.

'Yes, Dennis, I have. And it's final. I don't want any

bitching. I have a typed list, which I will show all of you tonight. I want you to memorise it because I will burn it.'

John Allen said, 'In Dandenong, you mentioned something about checking on the loot before collecting it.' '

'I did, and we will. The day before. It's approximately a two-hour walk to the motel. There happens to be a reasonably good path most of the way, part of a hiking trail. The actual track to the motel itself branches off this. I doubt if two and a dog have been down this second track in the last twenty years. The only other thing left to say is to relax for the next week and keep things cool.'

'That settles it then,' said Bob Pitman. 'Let's scale some fish.'

CHAPTER 13

Daniel awoke somewhat hungover on Boxing Day. There was too much Christmas cheer the day before. The thought of spending a week or more on something that moved was not appealing. He was relieved that none of the other rafters had been able to stay overnight; they all had family Christmas commitments. Now treading softly through the house to not wake anyone, he stole out to the workshop.

Daniel climbed onto the raft deck and sat near the edge with his feet dangling. He was relieved that the flotation test was over and the raft was complete. He checked his watch. Ten minutes past eight. What time had he told the others to be here? Nine. Fifty minutes to get some coffee into himself and freshen up. At least he felt vaguely human to greet his friends. He slipped off the deck and strode into the house.

After making a pit stop in the bathroom, where he used a strong mouthwash and swallowed two Eno tablets, he went to the kitchen and put the kettle on. He rustled up a quick breakfast and read the itinerary for the day, even though he knew it by heart. It was a list of the things that needed to be assembled before setting off for the lake. The thermoelectric fridge was in the garage and running, as were the three-way fridges, but the two coolers still had to arrive. Daniel finished eating and idly wondered who would be the first to reach. He assumed it would be Jeremy, who had been the driving force behind the raft trip.

As things turned out, Harry was the first to make an appearance. Daniel heard a car hoot and drove off. Moments later, footsteps on the drive and a large bag go by the window. He got up and went to the front door and had it open before Harry could ring the doorbell. 'There's a cooler on the front lawn, Dan,' Harry panted as Daniel helped his friend off with the pack. The two boys took the pack and the sleeping roll outside and placed them on the patio while they fetched the cooler. Then, they carried the lot into the workshop.

Harry and Daniel had been in the workshop for a few minutes when another car pulled up in the driveway. This time, the new arrival was Jeremy. He had gear like Harry's, plus one cooler. The three boys quickly brought everything into the garage. Harry organised the coolers near the thermoelectric fridge while the other boys organised the packs. The sound of yet another car in the driveway distracted them from their tasks.

The three boys watched as Sam and his father, talking nineteen to the dozen, got out of the car and began unloading Sam's camping gear. A minute later, everything was on the deck of the raft. Daniel switched on a ghetto-blaster, and Ed Sheeran invaded the workshop. Mr Dillon was keen to go and get the bulk of the supplies, as he had other things to do that day. Sam had a list, but Harry had the master list, which he guarded like it was a secret formula. Harry and Sam compared notes. It was decided that Sam and Jeremy would go on the food run with Sam's dad while the remaining boys would pack everything into Daniel's father's car.

While Daniel and Harry were busy organising the camping equipment, Mr Graham poked his head in the door and announced that he would get the trailer on which the raft would be transported. When he had departed, Daniel said it was break time, so the boys took a breather and went inside. They made it to the kitchen and found Megan having her breakfast. Harry said good morning and chatted while Daniel produced small bottles of Powerade from the fridge.

'My brother won't offer you anything to eat, Harry, so I will. Would you like some cereal or a muffin? I'm just about to put one in the toaster.'

'No thanks, Meg, I've had breakfast,' Harry said, rubbing his tummy. Daniel made nagging sister faces to the kitchen window while procuring the drinks. However, when he turned to take the brew over to the table, he found Harry spreading margarine on half a muffin.

'Thought you'd had something to eat'.

'I was offered. I couldn't very well refuse'.

With the timely arrival of Vince Dillon, Jeremy and Sam broke up the discussion. Daniel was grateful for the distraction. He suggested that he and Harry go out and lend a hand. The two boys traipsed out to the car and, placing their mugs on the driveway, began unloading bags and boxes. Harry took a large bag into the workshop and stayed in there to do the final organising. Sam's dad said his goodbyes to the four boys and left.

The utility with the trailer attached arrived soon enough. Jeremy and Daniel were relieved that the trailer had a small hydraulic crane. Mr Graham backed the ensemble expertly down the driveway. He could back up into the workshop with the cars out of the garage. Daniel busied himself unshackling the crane and, using the remote control on a heavy cable, swung the boom out and extended it so that its hook and chain hovered over the centre of the raft's deck. The other boys tied snatch straps through the heavy-duty eyelets in each corner of the raft and attached these to the hook.

With the whine of the hydraulic pump drowning out Ed Sheeran, Daniel manipulated the crane, gently lifted the raft's deadweight off the concrete and suspended it a few feet above the floor. Jeremy studied the vessel from every conceivable angle, his computer-like brain measuring stresses and strains. Then Daniel manipulated the levers to swing the load over the trailer bed and retract the boom. Daniel lowered the raft slowly onto the trailer with one of his friends in each corner. Tie-down straps came next, and the boys soon had them firmly in place. With the raft loaded onto the trailer and tied down, it was time to pack the utility with the supplies for the trip.

Everything had been packed into boxes and plastic crates, which made loading a breeze. In no time at all, the task was complete. Megan appeared at that moment carrying a plastic Tupperware container, which she presented to Harry. 'I've made a chocolate mud cake for the trip. Should last a couple of nights.'

Harry thanked her profusely while Steve Graham and the other boys checked the heavy straps that secured the raft to the trailer and climbed into the car. Mr Graham eased the vehicle and trailer out of the driveway and down the road. Daniel rode in front for the first part of the journey because he acted as a navigator, with street directory and road maps on his lap.

'Well, this is it, boys,' Steve Graham announced as they set off for Lake Eildon. Jeremy barely heard him; he was studying the trailer and its precious cargo. His face was a mask of concern. Daniel was watching him. 'Jeremy just about has kittens whenever we hit a bump', he said with a laugh, avoiding Jeremy's glare. Jeremy had nothing to worry about. Mr Graham was an excellent driver who prioritised safety.

CHAPTER 14

The journey from Dandenong had been uneventful, and Jeremy had stopped having apoplexy soon after the car left the bypass road and joined the main freeway. The boys settled into a routine of idle chatter and studying maps and charts of Lake Eildon and the surrounding area. They only vaguely listened to Mr Graham's commentary on every place they passed.

Jeremy worried about his underwater camera and sought constant reassurance from the other boys that it would be okay. The chain holding it to the raft wasn't going to be strong enough, the data cable would fray on some submarine object, or the lights would fail and they would get no image. To shut him up, Harry thrust a hand full of laminated menu cards into his hand and told him to review them. As the car left the toll road and entered the main highway to the lake district, the teenager's mood brightened. Sam and Daniel pored over a map of the lake, looking for potential swimming spots.

Daniel's father said they would stop for a break once they'd cleared the suburbs. This occurred in Healesville, where the boys bought take away coffee in Styrofoam cups and drank them by the side of the main street. Mr Graham ducked into the Grand Hotel for a bathroom break, so the boys kept his coffee warm. After depositing the empty coffee cups in a nearby rubbish bin, Jeremy had the bright idea of breaking into the beer stocks. Sam didn't need telling twice; he had the top of the beer cooler open and ripped open a six-pack of Sainte Moritz lager almost before Jeremy had finished suggesting the idea. The boys consumed their beers in the shade of roadside trees.

Mr Graham returned to the car, accepted his coffee, and the motorcade continued northwards. Jeremy had seemingly forgotten about the raft trailing behind, concentrating instead on a magazine displaying glossy pictures of Lake Eildon. The boys travelled in virtual silence, only vaguely hearing Mr Graham announcing that the next stop, if necessary would be Taggerty, where the road to the lake branched off.

The car met little traffic on the highway and only paused briefly at the T intersection at the road into Taggerty to yield to a timber jinker heading the opposite way. No one in the car felt the need to stop in the tiny town, so the cavalcade proceeded towards Lake Eildon. The car rolled through gently sloping farmland. The boys could see cattle dotting the hillsides and the occasional tractor ploughing a field. Soon enough, the Goulburn River came into view on their left, and the boys felt their excitement build.

Mr Graham said that there were two roads leading to the launching ramp and that he was going to take the road that partly went through the town of Eildon. The car proceeded over a bridge across the Goulburn River. Harry spotted an island to his left and made mental note to take the raft over and explore it. The road began to climb now, and Mr Graham explained that the lake itself was much higher than the river, and that the power station they were now passing used water from the lake to generate electricity. When Steve Graham pointed out that there was no physical connection between the main lake and the river, Harry's plans of using the raft to explore the island would have to be realised on some future trip.

The motorcade turned onto the road that lead over the dam wall and ultimately to the launching ramp. As the car crested the top of the dam, the lake stretched out before them, leaving the boys awestruck. Harry studied the OS map of the lake and to his delight, found another island North-West of the launching ramp. He cheered up immediately and was in very high spirits when the car slid into the turning area for the boat ramp.

'Well boys, here we are', Mr Graham said with a grin. 'I'll just manoeuvre into position so we can launch the Great Eastern'. Some expert reversing later, the trailer was axle deep in the lake. The boys piled out and began unloading coolers and bags. Jeremy and Daniel unstrapped the raft. When the car was relieved of all camping gear, Mr Graham continued to back down the ramp until the raft floated free of the trailer and bobbed on the surface. Sam had the main mooring cable in hand and guided the craft to the shore. He climbed aboard and locating the two mooring poles, rammed them into the muddy bottom of the lake at each end and made the raft fast to them.

Daniel and his father unloaded the last of the smaller bags and personal items from the car, while Harry and Jeremy transferred them to the shore, where Sam loaded them onto the raft. The other boys jumped on board and distributed the supplies so that there was enough room for the crew. Mr Graham announced that he was going to head back to Melbourne and shook hands with each of the teenagers. He gave his son a hug and walked over to the car, reminding the teens to be careful out on the lake.

The car departed with the trailer clanking behind and Mr Graham waving cheerily out the window. Jeremy was already busying himself with the generator, getting it going on the second rip of the cord. Harry set up the gas cookers and positioning his coolers and thermoelectric fridge, muttering to himself about food stocks. Sam and Daniel released the mooring lines and stowed the poles. With the generator idling now, Jeremy ducked into the cabin and flipped switches on the control panel and eased the main controller to DEAD SLOW ahead. He set the rudder to hard-a-starboard and eased the craft away from the shore and out onto the lake.

After a short distance, Jeremy swung hard left and headed for the dam wall. 'We've got to check the map and find a suitable place to camp. When I was checking it at home, I found an island. It's in the opposite direction to which we want to go, but it's not too far. Also, Harry really wanted to explore an island and his hopes were somewhat dashed with that other one not actually being on the lake'.

The boys agreed that they could fit this into the schedule. The raft motored closer to the dam wall. Jeremy brought the controller back to the stop and let the vessel drift. Sam set up the small table that would serve for meals as well as an ad hoc chart table. Daniel spread out the better of the two OS maps they carried, and the teens pored over the features and symbols. Using a fishing lure as a pointer, Sam selected a cove that had been formed by a re-entrant when the lake was created. 'That might make a good camping area. I know we're self-sufficient on this boat but we do need to touch land somewhere. Also, it's not too near civilisation'.

Daniel ran his finger down a swathe in the heavily timbered hills surrounding the lake. 'What's that?' he asked. 'That' answered Jeremy, 'is where the three-phase power lines are routed down through the hills to the suburbs.' He jabbed the map with his finger. 'The high-tension lines straddle the lake here. We'll sail straight under them on the way to the cove'.

The map was given a thorough perusal, but the teens finally decided on the bay that Sam had pointed out. 'It's got everything going for it except a Starbucks and its proximity to the old town makes it ideal'.

'It's close to something else too', Daniel muttered. Using his fore finger, he drew an imaginary line from the small cove to a point on the map marked with a hollow square and the word 'Ruin'. 'That's the 'Lakeview Motel' and I think we should give it the once-over.

'Sounds good to me', Harry replied, filling the kettle from

the small sink and lighting the single burner stove. 'How about coffee, lads?'

Jeremy spoke while setting the controller to half-speed ahead. 'Okay, that's our destination. The way I figure speed and time, we should get there at about seven tonight. So now we head over to this mystery island and then make our way to the cove. We'll be staying on board tonight, so it doesn't really matter when we get to the cove'.

The boys felt the raft surge forward and realised that their trip was really beginning. The lake was flat calm with only a slight breeze. Harry poured four coffees into paper cups and added a nip of Haig whisky to each. They made a toast to the raft and the trip and proceeded out on deck, except Jeremy, who was driving. Harry sat on a storage box and sipped his coffee. Sam wasted no time and grabbed a hand fishing reel. Checking the lure, he cast into the water, allowing the lure to be trailed behind the raft. Daniel studied the area with a pair of powerful binoculars. He concentrated on some object in the distance near the shoreline and called Jeremy: 'Hey, Williams, I don't think were the only raft out here'.

Jeremy pushed the controller up to three-quarter speed, and joined Daniel, who lent him the binoculars. He scanned the surface of the lake like a destroyer captain pursuing a sub. He too focused on the mystery thing that had grabbed Daniel's attention. He snorted: 'It's a raft alright, sitting lower in the water than we are, and it seems a bit smaller'.

'Otherwise, okay? Daniel asked. 'Maybe we should take a closer look. Harry, drive for a while. Head us in the direction of the mystery vessel. We'll have a gander on the way to the island'.

Harry didn't need asking twice. He ducked inside the deckhouse and brought the rudder telemotor control around so that the raft was now heading straight for the opposite shore. They were now in the middle of the lake and Harry checked his watch. Two-thirty in the afternoon. Jeremy had probably been right with the ETA at the campsite. It would be fun to arrive after dark, though. He sipped his coffee and imagined setting up the shore camp under the glare from the twin LED floodlights.

Daniel's voice brought him out of his daydream: 'Harry, come hard left. Don't want to make it too obvious we're checking 'em out.' Harry obeyed and the raft was once more pointing to the small island. Jeremy entered the deckhouse with the binoculars and further studied the other raft.

'Not quite so obvious in here', Jeremy said with a grin. 'Nobody would ever guess', Harry remarked.

'*Belleau Wood*', muttered Jeremy. 'It's got a French name. I wonder if they're French'.

'Offer them a croissant' suggested Harry, without taking his eyes off the water ahead. Jeremy countered: 'What do you hope to find on that island? Gilligan?'

'It would just be fun to land on an uninhabited island, that's all. Add to the sense of adventure.'

Harry steered the raft towards one side of the tiny island and then swung left, bringing the starboard side of the raft around to face the shore. He powered down and steered gently until the starboard pontoon scraped the lake bottom, stirring up a cloud of mud.

'Now let's do some exploring,' Harry exclaimed. 'Dan, run out the anchor, Jeremy, ram that mooring pole into the lakebed behind the raft.'

With these tasks completed, Harry, Jeremy and Daniel removed their deck shoes and climbed into shallow water. Sam refused to join in. The three boys waded ashore and stood on the gravelly beach, inviting Sam to join them. He still said no and went to a cooler, procuring a beer. When he returned to the rail, Harry suggested Sam put a message in the bottle when he had finished the drink. Sam said he would put Harry in the bottle if he didn't shut up.

Sam decided to soak up some rays while his friends explored the island. He had dropped off to sleep when he was awakened by water splashing on his face, courtesy of Jeremy. The other boys had hoisted themselves on board and dried their legs. Jeremy suggested they weigh anchor and Harry took orders for a round of hot drinks.

With the sun setting behind the hills and the tiny island in their wake, the raft settled on a South-Easterly course across the lake. Sam was at the helm, sipping his Sainte Moritz beer. His fishing endeavours had landed a rainbow trout and a Murray cod, both of which were being carefully prepared by Harry and Jeremy. He studied the GPS unit occasionally for the latest position. His eyes scanned the lake and the shoreline.

They passed the launching ramp and sailed under the low overhanging wires of the high-tension transmission line to

Melbourne. Jeremy briefly explained the concept of three-phase power to anyone who happened to be listening.

The raft passed the Jerusalem Creek Inlet and Sam brought it onto a North-Easterly heading. He beckoned to Jeremy, 'That's our second port of call down there?'

'That's right. The Jerusalem Creek campground. Looking forward to it. At least there'll be some facilities there. '

The boys took in this last piece of advice. They knew there were no facilities where they would be spending the first two nights. Daniel took over the helm and Sam put his empty beer bottle in the bin. 'I'm going to grab some shuteye for an hour or so,' he announced. He climbed into his bunk. He vaguely heard Harry say something about dinner being ready soon, and then nodded off.

Several small craft passed them going in the opposite direction. The raft felt the bow wash as each boat nuzzled its way across the lake. Daniel couldn't help noticing they all had their navigation lights on. He studied the control console, found the right switch and flipped it down. Jeremy looked up briefly and went back to helping Harry with their dinner, pan-fried rainbow trout and a Murray cod with chips, which were now deep frying in a saucepan. 'We'll need the headlights soon,' he said to nobody, staring out into the gloom that was enveloping the raft.

'Grub's up,' announced Harry. He passed two plates over to the table and began to pile strips of cod, trout and fries onto two more plates. Sam stirred himself and slid off his bunk and squeezed in at the table. Daniel positioned his plate on his knees and ate while he steered. Harry joined Jeremy and Sam and the four ate quietly, chatting about the good quality fish in the lake.

Jeremy checked the orange dial of his Doxa watch. Seven PM. With his mouth half-full of cod, he asked Daniel about their current position.

'Just about to make the final turn,' Daniel replied and brought the wheel over to the left. Opposite the Big River Inlet, mused Jeremy.

'We'll be there in about twenty minutes,' he told the others. 'There' was a place called Robin Bay, a re-entrant in the hills surrounding the lake. It didn't have a Six Flags amusement park, but Jeremy felt it would give them a chance to stretch their legs and touch solid ground. 'We'll anchor off the shore and use the dinghy to get ashore.'

The boys ate on in a silence broken only by the sound of water slapping against the pontoons of the raft and the monotonous drone of the generator. Harry collected the plates from everyone and put the kettle on. Jeremy took over the helm, his face bathed in coloured light from the control panel.

Jeremy hit the switch for the powerful headlights and the water in front of the raft was illuminated like day. He strained his eyes to see the shoreline for the break in the trees that would indicate the area he and his friends had selected as their first landfall. Several minutes later, Jeremy saw what he was looking for off the port side of the raft. He swung the wheel over to port and headed directly for the shore. In the glare of the LED light bar that served as the vessel's headlights, the boys could see where the valley in the surrounding hills swept down to meet the water. This had formed a small inlet that even at night, looked inviting.

Jeremy throttled back and announced importantly: 'There she is, lads.'

The other three boys gathered on the foredeck and stared at the ghostly, long-dead trees that ringed the shoreline and stood in stark relief under the glare of the headlights. Sam ducked back into the cabin and flicked the switch that turned on the main spotlight. Daniel swivelled it around so that the cove was bathed in the brilliant white beam. Harry was first to spot a wallaby, then another as the light swept around the small inlet. Jeremy glided the raft parallel with the shore and followed the land as it curved into the small bay known locally as Robin Bay.

'We'd better do some depth measurements so we can anchor,' Jeremy said, putting the controller at 'Dead Slow' as the raft slowed down to a crawl. Daniel and Harry removed the long poles from their stowage rack on the side of the raft and jabbed them into the water until they hit bottom. The poles were in fact crude yardsticks, with measurements drawn on them. Harry was the first to withdraw his pole and check the mark made by the water.

'Six and a half feet,' he called to Jeremy, who swung the wheel to the left and edged closer to the shore. He turned right and began the parallel course again. This time Daniel checked the depth and shouted 'four feet.'

Jeremy pushed the controller down to the stops and the

raft glided to a standstill. 'Let go the anchor, Sam.' The sound of chain rattling over the edge of the deck echoed around the small bay. Jeremy selected reverse and called: 'Daniel, ram your pole into the mud through the stern loop.' Daniel, who had worked his way around the deckhouse and now stood on the tiny rear deck, fed the tip of his pole through the metal bracket bolted to the side of the raft and rammed it firmly into the muddy bottom.

Jeremy stood in the opening to the front deck and looked at their new home. In the glare of a flood light mounted on the foremast, he announced: 'We'll stay on board tonight and go ashore in the morning. After settling at their mooring, the boys busied themselves with preparing the raft for the night. Harry chose to sleep on deck and do some star gazing. Jeremy suggested he light a moon tiger coil to keep the now rather annoying mosquitos at bay.

Later, having completed their ablutions, the four friends settled down for the night. As he was about to shut his eyes, Sam said sleepily: 'I bet nothing ever happens up here. I think we're in for a quiet, relaxing time.' The teen couldn't have known how wrong he was.

CHAPTER 15

tan Reed drew on his cigarette and toyed with the lightweight fishing rod that he had taken from the rack, practicing casting and retrieving, in the grassed area in front of the annexe. Dennis Hayne stood in the doorway to the annexe, looking for an opportunity to get past. 'Don't hook me there, Stan. I don't want to end up as bait. Just going down to get the papers.'

Stan put the rod down and Hayne strode out onto the road and trudged off in the direction of the front office. Les Truscott poked his head out of the caravan and asked Stan if he wanted him to make lunch for a few of the men who were going to explore the lake surrounds on foot. Reed nodded in the affirmative. Les disappeared and soon could be heard whistling in the kitchen. John Allen and Bob Pitman approached the campsite from the direction of the jetty. The two men had been checking the tinny and swapping an empty fuel tank for a full one. Allen had the empty fuel can in his hand and Pitman had some superfluous rope. They strolled into the campsite and stowed the boat equipment.

If Frank Taylor was conspicuous by his absence, it was intended. He left the caravan earlier and strolled down to the jetty, carrying some fishing gear. He returned the back way, hoping the couple in the mobile home next door hadn't seen him. He had drawn the short straw and was watchman while the others went out fishing and hiking. Stan wanted a presence in camp without anyone knowing. Frank was to stay out of sight in the caravan and keep an eye on things. 'I'll be able to catch up on these,' he said philosophically to John Allen earlier, patting a stack of *Popular Mechanic* magazines in a drawer.

'Don't let Stan see them, Frank. He wants eyes everywhere,' Allen had cautioned him.

'This is the thing I *really* don't want him to see,' Taylor said with a sheepish grin. Left-handed, he reached into a pocket of his jacket and produced a revolver. Allen knew enough about firearms to see it was a .357 Magnum with a four-inch barrel. 'This ought to do it for 'em.'

While John Allen was left wondering who 'they' were, Taylor decided to have a quick shower while the others waited for Dennis to re-appear with the papers. When he returned, each man grabbed equipment pursuant to the day's activities and paired up, Stan with Bob and Les while John went with Dennis. Bob Pitman made a show of closing the flap to the annexe and tossed a key into the air and caught it. Stan produces two small transceivers and handed one to John Allen, pocketing the other himself.

The five men trudged off down the road to the jetty, chatting and laughing about fishing and boating in general. The hikers would split off at the lake and walk around the shore in the direction of Robin Bay, enjoying the scenery but really looking for a place to bring the money when it was retrieved so it could be loaded into the tinny. As the men approached the jetty, they could see other morning boaters getting ready for a day on the lake. John Allen and Dennis Hayne bade the boaters farewell and made their way down a well-worn path along the shoreline.

The tinny crew made their way onto the jetty and placed the packs in the bows. Stan was in no hurry so the three men sat on the transverse seats, smoked and talked. Bob Pitman fidgeted in his back pack for sunglasses and chewing gum. He also let his fingers work around the heavy Colt .45 he kept in the base compartment, reassured by the cold gunmetal. Stan chatted briefly to a fellow camper about their chances for hooking the big one, while inconspicuously connecting the small transceiver to a microphone/ speaker inside his jacket. The jetty was quiet now and Reed made the decision to push off. The radio in his pocket crackled and John Allen's voice announced that he and Dennis Hayne were making good progress around the shore. Reed responded into the microphone fixed to the inside of his jacket and started the motor.

Stan used a barge pole to push away from the pier. The small boat putted out onto the lake, leaving a small V-shaped ripple in its wake. The three men settled in for the trip, thinking their own thoughts. Bob Pitman produced a small pair of binoculars and scanned the shoreline for the other men. Not seeing them, he turned to Stan, who read his thoughts.

'If you can't see 'em, it's because they're on a trail that leads directly to Robin bay. Doesn't follow the shore. It's part of the Eildon Nature Trail.'

Pitman could well imagine the trail festooned with greenies, hugging trees but turned his attention to the lake itself, more particularly the other boats that dotted its surface. He noticed that most of them had sailed due South and were by now congregated in a wide part of the lake known as the Goulbourn Arm. Bob and his friends intended to steer west and head more towards Eildon town. Stan opened his pack and produced plastic mugs and a Thermos flask. While he made coffee for everyone, Les cast his eyes over a laminated map spread out on his knees and checked his G-Shock. He said: 'We'll be there in twenty minutes.'

* * *

The hikers were making steady progress along the trail that had meandered away from the water and into the forest. The thick canopy gave welcome respite from the sun which was climbing higher into the sky. John Allen took a long drink from his canteen, to which he had previously added cordial powder and surveyed the scene. The path had gotten steeper in places, but this served to give stunning views of the lake between the Stringybark trees and the occasional Mountain Ash. Allen wondered for the hundredth time why he hadn't made the effort to travel into this area previously. Bell birds were making their presence known with the crystal-clear 'ping' sound. Not for the first time, Allen thought it sounded *like the sonar on a submarine.*

Dennis Hayne stopped to take off his jacket, mumbling something about the heat as he did so. Allen thought it was a good idea and removed his as well. Both men took in the scene while they stuffed their jackets into their packs. Allen produced a map from his pack and studied it. 'Stan thinks this unnamed inlet here might be suitable for our purposes,' he said, jabbing a finger at a feature on the shoreline. 'We should get there by lunchtime.'

Hayne grunted in agreement and the pair set off again. They met a lone hiker walking in the opposite direction, a young man who said he was walking the entire way around the lake. They trudged on, Allen giving the occasional progress report on the pocket-sized Motorola radio he carried, the twin of the unit Les Truscott had.

The sun was high overhead when the pair came to a fork in the road. John Allen slowed down, checked his map and indicated the left path. 'Downhill all the way now, Dennis,' Allen said with a grin. This seemed to please Hayne and the two men romped down the path, having to be careful where they stepped occasionally, for this path was not well used. After ten minutes, the water appeared through the trees in front of them, and the going got less steep, until they emerged from the tree line onto a flat area of hard-dried mud. Dead trees lined the shore, giving the area a post-apocalyptic look.

'Plenty of room here to bring the tinny into the shore,' Hayne said, echoing Allen's thoughts. The men walked around the shore of the small inlet, Allen probing the water depth with a broken branch. Hayne studied the shoreline of the inlet from every angle, the professional thief at work. Allen thought what great firewood the dead trees would make and suggested this to Dennis, who grunted in agreement. Hayne was stirred out of his painstaking examination of the area and raised a hand to signal that he had heard something that didn't fit in. Both men listened and the sound came again. A far-off tapping sound, as if someone was driving a stake into the ground somewhere.

'Probably the Parks and Wildlife people repairing some of those trails,' Allen suggested helpfully. Hayne seemed to accept this, having seen the condition of steps and retaining walls on the trek over. 'Oh, I almost forgot. I'd better tell the boys that we've checked this bay out and it looks suitable.' He produced the radio from his pocket and in clipped language referred to having arrived in a suitable fishing area. Les would understand this and presently replied with 'Roger' and further instructions to have a look at Robin Bay as well. Allen pocketed the radio and dug into his pack and produced a small alcohol cooker. 'Let's have a cuppa, Dennis,' he said cheerfully. 'I've opened the sealed orders, and they want us to go on to the next bay and check that out as well.'

Soon the men were enjoying steaming hot coffee and relaxing, Hayne telling Allen of the log cabin he would like to build at this spot. Allen checked his watch and stirred. 'We'd better get a move on, Dennis. Only about thirty minutes more. We'll have lunch there.'

The men departed the small inlet and made their way up and over the ridge separating the two inlets. The going was more difficult because there was no path through the scrub. They crested the spine of rocky ground, taking in the view of the lake as they headed down the slope towards the water. The going was better, but they had to watch for low scrub that became tripping hazards. As they got lower, the trees blocked their view of the bay and they had to get within eighty yards of the water to get an idea of what was there.

The view that greeted the men's eyes was not what they were expecting. A large houseboat was anchored offshore on the same side the two men now stood. On the opposite bank, some kind of raft was tied up to a small pier, near which several teenagers seemed busy on the shore. On the bank adjacent to both vessels, smoke from small campfires drifted lazily upwards.

Allen made his mind up quickly and beckoned to Hayne to follow him around the top of the inlet to the opposite bank. This would mean having to pass the teenagers near the raft, but it couldn't be helped. The two men ambled their way around the shore, commenting on the effect of the lake on the trees, which still stood sentinel after all these years since the creation of the lake. They approached the boys who appeared to be enjoying a meal. John Allen threw a jaunty wave and smiled while Dennis Hayne gave one of his trademark grunts.

The two men took in the campsite, the raft and the pier. Allen knew enough about carpentry for him to recognise quality work. Three of the teens eyed the men suspiciously, two tall lanky youths and a shorter boy of Asian appearance.

The other boy continued with his meal, occasionally stoking the fire, with his back to the men. The radio chirped and Allen told Les that the pickup point had changed. When the pair was out of earshot from the boys, he also added that the first bay was suitable for the pickup.

They traipsed out of Robin Bay and onto the shore of the lake proper. John Allen knew that the boat would be pulling into the shore in about thirty minutes, so he and Hayne found a shady place under a large spotted gum tree, out of sight of the raft and the houseboat, and had their lunch. Presently, Allen heard the sound of an approaching motor out on the lake. Thinking it sounded too big to be the tinny, he stood up to get a better view. Sure enough, a large houseboat ambled by with people on deck chairs and banana lounges soaking up the sun.

The sun had dipped behind the mountains when a familiar aluminium boat appeared, nosing its way around the dead gum trees to the shore. Hayne and Allen got to their feet and ambled down to the boat and the grinning face of Stan Reed.

'So, that bay is the place?' Reed asked, pointing. Big enough for the tinny?

'You could park the *Amoco Cadiz* there,' Allen replied. 'Dennis wants to build a little retreat there. It's perfect. Nice and quiet. No campers. There *is* a track branching off the main trail, however, but it's very overgrown and rather rough. Robin Bay is busy just now.'

The tinny reversed out a short distance and Les put it in

forward gear and motored slowly out onto the lake. 'Okay, so that nameless inlet is the place', Reed declared, making a small mark on a map with a pencil. 'While the hikers were checking out the land side of things, we boaters were sussing the lake itself. I have concluded that as long as the boat *looks* like a fishing boat, nobody gives it a second glance.'

'Can I ask the question that's on everyone's mind,' asked Les Truscott, not wanting to interrupt Stan.

'Go ahead, Les.'

'What day do we go and pick up the loot.'

'Sunday, which I believe is the thirtieth. Two of us will go up the day before to confirm that it's there. We take videos or pictures with our phones to prove to the others that it's there. Then five of us go and collect it on the Sunday. In the morning. We transport it to the unnamed inlet and hide it 'til night-time. Then on one of our evening fishing expeditions, we collect it from the shore hiding place and take it to the boat ramp, as per Mr Allen's idea.'

'Why only five to collect the money,' asked John Allen. 'Surely we don't need a watchman on that day.'

'I'm still a bit jumpy from the other night. I'll give it some thought, however. It would be nice to have everyone involved. Let's head back. I can hear a beer calling me.

The tinny left a V-shaped wake behind it that glowed in the setting sun. The men were all hungry and Les was lost in thought as to what culinary creation he would serve up tonight. For the five occupants of the boat, the countdown had begun.

CHAPTER 16

Harry Turner awoke first, with the morning sun already high in the cloudless sky. At first, his surroundings seemed unfamiliar. Then the trees and birds singing their morning songs made sense. He sat up and took in the lake vista. Jeremy had chosen their anchorage well. The teenager had never been anywhere so peaceful and the thought of eventually having to return to suburbia did not appeal. He unzipped his sleeping bag and crawled out onto the deck. He stood up and stretched before stooping in the doorway of the deckhouse.

He found Sam Dillon was also awake who greeted Harry with a sleepy 'hello'. Harry made for the galley and put the kettle on. Sam climbed out of his bunk and gave Harry a hand to get breakfast ready. The sound of cups clattering on the bench and the frying pan soon woke the other boys. Presently, steaming mugs of coffee were being consumed and the boys were talking excitedly about the day ahead. As was usually the case with Jeremy, the day's activities had been planned meticulously.

Over bacon and eggs, Jeremy reiterated the use of the camera when locating the sunken town of Rupertsvale. He stressed the importance of not attracting attention to themselves, so they all agreed that while two used the camera and GPS, the other two would fish from the raft, and when the town had been located they would swim near the raft. Sam, Harry and Daniel peppered Jeremy with questions about the condition the buildings were likely to be in and how they will appear on the computer screen.

Jeremy, however, was onto the next subject, the construction of a small pier to tie the raft to and walk ashore without getting their feet wet. As usual he had plans and the boys pored over these, getting the odd coffee ring, bits of fried egg and bacon grease on them as well, much to Jeremy's annoyance. They soon had the idea and finished their breakfast. Jeremy and Daniel got the small inflatable boat ready were soon on their way to shore armed with an axe and a bowsaw. Harry and Sam cleaned up after the meal and readied the raft for use in the construction of the dock.

Once ashore, Daniel and Jeremy soon found what they were after. Tall, very thin, straight trees, growing in large groups. Jeremy directed the cutting operation and the boys soon had eight long sturdy poles which they carried down to the waterline. They busied themselves removing the light foliage and making one end of each pole pointed, using the axe. Daniel beckoned to Sam to bring the raft up to the shore. The sound of the generator echoed across the small inlet. Harry removed the mooring poles and laid them in their storage brackets. Within minutes, the raft, freed from its moorings, motored to the shore. Luckily Sam knew what to do, weaving carefully between dead trees that ringed the shore, only applying full power briefly as the raft touched land, embedding itself in the muddy bottom, the front almost touching the reeds at the shoreline.

Jeremy drew a finger across his throat, the signal for Sam kill power. He had designed some circular supports, made from old scaffolding braces, for the uprights of the dock. These were made of two semicircular pieces of steel, joined by a hinge, one of which was to be attached to the front of the raft. The other piece was clamped to the first forming an 'O'. Harry and Daniel attached one brace each to the front of the raft.

'Make sure those bolts are tight' Jeremy reminded them. When this was completed, Sam stepped down onto the hard-baked muddy shore and helped Jeremy place the first of the newly hewn poles vertically into the port side bracket. This was followed by its counterpart on the starboard side.

'These poles here are obviously way too tall,' Jeremy addressed his friends. 'So, we cut them off at a manageable height, allowing to be stuck into the ground. The next two will be a bit longer and so on. There's only going to be five pairs of uprights, so we should get this finished today easily.'

'What about the horizontals,' Harry wanted to know.

'When we cut of superfluous timber, we'll use that. We will also cut notches in the uprights so everything can hold together better.'

Jeremy marked each pole with a thick marker and directed that this was the cut-off line. Sam attacked the first pole with a saw and after getting Daniel to hold the upper piece, soon had the first upright cut and ready to be driven into the ground. This was undertaken by Jeremy using the back of the axe. When the first two poles were in the ground, the raft was released from the poles by undoing the brackets, allowing the raft to slip back and be positioned for the next two uprights.

The boys installed three sets of uprights and had a break. They drove the raft ashore, using a mooring pole at the back to secure it. Daniel gathered some dry twigs and light branches and soon had a fire going. Sam produced the kettle and mugs from the galley. Daniel used some rocks to complete his fireplace and presently, the kettle was boiling merrily.

Harry made coffee and salad rolls for the group, the sound of passing boats on the lake echoing around the small bay. While the boys relaxed, a large houseboat meandered into view and made its way to the other side of the inlet. The sound of an anchor chain rattling out was heard.

The sun was high overhead now and the water looked very inviting. Sam said: 'How about a dip before finishing the Tay Bridge?'

Jeremy was adamant. 'When the dock is finished. It'll only take another hour or two if we all work at it.'

As was so often the case, common sense prevailed. The boys got back to their task and soon enough, the job was done. The horizontals were screwed to the uprights and two long, plastic decking panels were laid on them, end to end and fixed with galvanised screws. With the raft tied to their new creation, Jeremy announced it was beer o'clock. Sam did the honours and soon the four boys were enjoying cold cans of Sainte Moritz beer. 'You do realise that when we've gone through these beers, that we won't be able to replenish them here. There's no way that the local store is going to have this brand.'

Jeremy was about to reply when he noticed something had caught Daniel's attention. He turned his head to see what it was. Two men were ambling through the brush and low scrub near the shore and heading in their direction. 'Hikers,' he muttered to himself. As the men passed their campsite, one threw a cheery wave. The other seemed to glare at the boys. Sam who had been stoking the fire, didn't pay attention to the hikers, but asked for a description anyway.

'One looked like somebody's favourite uncle,' Harry told him, 'but the other one looked like he knew where the Beaumont Children are buried.'

The next hour was spent lying on the deck on beach towels, soaking up the summer sun. Jeremy checked his dive watch. Three-thirty. 'Time for a swim,' he declared. 'Harry, get the ball.' The other boys roused themselves from their slumber, muttering curses but after easing off the deck into the water, they soon began to enjoy the cool embrace of the lake. They swam and played ball games in the water for the next two hours until Harry decided to get their dinner organised and Daniel thought it was beer time again.

As the sun went down behind the mountains, casting a shadow over the small bay, and bringing welcome respite from the baking heat of day, the boys ate their dinner and

Jeremy announced that they should set up a basic camp area onshore and store some of the less needed items there, freeing up space on board. He reminded them that this would be appreciated the next day when the underwater camera was being used.

The evening was spent transferring boxes and other items to shore, setting up a simple shelter with a tarpaulin, playing cards out on deck, and drinking hot chocolate. Later, as they settled into bed, Jeremy found sleep elusive. His mind was filled with thought of what they would find lurking under the water the next day.

CHAPTER 17

Despite his best intentions, Jeremy woke last the following morning. Sam had instructed the others to let him sleep in to give his overloaded brain time to cool down. Harry made breakfast for those that had risen and they ate in peace out on the deck, mulling over the day ahead, wondering who would be doing what. One thing was for sure; Jeremy would have all the answers.

The boys were tidying up after they finished their breakfast, when Jeremy finally woke and climbed out of his bunk as if he hadn't slept very well. Harry didn't ask what he wanted; he made a mug of rather strong coffee and rustled up bacon, black pudding and eggs. Jeremy glanced at his Doxa dive watch. The large hands said ten-thirty. 'You guys should have woken me,' he scolded. 'I wanted to at least get started before the day got too hot.'

'The town isn't going anywhere,' Sam shot back. 'Besides, we thought you could do with a sleep in.'

'Yeah, we can cool off in the water whenever we want,' Harry chipped in.

'Okay, let me finish this and we'll get down to cases.' Jeremy consumed the last morsels of food and wiped his plate with a slice of bread. Pushing his plate aside, he got up and stepped through to his bunk and grabbed a laminated A4 sheet covered with diagrams and notes. 'Dan, can you get the camera and battery pack out, please. We'll set it up on the deck and I'll show all of you the ropes.'

Daniel lifted the lid on the large plastic trunk that was fixed to the deck. He rummaged for a few seconds and produced a grey plastic box about the size of a facial tissue box, an SLA battery with a short lead and an inline switch, and a length of cable. The box had a handle on top to which a short length of light chain was attached. The cable fed into the top of the box through a waterproof gland nut. One end of the box contained two glass windows, the lower one through which a small camera was visible. The camera appeared to be set pointing at an angle downwards. The upper window allowed a small auto driving light to shine through. The side of the unit contained a similar window and here a small panel containing LED lights could be seen. There were no switches or other controls on the outside of the box.

The other end of the cable branched into two smaller cables. Jeremy explained that these were for power and the audio and video signals. The signal sub-cable ended in a normal A/V plug. The power cable terminated with an Anderson connector. At Jeremy's request, Sam reached under his bunk and produced the laptop and set it up on the table. Jeremy plugged the A/V lead into a port on the laptop and the power plug into the battery. Sam fired up the computer and seconds later an image of the inside of the cabin appeared on the screen. The boys saw each other on the screen and made various uncomplimentary comments. Then Jeremy flipped the rocker switch on the battery and the box emitted a bright light which dazzled the boys.

'Well, that's it in a nutshell,' Jeremy said. 'The only thing still to add is the counterweight, which will give the box a bit of weight allowing it to sink properly and keep the correct orientation. We slow right down when we get to the approximate site and lower it over the side. Sam will be on the monitor and Daniel in charge of the depth readings, which are marked on the chain. We can mark where we've been on the GPS so we don't go over the same ground. That's my job, Harry won't be left out. He'll be taking over from Sam in addition to keeping us supplied with drinks.'

Jeremy studied his watch. 'It's now eleven o'clock. I think we should just get out there. I'll show you where 'there' is.' He unrolled a map of the lake and pointed to an area at the entrance to Rupertsvale Bay. There was a small X on the map at that point, but Jeremy added a heavy circle with his pencil. 'That's where we'll be for the rest of today. We will probably get back here late tonight.'

With that said, Daniel and Jeremy fitted the weights to the camera unit, while Harry tidied up the galley and Sam organised the table for the computer. Harry darted ashore to the shelter, to get last-minute supplies. When Jeremy's Doxa watch said eleven-thirty, Sam started the generator and Jeremy engaged the electric motors. Daniel and Harry cast off and the raft slid away from the pier and out into the inlet.

Daniel, out on the foredeck, glanced over at the houseboat

moored on the other side of the inlet. The occupants were relaxing on the top deck, enjoying the morning sun. Some waved and Daniel waved back. With Jeremy temporarily at the controls, the raft slid out of Robin Bay and out onto the lake proper. Sam took over driving while Harry made a round of drinks for everyone. Daniel sat on the edge of the deck and let his feet dangle in the water. The lake stretched out before him, glistening in the morning sun. Sam was keeping a steady pace, and the light breeze was refreshing. He hoped they found the sunken town quickly so he could spread out a towel and relax.

Harry appeared on the deck with two mugs of coffee and, handing one to Daniel, sat down next him. Both boys took in the scene, Harry's feet not quite reaching the water. Harry said, taking a sip of his drink: 'This old town better have a bank full of gold. What with all the detailed planning Jeremy has put in.'

'I was thinking more along the lines of a 1930 Pierce Arrow that is somehow in restorable condition.'

'I don't mean to rain on your parade, but we'd never be able to get it to the surface,' Harry suggested practically.

'What about your gold. Same there.'

'Drink your coffee.'

The boys encountered more boat traffic as they neared the location picked out by Jeremy. Fry's Bay, which appeared on their left, had half a dozen houseboats moored in and around it. Jeremy wandered out onto the deck, a pair of mini binoculars around his neck. 'Knowing our luck, there will be a dozen fishing boats just where we want to go,' he muttered more to himself than anyone else.

'How about we do a test run with the camera system before we get there,' suggested Harry. 'I'm dying to see how it works.'

Jeremy stared at Harry. 'That's the best idea I've heard yet.' He ducked into the deckhouse and told Sam: 'Dead Slow and hug the shoreline.' Then he was out again, barking orders: 'Harry, help me with the camera and cable. Daniel, keep watch aft, I don't want any boat to run up our arse.'

Five minutes later, Harry stood on the starboard side of the raft with the grey box at his feet and light chain draped around his shoulders. The box now had rectangular blocks of stainless steel attached to its base; one end of the chain was firmly bolted to a steel eyelet on the deck. Jeremy was in the cabin, stooping over the laptop computer, satisfying himself that all was working properly.

'I'm just going to test the spotlight,' he called out to Harry, flipping the rocker switch. Harry yelled back that the light was on. He flipped the switch back to the off position. 'Okay, lower it in, Harry.'

Harry picked up the box and eased it into the water. He began to let out the chain/cable, watching it snake across the deck and over the side. Jeremy's eyes never left the screen. He watched intently as the natural light faded. He wanted the raft to go even slower, so he suggested to Sam to switch off one of the electric motors. Sam did so and the raft crawled along. When Harry shouted that he had played out about fifteen metres of cable, Jeremy told him to stop. The screen was almost dark. He flicked on the light. Immediately, objects appeared in view. Gnarled trees swam out of the murk and seemed to almost collide with the camera. Jeremy knew that controlling the camera's sideways movements was going to be almost impossible.

'Sam, this is how we're going to do it.' Jeremy's voice was firm. 'Steer and keep speed to my exact instructions. This camera box has the aerodynamics of a house brick. In a nutshell, where the camera goes, the raft goes. So, in effect, you're controlling the camera, Sam.'

Sam got the picture. Harry received clipped instructions to at least try to swing the camera around so that it was facing ahead. When everything seemed to be in synch, Jeremy relaxed a little. Daniel was relieved of his rear-guard duty and took over from Harry, who was now on lunch duty. Sam found it best to look at the computer screen and steer accordingly. The sound of beer cans hissing open permeated the deckhouse. Jeremy was satisfied with the operation of the camera and monitor and told his friends so. Daniel laughed, saying he sounded like Blofeld from the 007 books. Harry said the only thing missing was a furry cat on his lap. Predictably, Jeremy ignored them both.

'I think we should go deeper,' Jeremy announced, taking a large gulp from his can. 'Steady as she goes, Sam. Dan, let out a few more metres.' The sound of chain rattling on the wooden deck was heard and the boys studied the monitor more intently. Jeremy gave some directional directives to

Sam and got Daniel to let out more chain. The camera was now following the contour of the lake bottom. 'I'm getting a good feel for this, lads,' he exclaimed. His friends were pleased for him though they had had to endure his long-winded explanations about it and the use it could be put to.

Soon the muddy bottom of the lake appeared, speckled with small rocks and debris from human habitation. Old bottles, cans, the odd tyre, even an aluminium saucepan. Then fish appeared, at first curious about the box with the light, then they swam away, disinterested. Jeremy guided the raft out into deeper water and the lake bottom fell away. He navigated, using the camera alone, this way and that before Sam pointed out that they might be a menace to other boaters.

Jeremy decided that the test was a huge success, and it was time to haul up the camera and make for the target area. Daniel started gathering the chain and cable and Sam connected all the motors and put the main controller to full. The raft lurched ahead. Sam was relieved to be able to give it the gun at last. Jeremy shut off the image from the camera and focused on playing back the footage they had captured. Harry filled the kettle and placed it on the gas stove before slicing bread rolls and asking what everyone wanted on their hot dogs.

Daniel had by this time coiled the cable and chain neatly on the deck and disconnected the grey box, which he took into the deckhouse. Harry threw him a dish towel to dry it off, before placing it on the table next to the laptop. Jeremy ran his hands over it, pleased no end with his baby. 'If you ask nicely, he'll re-run the test video,' Harry said, sipping his beer.

'Target area coming up, Jeremy.' Sam's voice broke in. Jeremy detached himself from the table and came over to the steering position. The small GPS unit displayed an image of the lower part of the lake. Two objects were visible on the 'lake': a small red X and a green dot. The dot represented the raft, the cross the town. 'We've probably got about ten minutes.'

'Okay, let's have lunch now. When we get over the old town, we'll stop and pretend to fish. We'll have a cuppa and then really start exploring Old Rupertsvale.'

'Here it is, guys,' Harry exclaimed, setting plates containing long bread rolls with hot dogs and mustard down on the table. The boys ate in silence, reviewing the video footage taken earlier. Jeremy paused every time a fish came into view, much to Harry's annoyance. Sam ate with his plate balanced on his knee, his eye on the GPS unit. As they were finishing their lunch, the raft slowed down and Sam announced: 'We're here.'

Jeremy leaped up and studied the GPS, as if he didn't trust Sam's judgement. 'Okay,' he announced, 'Daniel, deploy the camera and let out thirty metres of cable. Harry can help you. Sam, hold the raft as straight as you can and keep the speed to a crawl.'

Everyone went to their battle stations and Jeremy adjusted the laptop to receive the latest video footage. Harry and Daniel wrestled with the cable and got the grey box lowered over the side before Jeremy started getting impatient. Sam got the raft going at a crawl, awaiting the next round of directions. Harry yelled: 'How much cable do we let out?'

Jeremy consulted a laminated A4 sheet. 'Old Rupertsvale was built on the shore of the Goulburn River. While the maximum depth of the lake is in the region of eighty metres, the town is only about forty metres down. So let out about thirty-five metres.'

Harry and Daniel gave each other knowing looks and began letting the chain and electric cable run into the water. Jeremy switched on the camera light and watched the odd fish go by on the camera's decent. Daniel called out the depth, mentally keeping tabs on the number of red markers on the chain as they went under. When he reached thirty metres, Jeremy called out to slow the rate of decent.

As he watched the laptop screen, Jeremy saw solid objects drift into his field of view. At first it was the gnarled and twisted trunks of long-dead trees. Then something definitely man-made appeared. It was a cruciform shape with small projections on the horizontal piece. The penny dropped. It was a telegraph pole. The pole leaned drunkenly to one side, with the pathetic remnants of wires draped from the cross-arm. 'We've got something, lads,' Jeremy muttered. Other ghostly shapes glided into the light. 'Go lower, Harry.'

Harry and Daniel carefully played our more cable. 'That electricity pole meant that we were at or near a road. Now we are viewing from about ten feet up. It appears that we have crossed the road and are now over a property on one side. Sam, steer right a few degrees.' Sam spun the wheel and straightened up. He said: 'Now what do you see?' Jeremy shifted the computer, so Sam had a better view.

Both boys watched in silence as the grime covered remains of an old car materialised out of the gloom. One still intact headlight, caught in the bright light, shone as if left on by the car's long ago forgotten owner. The glassless windscreen cavity stared back emptily, revealing rotting seats and rusty steering wheel. The camera glided over the vehicle, only to reveal another one a few metres behind, in a similar state of decay. Sam was getting the hang of navigating by watching the image on the laptop. He began to get creative. Realising that they were heading down a road, he veered right and as he anticipated, the boys had their first glimpse of the first remnants of Old Rupertsvale.

An old house with its windows gone, and a caved-in corrugated iron roof, emerged from the murkiness. As the camera glided over the remains, Sam had to turn sharply to avoid a chimney which still stood sentinel, a rusted television antenna somehow clinging to the top. 'Keep the camera at this height,' Jeremy commanded, his eyes glued to the screen. 'You can speed up a little, Sam, but not too much.'

Sam nudged the throttle up a notch and set the GPS to produce a red line over their current path. This would enable the boys to know exactly where they had been. Jeremy told Harry and Daniel to tie off the cable and chain and watch the scene below them. They didn't need telling twice and presently the four boys were watching without breathing. Harry muttered something about beer and ducked into the galley, reappearing with four Sainte Moritz cans.

'We'll have to start doin' the search a bit more scientifically,'

Sam suggested, 'like they did when searching for the Titanic.'

'What we need to do is find the perimeter of the town, mark it on the GPS and go from there,' Jeremy replied. As he spoke, more drowned remains drifted past the camera. Picket fences, sheds, concrete paths leading nowhere. Jeremy took over the helm and continued in a straight line. His intention was to keep going until the came to the last of any structures or remnants of any kind, mark that place and swing around and follow the edge of the town. He told the boys and admitted it wasn't going to be easy.

All manner of objects passed by the camera. Sam, now sitting at the table, pointed out an old rotary clothesline, wireless now, one arm hanging awkwardly down. Another picket fence and nothing until a circular hole with some kind of frame over it. 'A well,' Jeremy mused. Then the penny dropped. 'There wouldn't be a well in the town would there?' he asked. Daniel said: 'No, but there would in a paddock.'

'So that fence back there was the edge of town. I'll get us back there and we'll follow an alignment from that point, say, going west.' He turned the wheel to the left and then came right and made a lazy turn back onto the track they had made over the town. Presently, the well appeared to the right of screen and shortly after, the decaying picket fence. Jeremy came hard right and managed to have the camera glide along the fence.

'We'll come to that road shortly. We'll go along it to the north then turn west again. When we're going along what we think is the boundary of the town, we'll just mark it in the GPS.'

'Let me have a go driving,' Harry's voice was impatient, a rare situation. 'Cool your brain off and make dinner. The recipe card is there.' Jeremy reluctantly left his post and let his friend take over. Harry got the hang of co-ordinating the camera quite quickly and was enjoying himself. The same could not be said for Jeremy, who, despite Harry's brief cooking lessons, was not at home in a kitchen, even one on a raft. He used the gas stove, not daring to light the kero stove. However, he soon got into the swing of things and not long after, the boys smelled delicious aromas emanating from the galley.

The day continued with Harry receiving steering directions and Daniel or Sam plotting waypoints in the GPS. They found the original course of the Goulburn River and the other boundaries of Old Rupertsvale. By this time, the sun had gone down behind the hills to the west, and it began to get dark rather quickly. Harry flicked on the navigation lights and the interior red lights.

With the town co-ordinates in the GPS unit, Sam suggested they take one more run over the town and head for home. Daniel took over from Harry, who was only too keen to get back to his galley and see if there was anything left of it. He gave Jeremy a hand while Daniel and Sam co-ordinated the camera between ruined buildings and other debris.

After traversing the town, Sam decided to call it quits. He stopped the recording function on the laptop and shut off the underwater light. Then he made his way out onto the desk and began hauling up the chain and cable. He neatly coiled it on the deck and when the grey box finally appeared, he placed it carefully on the deck, disconnected the cable and chain and carried the unit inside.

Jeremy and Harry carried plates laden with food to the table. The camera unit was placed on the deck and the four boys ate hungrily, Daniel sitting at the helm. It was dark now and he had the powerful headlights on. With both motors on, the raft glided across the water, passing the occasional small boat heading back to Rupertsvale or at anchor fishing. The sound of laughter and yelling rolled out over the water from Fry's Bay as the houseboats moored there prepared for the night.

The GPS unit made finding Robin Bay a breeze and the raft coasted into the small inlet at ten minutes to nine. The houseboat was still there, a small group on its upper deck, the occasional chink of glass carrying across the water. The raft bumped against the jetty and Harry tied her off. Jeremy and Daniel cleaned up after dinner, while Sam hung the coiled chain and cable up to dry out. The cabin was made ready for sleeping and the boys went about their ablutions before climbing into their respective bunks.

The boys chatted for a while. Jeremy announced that the next day would be a rest day. Buoyed with this news, Daniel and Sam said that they were going hiking up to some ruins in the area. 'Harry and I will probably fish,' Jeremy said. 'Won't we, Harry?'

If a reply was expected, it wasn't forthcoming. Switching on his flashlight, Jeremy aimed the beam at Harry's sleeping position. The boy was fast asleep.

CHAPTER 18

John Allen was going stir crazy. He swore on his late mother's eternal soul that if he had to look at another fish he would go berserk. He stood, coffee mug in hand, outside the annexe, gazing towards the lake. He thought of the people who came up here for a holiday. *They* seemed to be having a good time. He wasn't the only one beginning to go loopy. He could see that Stan was having trouble keeping the calm and businesslike façade up. Only Bob Pitman seemed to retain his cheerful disposition.

Bob talked mainly about his car mechanical repair business. This was fair enough. It had provided him with a good living and more importantly kept him out of trouble. His latest gripe was keeping up with the latest industry standards regarding chemical handling. He said at breakfast, 'Did you know there are these things called PAHs? Don't ask me what that stands for, but they're bitching like mad about them now.'

Allen had thought of going for a walk and sneaking up to the old motel, but that presented a problem. He didn't know which room the loot was in (indeed, Stan hadn't told any of them), and he was sure Stan would know if someone had been poking around up there. The latest modification to the plan, that of leaving the loot hidden on the shoreline of the unnamed bay, seemed logical. It meant that on the night, handling the money involved fewer people.

Allen decided to go for a stroll anyway. He strode into the annexe and entered the caravan. Placing his empty mug in the sink, he briefly told Stan that he was going to get some fresh air. Then he went out to his bunk and retrieved a beach towel and a compact pair of binoculars. Pocketing the binocs, he left the campsite. He was relieved that nobody had offered to go with him. He really needed some quiet time.

The couple next door were out the front of their trailer and John Allen gave them a cheery wave. The woman responded with a smile, but her husband only stared. As he turned down the gravel path to the water, he dismissed them from his mind. The lake looked calm and inviting, with the sound of children yelling and splashing and the drone of outboard motors.

Turning to the left at the water's edge, Allen strolled along the shore until he found a grassy area bounded on two sides with wind breaks, which shielded him from view of the trailer park. He set the towel out on the grass and removed his shoes. Lying back, he decided to soak up the morning sun for a while. Then he would do what he in part came here to do. Study the comings and goings of the lake, particularly the jetty.

While Allen lay there, Bob Pitman and Dennis Hayne left the caravan park in the Commodore utility and drove over to the launching ramp by the dam wall. Stan had told them to get the geography in their heads to make things quicker at night. When the men pulled into the gravel apron, there were several cars parked by the main launching ramp. The two men parked their vehicle on the opposite side of the carpark and wandered about on foot, occasionally making comments about the fishing. When they had finished their recon, they drove into Eildon and had a few cool ones at a local pub before driving cautiously back to the holiday village.

As they pulled up outside the caravan, they saw John Allen strolling towards them. As he approached the campsite, Bob Pitman asked, 'How's it goin', John? What's the lake looking like?'

Allen paused and leaned on the windowsill. 'Well, the jetty is out. There's going to be quite a bit of action there tonight and the next few nights. Seems that everyone's into night fishing.'

If Dennis Hayne's nose was out of joint at John Allen being right again, he didn't show it. He merely grunted something and got out of the car.

Stan spoke to everyone briefly that night, timing his homily to conclude before the Broncos and the Rabbitoh's match. The day's reconnaissance had gone well, reinforcing the changes to the plan. To conclude, he said, 'Tomorrow the party to go and check the money will consist of me, John and Dennis. One of us will take pictures of the loot and the general area. We'll head up there at about midday. That'll give us plenty of time to do what we must do and get back here. Well, that's about it, chaps. Drink up and enjoy the game.'

CHAPTER 19

Daniel backstroked away from the raft until he was in the middle of the small inlet known locally as Robin Bay. From here, he could still make out the cheeky iron rattle of the small air compressor that Sam was using to inflate a large beach ball. Harry and Jeremy were in the water, yelling and splashing about. 'Come over and join us, Dan,' Harry hollered across the water. Daniel waved with his hand but was surreptitiously positioning himself closer to the large houseboat moored on the opposite side of the bay.

He had spotted a girl, approximately his own age, sunbaking on the top deck of the houseboat, and was trying to get a closer look. She had waved to him the day before when he was standing on the raft, so he decided to spend the morning investigating further. The remainder of the day was planned with Jeremy's usual detail, so, he thought to himself, he didn't have long. Sam's voice made him look over to the raft. Daniel saw his friend kick the beach ball high into the air. 'Catch this, Dan,' Sam shouted. Daniel had no hope of doing so for the ball flew high over his head and land with a splash, about ten feet from the houseboat. He couldn't believe his luck and swam powerfully over to retrieve the wayward ball.

Daniel felt his feet touch the muddy bottom of the lake and he walked awkwardly the last few metres to the ball. As he grabbed the ball, a movement on the deck of the houseboat caught his attention. Daniel looked up and was pleasantly surprised to see the mystery girl, towel draped around her shoulders, leaning against the handrail, glancing down into the water. 'Just retrieving our ball,' Daniel stammered nervously.

That's okay,' the girl replied. 'That's a nice boat you've got there. How many of you are on it?

The girl's interest caught Daniel off guard. 'Er.. Oh, there are four of us. Four teenagers and we haven't driven each other mad yet.'

The girl laughed. 'Since we're camped almost on top of each other, I'd better introduce myself. I'm Allison. There's two groups of us on this boat. We've hired it for a fortnight.'

Daniel, realising that his friends must be getting impatient, served it volley-ball style back in the direction of the raft. 'I'm Daniel and these are my fellow rafters. We built it in my dad's garage. Today two of us are taking a break from sailing and going hiking. What's on the cards for you?

'Sunbaking, mainly. Hiking sounds like fun,' Allison said. She turned and made a hand gesture to someone unseen. Turning back to Daniel, Allison excused herself and ducked out of view. Daniel paddled back to his three friends.

'Sorry to disturb your social life, but we were wondering if you were going to re-join us,' scolded Jeremy.

'My apologies, but it isn't every day you meet a cute bird like Allison.'

'Especially while standing waist deep in a lake,' chimed in Harry.

'It would have been neck deep if it had been you,' Daniel was quick to respond.

'First name terms now is it,' enquired Sam.

Changing the subject, Jeremy said, 'It's five past midday. We'll play ball for a while longer then Sam and Dan had better head off if they want to spend any time at this ruined building. Harry and I are going to explore more of Old Rupertsvale.'

The boys played their water ball game until one o'clock, when Harry decided it was time to make the travellers some lunch to take with them. After re-boarding the raft and drying off, they set to their various tasks. Harry made sandwiches and organised bottled water. Sam and Daniel dressed in their hiking clothes, checked backpacks and donned sun block. They packed the lunch that Harry had prepared and stowed the water. Jeremy had one more item for them. He handed Sam a small FM transceiver.

'I've got the other one. Keep me posted on the way. You guys also have the GPS. What I'll get you to do is every now and then give me your location and I'll check the signal strength. Everything okay, Dan?'

'Just doing some last-minute checks,' muttered Daniel. He rattled off a few items and Sam assured him that they had them. The boys stepped onto the jetty and with cheery waves; they headed off, past their shelter and fireplace and into the thick Australian scrub.

CHAPTER 20

Jeremy and Harry watched their friends disappear into the bush, and then it was action stations aboard the raft. The boys tidied up the deckhouse and organised the camera box and the cable. Harry checked the fuel level in the generator and topped it up. Occasionally the radio would crackle, and Jeremy would answer.

To say that Jeremy was keen to get out on the lake would have been the understatement of the millennium. He fidgeted with the laptop to get it just right and checked and re-checked the camera box. He asked Harry to drive so he could spend time with his 'baby'. Harry was quite happy with the arrangement and while Jeremy untied the mooring lines, Harry checked the controls and backed gently away from the jetty.

The raft glided out of the inlet and picked up speed, with Jeremy giving directions. Jeremy stepped over to the galley to make a round of hot drinks and soon Harry watched him cursing and swearing as he struggled to find what he was looking for. Soon though, Jeremy had a mug of hot coffee for each of them and he relaxed a bit as they neared the old town. Although he kept his eyes glued to the GPS screen, he gave no course change instructions, much to Harry's relief.

Jeremy was studying an A4 sheet map of the old town. 'Today I thought we'd explore the southern part of the town and then try to find the church. It'll be interesting to see what's left if anything.'

'What denomination was it?'

'Presbyterian. If it was a Catholic church, there'd be nothing left behind. Tight as a duck's arse they are.'

Harry looked around as if he expected the raft to be struck by lightning at any minute. 'If you *do* find anything, such as a gold chalice, how are you going to retrieve it?

'If it's lasted this long underwater, we would have to come back here later on and pick it up with some grabs that I have yet to develop.'

'I like how you say *we*,' Harry remarked, sipping his coffee.

Jeremy was offended. 'You guys would help me, wouldn't you?'

Harry suddenly felt dreadful. He decided that he would help, even if it meant diving down and retrieving the object himself. That, however, was several steps away. They had to find the church first.

Jeremy nodded at the GPS. 'Nearly there. I'll tell you when to stop. When we get to the point we started at yesterday, slow down and turn right. That will take us into the southern part of town, here on the map. I'm going to get the camera ready.'

Harry scanned ahead of the raft and realised that there was a small boat right in their path. He pointed this out to Jeremy, who wasn't perturbed. 'We've got the GPS, we can easily get back onto the right course' he reminded Harry, who brought the wheel over to the right, giving the small tinny a wide berth to the port side. The man and woman occupants waved, and Harry waved back. Jeremy signalled to halt, so Harry brought the controller to the OFF position. The raft glided gently to a halt.

On the foredeck, Jeremy let out chain and cable until the thirty-five-metre mark, and then tied it off to a cleat. He stepped into the deckhouse and adjusted the laptop computer. A submarine image leaped into focus. Grabbing the GPS unit from in front of Harry, he studied both and gave short commands for speed and direction.

'The camera is a bit off to one side. You'll have to compensate for that.' Having done that, Jeremy sat back at the table and stared at the monitor. Presently, familiar objects came into view, gnarled, twisted trees, a picket fence and even another old rotary clothesline, this one intact, but leaning drunkenly to one side.

'We're over a house block. Let's try to find the house. I think it's dead ahead.' Sure enough, just within range of the light, a dark shape materialised through the murk, and as they crept closer, an empty window frame stared back at them. Harry guided the camera expertly up to the cavity and both boys peered in. They could make out fallen timbers from the roof and sheets of rusty corrugated iron. An interior door frame appeared, and the light shone through into a hallway. Also caught in the beam was a dresser, with a shade-less lamp on top.

The boys stared at the screen in silence as they invaded the long-forgotten dwelling and thought of the people who had once called this now-ruined place home. Harry manoeuvred the raft to the left, following the outside wall of the house, but inadvertently caught the cable in the branches of a crooked tree. He selected reverse and backed out of the tangle of branches.

'I think we'll get away from this house and get over to where the church is. It should be here,' Jeremy said, pointing to a rectangle on his map. 'We'd better make tracks too. It's getting late. While Harry familiarised himself with the layout of the town, Jeremy hauled the camera up a few metres and gave Harry directions to steer. Jeremy watched the screen as the camera appeared to fly over the ruined house, up high enough this time to avoid any chimneys.

A debris field drifted by in the light, forty-four-gallon drums, car parts, an old ladder and an assortment of other discarded junk. More picket fences, another house, completely roofless this time. Then Jeremy's sharp eyes spotted something. A small object standing upright, about four feet high. Then another. Then one in the unmistakable shape of a cross.

'This is it,' Jeremy exclaimed.' We're over the cemetery now. Somewhere very close is the church.' The radio crackled. Sam's voice came over the air. It sounded urgent. Harry took the call. Jeremy heard Sam asking for him. Harry handed him the radio. Jeremy went pale.

'Some of those men are at the motel,' he told Harry.

'We've got to help the lads. We can look for the Holy Grail tomorrow.'

Jeremy responded to Sam, 'Okay. Got that. Harry and I will return to shore and be ready to assist if need be.' He turned to Harry. 'Let's get out of here. I'll haul the camera up.'

'What's up? How much trouble can two teenagers get into doing a bit of urban exploring?

'Those guys that wandered past the camp yesterday are now up at the ruined motel. Daniel can smell a rat the size of a greyhound. So, I think we should be ready to help.'

While Jeremy hoisted the chain and cable onto the deck, Harry made sure both motors were engaged and turned the controller to the stops. Spinning the wheel to the right, he set a course for Robin Bay.

CHAPTER 21

Frank Taylor was the first of the gang to surface the following morning. He had plans to do some lure fishing, but he would need someone to drive the boat for him. So, while he decided who that person would be, he strolled out of the annexe and chose several fishing reels that he would likely use that day. As he compared one reel to another, Stan poked his head out of the tent flap and with his ubiquitous grin.

'How would you like to go and get the papers?'

Frank didn't need asking twice. A chance to escape, even if only for a short while, was a gift. He would willingly have walked back to Melbourne for them.

'Sure. I'll just put these away. Does anyone want something at the kiosk?'

Stan retreated into the annexe. He reappeared a minute later. 'Yeah, Dennis 'll have a pack of Peter Stuyvesant. I've still got plenty of rollies. And we have at least six litres of Aker Bilk.'

Frank smiled at Stan's rhyming slang. He was getting fluent in it himself. 'I'll just go in and get some Bugs Bunny.'

Emerging from the annexe, Taylor strode out of the camping area and down the road, his shoes crunching on the fine gravel. He breathed in the cool morning air while he still could, knowing another scorcher was on the way. He followed the path as it meandered between he trailers and cabins, children playing in the small front yards, their parents applying sun block in anticipation for the day ahead.

Several cars were parked outside the kiosk and office area when Frank arrived. He stepped up onto the veranda and entered the cool embrace of the interior, which seemed dark after the bright morning sun. He picked up copies of three different newspapers and selected some sweets before joining the line at the cashier, behind fathers and their sons stocking up for a day out on the lake. He remembered Dennis's cigarettes when it came his turn and gave the pretty girl behind the counter several winning smiles.

Frank stood by a rod and tackle stand, organise the papers and deposited the cigarettes into a pocket. He peered out into the bright morning sun. He stopped cold. His next-door neighbour was standing outside; talking to a man whose face rang a bell in his mind. Due to the clatter in the shop, Frank couldn't hear what was being said. He thought quickly. He rummaged in his trousers pocket for his mobile phone. Pretending to look through a menu, he selected the camera. Positioning himself behind a rack containing inflatable soccer balls, Frank snapped off several photos of the pair outside the shop. Stan would be very interested to see these.

Taylor waited until the men had dispersed before he left the shop and took what Stan called the Great Circle Route back to the caravan. When he arrived, he gave a grateful

Dennis his cigarettes and placed the papers on the dinette. He found Stan and held up the phone.

'I think you better see these. Our friend next door has contacted a mutual friend of ours.'

The two men went into one of the bedrooms in the caravan where Stan kept his laptop computer. After booting the device and connecting Frank's phone, the men waited until the file directory appeared. Stan selected the phone symbol and the images from the phone appeared on screen. Stan studied them like they were precious art. Finally, he sat back and stroked his chin.

'This is the second time we've caught Granddad talking to someone. First it was over the phone, now it's to a bloke we all know well. Okay, over lunch we'll have a bit of a chinwag about it. We'll make whatever changes are necessary to the plan. Meanwhile, you might as well go fishing. Take a radio with you. Somebody'll call you for lunch.'

Later at lunch, when the men were seated at the dinette, and Les had produced a plate laden with toasted jaffles, Stan cleared this throat. 'Gentlemen, we are in a state of emergency. Frank has produced some fine pictures of our next-door neighbour talking to an old friend of ours. None other than Jack Slipper.'

There was total silence around the table. The name conjured memories of 'Slippery Jack' across interview tables in various police stations. That the man, whose real name was Jack Coburn, was well-known to the group was an understatement. Frank and Dennis knew him better than the others due to their stints in jail. His presence here was a thoroughly unpleasant surprise.

Stan continued, 'Pops has talked, and Uncle Jack has done some probing. This has changed the plan substantially. I think that we go to check on the money as planned. Then tonight, or more accurately, in the wee hours of tomorrow morning, we collect it.'

'Do we still hide the loot in that bay,' asked Frank Taylor.

'Yes, Frank. That part of the plan hasn't changed. We are merely bringing it forward by twenty-four hours. So, I suggest we have lunch and at two o'clock the checking party heads off. We'll go via the jetty, carrying rods to look like we're going fishing.'

Later, Stan, John & Dennis, armed with fishing rods and tackle boxes, trudged down the gravel path towards the jetty, making small talk about the best areas on the water to hook the big one. Once down by the jetty, the fishing gear was handed to Les Truscott, who has been sitting in the boat, organising reels. The four men made conversation until they were certain nobody was watching the area. Then the three men, sans fishing gear, headed off along the path that would take them into the hills.

Daniel reached the top of the incline, pushing the thin branches out of his way and as the ground levelled out, paused for a breather. Somewhere, he heard the metallic tink of a bellbird. He took a long drink from his canteen and placed it back on his belt. He heard twigs snap behind him and glanced around to see Sam trudging through the undergrowth, brushing away an annoying fly. Sam stopped next to Daniel and, from a pouch on his belt, produced a folded A4 size map which he unfolded and studied. 'There's a minor hiking trail just through there,' he said, pointing. 'When we cross that, we're half-way there.'

Daniel took the map and made some rough estimates of distance before handing it back to Sam. He checked his G-Shock watch and remarked, 'We're making good time. Okay, let's go.' The boys trudged on, the ground getting steeper now, and the scrub denser. Daniel griped, 'You said the trail was just ahead, I wouldn't know if the M25 was ahead.' Sam laughed and gave his friend a pat on the back. 'You'll make it.'

The dense bush opened out onto a well-worn but narrow trail, complete with the ubiquitous fast-food wrapper, the well-known symbol of human habitation. Sam remarked,

'Luckily Jeremy isn't here. Speaking of which, we'd better call him.' He produced the small transceiver from his belt and called the raft. Jeremy's voice, surprisingly clear, came back. 'Roger, reading you loud and clear. Heading out onto the lake.'

Sam gave signal strength and location details and signed off. Pocketing the radio, he caught Daniel's arm. He beckoned down the track. Daniel turned to see two girls, weighed down with packs, walking towards them. The boys busied themselves with their own daypacks until the hikers were even with them. The girls said hello and the four made small talk briefly. The girls said that they were going to make camp at O'Grady's Gulch campground. Sam procured his map out of thin air and the small group studied it. 'We're just on a short day-hike to Rourke's Drift mining area.' He glanced at Daniel who nodded at his lie.

The four said their goodbyes and parted. The boys wanted to make up lost time, so they jogged the next few hundred yards. They slowed down as the terrain became tougher. Forty-five minutes later, Daniel spotted something man-made. He pointed and Sam saw it too. The unmistakable alignment of a flat roof and as the boys edged closer, painted brickwork became evident. The underbrush thinned out and the came to the remnants of a post and wire fence. As they entered the motel grounds, a dove, pecking the ground, fluttered skywards.

The motel was a desolate ruin. It consisted of two long buildings set at right angles, the windows of which faced the lake, hence its name. Sam and Daniel walked between the ends of the two main blocks and saw a swimming pool set in the center of the paved square area formed by the accommodation blocks and an administration building, which appeared around a clump of native scrub that had once been a garden. The pool held a few feet of green stagnant water and a variety of plant life. Daniel noticed that there was no evidence of a pool fence, itself an interesting relic of the times.

Sam pointed at the administration building. 'Let's start at the admin block. Never know what we'll find.'

The administration block almost formed a third side to the paved hardstand where the pool was located but was too short. The rest of the alignment was taken up with a garden that separated the paved area from the gravel, weed-infested carpark. Before entering the office, Sam produced an extendable baton from a side pocket in his pack. 'Just in case,' he said with a grin, flicking the weapon out. Surprisingly, the door handle yielded when Daniel turned it. The musty smell of abandonment invaded their lungs as soon as they stepped in to the decrepit reception area.

Although it was almost midday, the interior was subdued. Daniel soon saw the reason: the windows were covered in three decades' worth of grime. Both boys dropped their packs and produced torches, Daniel's a hand-held and Sam a headlight model. By the bright white light of these, the boys made a thorough inspection of the building, finding motel records, room menus, advertising literature and assorted odds and ends, including a layout plan of the motel.

'This place is like a time capsule,' remarked Daniel. 'Everything just frozen in time, still exactly where it had been left.'

'Yeah, and one other thing; no graffiti or damage anywhere,' Sam offered. He entered what must once have been an office and sat down in an old, dust covered swivel chair.

'Welcome to Sam's Motor Lodge.'

'All you need is a cigar,' Daniel remarked.

'That's right.' Eyeing a key press on the wall, he added, thinking aloud, 'So this is where they kept the keys to everything.' The boys noticed that most of the original room-keys still hung on their respective hooks. 'Unbelievable,' he muttered, 'only three missing'.

The boys continued with their exploration of the administration building for another hour. Daniel studied his watch after a while and suggested that they move onto the rooms. Sam, who had souvenired a stainless steel teapot, agreed and collapsed his baton. They left the way they had entered and, studying the plan, Sam suggested they start the room exploration near the office. The first room in the block was, like the office block, unlocked. The pair walked into a short hallway with a door on the right.

'Must be the bathroom,' mused Sam. They continued into the main room. This too was devoid of natural light, despite having large windows at one end of the room. In the gloom, the boys saw a single bed, a bedside table and on the opposite side of the room, a small fridge with a kettle on top. Daniel flicked on his torch and went through the bureau drawers one by one.

'Look what I've found,' he exclaimed, holding up a Gideon's bible. 'Here, you could use a dose of this.' He pitched the book to Sam who set a new world record for reading the bible and tossed it on the bed.

Sam was focused on the windows at the end of the room. He strode over and tried the latch. Surprisingly it came easily. He pushed the door open and stepped out onto a small terrace, above which hung an ivy- covered trellis. The view from the terrace was totally blocked by native scrub. No wonder the room was so dark, Sam thought. He studied the wooden trellis. It sagged in the middle from the weight of the thick ivy growing over and through it.

'If I sneeze out here, this whole lot's going to come down on me,' he declared to Daniel.

'So much for Sam's Motor Lodge,' Daniel remarked, sweeping his eyes around the room. 'You should keep up the maintenance. And you of all people, a carpenter.'

'I wish I'd never mentioned it. Anyway, good staff's hard to find.'

Daniel stepped out onto the terrace, briefly glanced around and said to Sam, 'Let's go explore some more rooms.'

Sam didn't need any encouragement. The boys made for the door. They stepped onto the covered porch that connected all the units in the block. The boys tried the next room, finding it similar. Sam suggested they have lunch, so they placed their packs on the bed and opened the sandwiches that Harry made for them. Sam rigged up his alcohol stove and soon had water boiling for coffee. The teenagers sat back on the bed, glad to take a break. They sipped their coffee, glad that it was a downhill trek back to the raft.

'It feels weird being the only ones in this place,' Daniel commented.

'Yeah. I wonder if anything exciting ever happened here.'

CHAPTER 23

It was quite the worst time of day to contemplate physical activity of any kind. The men were grateful when they came to the thick bush, with its heavy overhead cover. However, this presented a new predicament. Bugs of every description. Mosquito repellent was passed around, but then there were dragonflies the size of biplanes, the repellent for which had yet to be invented.

'Has anybody got a flame-thrower?' John Allen mused, more to himself than anybody else.

'Could sure use one,' Stan chuckled, studying a small map. 'We may as well stick to the trail. No point diverging from it. The only time we'll have to be careful is when we come to the track that leads to the motel. If we happen to get some company approaching the divergent point, we'll just stop and make a brew or study the map. Our official destination is Rourke's Drift mining area'

The men trudged on, the terrain getting steeper. They reached a point where the track levelled out. A minor track diverged to the left. They walked along straight ahead, each man lost in his own thoughts. Suddenly, Stan held up a hand; the two following stopped. Reed turned around and spoke softly, 'There's two hikers just ahead. I think they've heard us so we'll just lag behind. If they want to join us, that's fine but I'd rather not let it get to that.'

The three men started off again, but this time at a slower cadence. The small group ahead began to extend the distance and eventually disappeared around a bend in the track. This routine was kept up for the next hour. Stan produced his map and announced that the trail to the motel was approaching. 'I'll go ahead just to make sure there's nobody about. John, keep watch on the rear.'

With nothing to do, Dennis Hayne sat down and rummaged through his daypack for a candy bar. Stan walked at a brisk pace until he was out of sight around a corner. Hayne got to his feet and he and Allen set off to catch up. Soon enough, Stan appeared around the bend and indicated the left side of the track as Hayne and Allen viewed it.

Sure enough, there were the vague remains of a trail leading off into the scrub. Two large trees, lying across the path, blocked passage to anything but hikers. However, it was immediately obvious to all three men that nobody had ventured down this path in decades. The men conferred. 'The best thing to do is sneak through the bush to the side of the entrance. Nobody will think to look there,' said the ever-cautious Stan.

With one more visual sweep of the area, the men set off into the scrub; all wishing a machete had been packed. Finally, they stepped out onto a path that, while not clear, was easily navigable. The formation of this new trail was as wide as the path they had just left. Stan held up a precautionary hand. The sound of voices drifted through the trees. Hikers on the main trail. The sound got fainter and the men moved off. Stan had said during the planning stages that it was about one-and-a-half kilometres to the motel.

When the group had gone a hundred yards down the trail, Stan produced a radio and contacted the boat. Bob Pitman's voice came over the airwaves. Stan gave a sit rep and switched the unit off. The trio tramped on, the going easier now, down a slope. The infestation of bugs had almost ceased; the ones that were about weren't paying the men much attention.

It was John Allen who spotted the rusty galvanised iron roof of the once proud motel. 'There she is chaps,' he exclaimed. Now the men entered a steady trot the last hundred yards or so. The path levelled off and widened out into a weed-infested gravel carpark. To the left-rear of the carpark, there stood a brick building which even Dennis Hayne could have guessed was the office. The rest of the motel was out of sight now, behind a garden which followed the alignment of the building.

Stan, diagram of the motel layout in hand, paused to get his bearings. He pointed towards the end of the garden. 'We go this way,' he declared. Dennis and John followed their fearless leader across the weed-infested gravel carpark and through a thin patch in the weed choked garden. When they emerged, the motel was spread out before them. Now they were on a crazy paving hardstand which spread out all the way to the two long buildings set perpendicular to each other. In the center of the paved area was the pool, which now contained a few feet of stagnant green water.

Allen pricked his ears up. A sound, rather like a door closing, floated across the paved area. He looked about. The empty rooms stared back. John Allen noticed that the buildings themselves seemed to be in fair condition until he saw the result of a large tree that had fallen across one end of one of the buildings. The men traipsed past the pool towards the far end of a block. Stan spoke, 'The room we want is the last one. I've got the key. I locked it when I came here last. I also locked two other rooms with keys I found in the office.'

By this time, three-thirty by Stan's watch, the trio had reached the covered veranda that ran along the front of the building. Stan dramatically produced a key from his pocket and walked up to the last door in the block. He turned it and the door opened silently. He and Hayne entered but Allen remained outside for a moment. Something else had caught his attention. The veranda was covered in dust and the men had made footprints. But here there were clearly other sets. And another thing; they looked recent. Hikers, he thought. He decided not to tell Stan.

CHAPTER 24

The boys wandered in and out of each room, Daniel taking photos by the dozen. They found two of the rooms locked but didn't get too concerned.

As the sun began to go down behind the hills to the west, creating long shadows, the teens had reached the last room in the motel which they also found locked. Daniel tried the door several times, just to make sure, but it was locked all right. Had the teenager studied the lock more carefully, he might have noticed minute traces of graphite powder in the keyway, a sure sign of recent use.

As they walked back along the covered way, something over near the office caught Daniel's eye. He instinctively grabbed his friend and shoved him through an open doorway of one old room. Sam let out an exclamation as Daniel shut the door rather hard with his foot. Daniel peered out through the dirt encrusted window next to the door. He was joined by Sam. They saw two men and then a third traipse through the weed-infested garden next to the former carpark. The trio made their way across the back of the pool area almost towards the boys, then over to the far end of the block.

Both boys watched through the grimy window. From their vantage point, they could just make out the men loitering outside the end room, as if having a discussion. The teens heard voices and the sound of laughter. Then, as the teenagers looked on, the men disappeared. Seconds later, they heard a door shut. Daniel let out the breath he had been holding and turned to Sam. 'We'd better tell the others. I think I know two of those guys.'

Sam took off his pack and rummaged through it for the radio before remembering that it was in his pocket. He produced it and called Jeremy. Harry answered with a cheery 'Hi lads. Guess what we're doing?'

'Put Jeremy on, Harry.' Sam's voice was urgent.

There was a silence then the radio crackled. Jeremy sounded quite close, 'What's up? You sounded urgent, Sam'

'It is. We've got company. Remember the two guys that passed our campsite? Well, they are here at the motel, with another man.'

'Okay. Got that. Harry and I will return to shore and be ready to assist if need be.'

'Roger that. I'll call back when I can.' Sam switched the radio off, thankful that their nerdy friend could switch to a dead-serious mode when required and stared at Daniel. 'What do we do now?'

'For a start, lock that door. Keep away from the window. I'm going to try the back door of this room and see if I can creep across to that room they're in. Maybe I'll be able to hear something.' Daniel reached into his pocket and produced a pack of chewing gum. Offering Sam one, he put the stick of gum in his mouth and dropped the wrapper on the floor.

Sam was about to disapprove of Daniel's plan but gave up. Instead, he handed Daniel his baton. 'You may need this.' Daniel grabbed his camera, figuring he might at least be able to record sound. Then both boys moved to the end of the room and Daniel opened the door as quietly as he could. Not having been opened in over thirty years, the hinges groaned and then squeaked. The boys dared not breathe. Sam stood back and unwrapped his chewing gum, similarly disposing of the wrapper.

There was enough of a gap for Daniel to squeeze out, and he did so, stepping out onto the small porch. He looked about. These small concrete areas were divided off from one another by wooden trellis. Like the first room the pair had seen, there was a light structure over the top, extending out from the building for about six feet, creating a shaded area. Daniel couldn't help thinking how it must have looked in the motel's heyday. The boy crept over to the dividing screen and peered through into the neighbouring terrace. Empty. He could just make out voices, so he concluded that they were emanating from the end unit, two units away.

Now was the difficult part. Daniel saw that the screen separating the last room from the one next to him was almost totally gone, just the frame remained. If he climbed onto the neighbouring terrace, he could easily be seen. But he wasn't finding anything out staying here. He decided to take the risk. Creeping along the low, vine entangled fence, he found a place where the vine was thinner, and he could get through. Daniel put one leg through the creepers and pushed the infernal things out of his way so he could see properly. Not seeing anything to give concern, he touched ground with on foot and hauled himself through.

Crouching in the weed-infested yard, Daniel could hear the voices clearer now. He decided it was now or never. He was worried that his long afternoon shadow would be seen, or his outline against the setting sun. Crawling on his belly, he made it over to the opposite fence, and stole towards the building. From here, he could just make out the back windows of the next room. He prayed that he was right about which room the men were in. The rear windows and door of the room he was now outside were just as filthy as any he had seen in this forgotten place. It would be hard to spot him from the inside but what if one of them opened the door?

As if on cue, Daniel heard a door open. Out the corner of his eye, he saw the door of the next room swing out and a man step onto the paved terrace. A voice from inside said, 'What you doin', Dennis?

'Just havin' a leak'.

'I was just tellin' John. Twenty bags. Five of us. Should be a piece of cake. But it's getting late now, so I say we leave now and come back tonight.'

There was a grumble from the man outside and a monosyllable answer from a third voice inside the room. Daniel heard the rear door of the room close

Daniel retreated from his position as quietly as he dared. His mind was in a spin. Bags? Bags of what? Twenty of them? Was it drugs? The teen assumed so. He had to tell

Sam. As silently as he could, he retraced his path across the weed strewn area and through the dividing vines. He tore over to the door which Sam had left opened, to avoid noise. Breathing hard, Daniel burst into the musty room and flopped down on the mattress.

'They've got bags of something in there. I don't know what. Whatever it is, they're not taking them away now. They're going to come back for them.'

Sam leaned against the wall, staring off into space. 'No, they're not.'

CHAPTER 25

Beatrice White could feel the excitement welling up in her husband like Mt Vesuvius about to explode. She retreated to a safe area of the living room in the trailer and watched Ray pace the floor. He punched one hand with the other and repeated over and over, 'I knew it, I knew it. Didn't I tell you, Bea?'

Beatrice said patiently, 'You did, dear, several times. I knew Jack Coburn would deliver the goods.' She remembered only too well the muted conversations at three in the morning on any given morning when Ray and Jack had discovered something that was going to nail the lid on the coffin of some Melbourne low-life. Figuratively speaking, of course.

'The trouble is that we've only got the nitty-gritty on four of them, and there are six. I may have to call on your surveillance skills, Bea. But we're going to have to be careful. Four of these guys are pros. They have a nasty habit of spotting surveillance a mile away. So, I thought I'd use the little cube camera.'

'The one in the flowerpot?'

'That's the one. After we've had a cuppa, distribute similar pots out the front. One will contain that cube camera we bought on the internet. Naturally, only water the ones without the camera!'

Beatrice gave her husband the 'no kidding' look. 'I'll get coffee going and you can get out the pot and the camera. Show me how it fits together. '

Over a steaming brew, Ray and Beatrice discussed the morning's activities. Bea mentioned that one of the robbers had walked off in the direction of the office. This was clearly news to Ray. His mug stopped halfway to his mouth. 'Which one? I didn't see any of them when I was talking to The Slipper.'

'Well, he must have gone to the kiosk because when he returned, which was about ten minutes after you, he had the papers and was chewing a Mars bar. He walked with a slight limp.'

Ray stared into space. He suddenly realised that he had made a dangerous and silly mistake. He had spoken to Jack Coburn out the front of the kiosk. The man his wife mentioned could only be Frank Taylor. Frank was a dangerous and cunning criminal. Ray had had dealings with him. But The Slipper knew him better. Coburn had been in the background at Charlie Munroe's funeral. And there, large as life, was Frank Taylor. Standing next to him had been Les Truscott.

'They're up here for something. I can smell it. The Slipper thinks so too. But what?' Ray continued sipping his coffee and staring vacantly at the opposite wall. Beatrice brought him out of his daydream.

'Has Jack gone through any recent unsolved cases?'

'What do you mean?'

'Robberies. Maybe they're up here to collect something.'

'That makes more sense than anything so far. The Slipper and I were working on the theory that they'd come up here to settle an old score. Although, with Shane Hill very much out of the way, I just can't think who the likely target would be.'

Bea was keen to set up the clandestine cameras and said as much to Ray. They carried their coffee mugs out onto the front porch. Ray walked over to a cupboard, unlocked it with a small key and produced a realistic looking marigold in a red pot. Using a fingernail, he opened a small door in the side of the pot, pressed some buttons and watched LED lights do their thing. Satisfied, he carried the 'plant' over to Bea, who had some of the real variety in her hands. Stepping out onto the lawn, the pair positioned the pots along the perimeter of the site.

'I just thought of something,' Bea said suddenly, looking around and keeping her voice low. 'It may not be important but the day after that mob moved in; I saw one of them place a Christmas tree box under the caravan. He was being very careful carrying it. And I've seen no evidence of a Christmas tree set up in the caravan or annexe.'

'Not meaning to sound like a charity, but every little helps. When we know that their campsite is empty, I think you and I have some detective work to do.'

CHAPTER 26

llen entered the short passage and heard the other two in the bathroom. He peered in. The bath itself had been lifted at the front, revealing a cavity underneath that should have been empty. It was not. Into every crevice white heavy-duty bags had been stuffed. Stan wrestled with one and lifted it out. He and Hayne hefted the bag onto the vanity unit. Reed fidgeted with the drawstrings and half a minute later, had the bag open.

In the golden light of the setting sun, Dennis Hayne and John Allen stared open-mouthed at the neat bundles of one hundred-dollar bills that almost burst out of the canvas sack.

John Allen recovered first. He picked up one of the bundles and flipped through the bills with his thumb. It amazed him that although he had helped steal this money over six years before, this was the first time he had seen it.

'I gotta have a leak,' Hayne mumbled.

'Yeah, well go out the back.'

Hayne trudged out of the bathroom and across to the rear door. He fumbled with the lock and was surprised to find the door opened easily. Stepping out onto the patio, he was invisible to those inside. Allen replaced the bundle of banknotes in the sack and Reed tied it up. He placed it rather haphazardly in the cavity and took out the stick supporting the bath. The two men lowered the tub down but found it didn't sit flat. Stan wasn't worried.

The two men left the confined space of the bathroom. Stan pulled the door closed and walked over to the dust covered bed. Sitting on the old mattress, Reed produced a small tin that contained several hand-rolled cigarettes. Left-handed, he worked one out of the tin and placing it between his lips, lit it and lapsed deep into thought. Suddenly he came back to earth. 'Yeah, that's what we'll do. Get up here tonight. Get the bags down to the lake. The problem remains as to whether we collect them tonight or leave that part until tomorrow as planned.'

'I think we *should* take them down to the lake tonight,' Allen confirmed. 'That way, we only need the tinny to collect it. Much neater.'

'You're right, John.' Turning to the open back door, Reed called out, 'What you doin', Dennis?'

Allen heard Hayne reply but didn't catch what it was. He had, by that time, moved away from the bed to the front door and was peering out. Nothing. But the footprints and the door closing sound bugged him. He looked around in time to see Dennis step in from the terrace and close the door. Stan roused himself from the bed and mustered the troops.

'Okay lads, let's go. Everything's as it should be. Last one out, pull the door closed. It'll lock itself.'

CHAPTER 27

For Stan Reed, Dennis Hayne and John Allen, the walk back to the holiday village was surprisingly pleasant. Hayne and Reed smoked and all three even talked in normal voices, not bothering to be quiet. They left just after four-thirty that afternoon, spirits high, and made good time on the way. Reed spoke while brushing a mosquito away, 'We'll do a pub run when we get back. I can hear a bottle of Black and White calling me.'

John Allen studied the big dial of his heavy Citizen diver's watch as the men walked along the familiar and welcoming gravel path past the jetty, bathed gold in the setting sun. Just after six, he noted. Les Truscott was tidying the tinny. He held up two enormous fish, grinning like a Cheshire cat. Stan headed down to the jetty, telling his companions he would join them later. Allen and Hayne scuffed along the gravel in the direction of the caravan, Hayne remarking how peaceful the place seemed. Most park residents were indoors now, the aroma of cooking oozing from every trailer they passed.

'I hope Les doesn't do those fish tonight,' John Allen remarked as the pair neared their trailer, 'I don't think I could look at another fish.' He added a cheerful 'Howdy' to Beatrice White as they drew level with the next-door trailer.

'Yeah, I see what you mean,' Hayne said. 'I might even give cooking a go myself, one night.'

'We'll discuss it with Sir Les when he gets back,' Allen added. 'Meanwhile I could murder a beer.'

The clatter of dishes in the sink signalled the end of another hearty meal, contributed to this time by Dennis, who had whipped up a fine potato salad. He helped Frank Taylor clean up while the chatter from the annexe permeated into the trailer. The television was on the day-night cricket match from Sydney, but the two men seated on the couch paid no attention. They talked mainly about the job ahead. Outside the annexe, Stan Reed enjoyed a quiet cigarette, and John Allen used a bottle opener on his keyring to remove the cap on a bottle of Carlsberg. The two men chatted, in muted tones, also about the night's task. The topic changed to fishing when evening strollers went by. Stubbing out his cigarette, Stan said, 'I'll get 'em all together soon, John. Sort out who's doing what.'

Allen nodded in agreement and the two men enjoyed what was left of the day's warmth before returning to the annexe.

Stan stepped up into the trailer and asked Frank and Dennis to join the others in the annexe. When everyone was assembled, Reed drew a small notebook from his pocket and cleared his throat.

'In accordance with what Charlie Munro wanted, I have made a schedule for tonight. It's quite simple. First up, I'm putting you in the boat, Johnny. I think Les must be getting sick of it by now. Plus, you've already been up to the motel.'

If Allen was annoyed, he didn't show it. He merely said, 'That's fine, Stan.'

'Everyone else is going up the hill.'

CHAPTER 28

In the old motel room, Daniel and Sam crouched rest to the still open back door in total silence, scarcely daring to breathe. Daniel glanced at his G-Shock: four-thirty-five. Finally, Sam summoned the courage to move over to the front window and peer out. He made as small an outline as possible, lest the men out on the paved area glanced back. He watched the trio retrace their steps past the pool and over to the overgrown garden. Once through the gap in the shrubs, they disappeared out of sight.

Sam whispered to Daniel, 'Give me the binocs.'

Daniel produced a compact but powerful pair of binoculars from his pack and crawled across to Sam's position. Sam took them and made a thorough study of the area, in particular the garden through which the men had appeared. Seeing nothing amiss, he turned to Daniel. 'I think we'd better go and find out what those guys were hiding in that room.'

'Right, we'll go out the back way. I'll lock the front door, just in case. We'll go the way I went. Hopefully they haven't locked the back door of the room they were in. Might have to break a window.'

The pair repacked any loose gear into their packs and

made for the back door, which was still ajar. They slipped out onto the terrace and over to the fence and the hole Daniel had used. Daniel went first and waited for his friend to burst through the vines and creepers. Both boys, keeping a low profile, made their way across to the missing trellis panel and stepped through into the neighbouring terrace. Stealing across to the door, Daniel tried the handle. This was the moment.

The weathered electroplated handle turned easily, and the sweating teen pushed gently. The door swung <u>in</u> silently and revealed the dark interior. Sam, who had brought his baton with him, extended the weapon with a flick of his wrist. Daniel let him go into the room first, baton held in the striking position. Sam's eyes darted everywhere, and he beckoned to Daniel to follow him.

The teens began a methodical search for anything resembling sacks stuffed with contraband. They searched cupboards, drawers and under the bed. Sam even produced his hunting knife and turning the mattress over, sliced a gaping hole in it. Finding nothing, the boys returned the mattress to its original place. Sam indicated the bathroom. The pair headed over to the door. This time Sam did the honours. It swung open to reveal a bathroom identical to the others the boys had seen.

Almost identical. Sam's trained carpenter's eye notice immediately the bath wasn't sitting right. Curious, he stepped over to it while Daniel went through the vanity unit. He worked his fingers under the edge of the tub and lifted.

To his surprise, it came up with only a small amount of effort. Seeing what was underneath made him drop it with a bang. Daniel just about had kittens there and then.

'Jesus, Dillon, what are you trying to do? Scare me to death?' Daniel gave his friend a reproachful look, and then noticed he had gone pale.

'What's wrong, Sam?'

'I'll show you. Help me lift this.'

Daniel grabbed on end of the bath and Sam moved along to the opposite end. Both strong boys hefted the heavy tub until it was against the tiled wall. Only then did Daniel look down. If Sam hadn't been holding the unit, it would have crashed down for a second time. He tightened his grip and simply stared at the bulging canvas sacks.

W..What's in them?,' he stammered.

'Money' said Sam, stating the obvious. 'Most probably stolen. Bank job, I'd say, judging by those bags. Well, we'd better get the others up here fast. We've got to get this fun ticket out of here.' Looking about the bathroom, Sam noticed a length of timber leaning against the wall. Grabbing it, he wedged it between the top of the bath enclosure and the underside of the tub. He and Daniel let go.

Sam reached into his pocket and produced the radio. He spoke as softly as he could into the small transceiver, 'Jeremy, Harry, it's Sam. Dan and I need you both up here pronto. Can't tell you why now.'

He waited for a reply from the raft. Daniel stared at the radio, willing his friends to answer. Finally, there came a crackle then Jeremy's voice came over strong and clear, 'Got that, guys. What's up?

'We've got some stuff to take back to the raft. Can't talk now. Get up here and leave a Glowing Trail'

A glowing trail was Daniel's idea to enable hikers and urban explorers to retrace their steps. Simply, the lead hiker places chemical lights at strategic positions along a trail. The boys had used glowing trails when exploring mines and urban exploring. In this instance however, the idea would be used for the return journey. Sam didn't fancy being lost in the rugged Australian bush carrying bags of money.

Sam rang off and placed the transceiver on the vanity unit. Daniel's eyes brightened.

'I've got a better idea. Why don't we take at least *some* of the bags down to the raft? Then all of us can come back up and get the rest. I don't fancy weighing Harry down with too many bags. He's just a little guy.'

Sam smiled when he thought of his pint-sized friend. 'Okay, I'll tell the others that the plan has been changed.' He picked up the transceiver and got through to Harry. The raft's cook sounded somewhat bewildered but understood the message. Sam looked at Daniel and said, 'Let's get out of here.'

The boys hefted two bags each and made their way out through the back door. Once outside, they went through to the neighbouring terrace and from there, out the back of the motel and down the slope towards their original track. The going was slowed only by the thick scrub, but the boys managed the extra load well. They crunched the underbrush with their hiking boots, pausing only to drink from their canteens.

When they reached the minor track, Daniel checked his watch: half past five. Sam contacted the raft and gave a sit rep. Jeremy answered and told Sam that he and Harry were ready to make the trek up. They had a visitor briefly - the girl from the houseboat moored on the other side of the bay, looking for Daniel.

As the boys made their way down the draw, Daniel voiced his concerns about the fading light. Here, between two hills, the area was darkening quickly, although the lake itself was still bathed in warm sunshine. Soon the darkness would be absolute. Sam reassured him to keep going straight down. Jeremy's voice crackled out of Sam's pocket; the raft floodlights would be on to assist the hikers. Occasionally, a glimpse of the lake appeared through the trees, the far hills now in semi-darkness.

Daniel saw it first; a shaft of light stabbed through the forest. Heading straight for it wasn't possible, with the thickness of the scrub; the boys had to take a slight diversion and ended up bursting out of the trees very close to their neighbours. The raft was tied to the jetty, deck floodlight on and illuminating the campsite. Sam and Daniel tried to play down the fact that they were each carrying two large bags stuffed with cash. The pair felt as if everybody on the houseboat was staring at them. Jeremy appeared on the raft's deck: Sam whistled, and Jeremy waved. He ran down the jetty and around the shore to greet his friends.

Grabbing a bag each from Sam and Daniel, it was on Jeremy's mind to tell the hikers about using the underwater camera. He realised, however, that they were tired and not looking forward to a return journey that night. They made their way over to the jetty and climbed onto the raft. Harry hugged both his friends and relieved Daniel of his load. The canvas sacks were taken into the deckhouse and heaped them onto Sam's bunk.

'I'll open one and show you what's inside,' Sam said after Harry thrust a beer into his hand. 'Then Dan and I have a rest and all four of us head back up.' He placed his beer on the floor and reached for his pocketknife. The cord securing the HVP came away easily and the sack yawned open. Harry and Jeremy were too stunned to say anything. They just stared. Jeremy managed to mumble, 'How much is there?'

'I don't know. But I'd say it came from a bank job. The important thing is that there are more where these came from. Dan heard on of the men say something about twenty sacks. We took four. It doesn't take Euclid to figure that leaves sixteen. Four each. It will be hard going for Harry. So, I suggest two courses of action. One, we take the lot to a waypoint in the forest. We can leave the GPS tracker with the bags. And collect them later. Two, we bring the whole lot back here, hide them on the raft, call our parents and the cops and get over to the launching ramp. We can anchor there until the police arrive.'

'I think I'll be able to manage, Sam,' Harry said. But Sam wasn't convinced. 'Dan and I will rest up a bit. I think we should get the rest of the money later tonight. So, we'll finish these beers and get going in a couple of hours. Dan, have you got anything to add?'

'Yes. Torches everyone. Hand-held. Red or blue filters. Soft shoes if you've got them. Mobile phones get left here. When we get to the motel, absolute silence. One of use goes ahead and gives a sit rep. These people could be up there now. We don't know their timetable. It suffices to say that if we get caught, they won't just cross us off their Christmas card list.'

A light snack and some shut-eye later, Sam stood up and checked his watch. Five past eight. 'Okay, that it. Let's get ready and we'll be off.' The raft became a beehive of activity. Fifteen minutes later, the four boys trooped along the jetty and made their way as quickly as they could into the scrub. From there the group turned right and headed north. Sam led with the GPS unit. The four separate beams of the boy's torches shone ahead of them in a kaleidoscopic dance. Daniel remembered to bring his small machete and scythed through the overhanging scrub with ease. Jeremy had a pocket full of chemical lights and affixed them to trees at periodic intervals.

When they reached the minor track, Sam stopped the group and checked everyone was okay. He cautioned them about excessive noise from now on. The small party crossed the trail and headed up the steeper slope, barely able to see each other in the darkness. When the terrain began to level off, Sam paused again and conferred with Daniel. Sam faced the group and whispered, 'It's just ahead. Being familiar with the place and second smallest, I will go and check the place out.'

The four boys began moving forward, this time with only one torch lighting the way. Presently this was switched off and the last few yards were by moonlight. Ahead, Sam could make out the broken-down fence that once bordered the motel. Then, as the moon came out from behind a cloud, the buildings appeared, chalk-white in the light. Sam crept up to the fence and crouched beside a forlorn post. He gave a signal to come forward quietly, and the boys gathered silently around.

Sam whispered that he was going to have a look around and, like a shadow, slipped away towards the closest building. The boys saw him dart between the two blocks and along the covered verandah. He was out of sight for no more than ten minutes, which seemed more like an hour to the waiting teens. He reappeared from the back of the western building, panting and excited.

'Well, it's still there. I say we move it to the edge of the tree line, take a breather then move the lot in short bursts, down to the raft. It's eight minutes to nine so I think we should move now.'

Daniel was the first to his feet. 'Okay, no lights. We use the moon. Quiet as possible.' The four stole across the flat ground and around behind the motel building. Daniel led the way, pausing now and then, listening. Satisfied he moved on until the four boys were opposite the end room. Somebody's watch chimed the hour. Daniel told them to wait and crept forward, over the grass area to the terrace outside the dark windows. Hearing nothing, Daniel signalled to the three waiting boys to join him.

When all four teenagers had gathered on the back terrace, Daniel slowly stood and gingerly opened the door. He peered through the moonlight into the blackness, trying to make out the features of the room. Fidgeting for his torch, he turned it on and swept the red beam over the floor. 'Okay,' he whispered. 'Let's go.'

The four teenagers entered the room like ghosts, Daniel making a beeline for the bathroom. He played the light onto the bath, still in the raised position. The cavity bulged with white canvas bags with black stencilling. Daniel wasted no time, 'Two bags each down to the tree line. Drop them and return. Harry, here's a pay rise.' He grabbed two bags and dumped them on the floor. Harry picked them up easily enough and squeezed out the door into the short hallway. Sam was next and departed with his load. Jeremy just stared at the canvas sacks when Daniel retrieved them from the bath cavity.

'Hurry up, Williams. You're not in the supermarket, you know.'

Jeremy snapped out of the trance he was in and picked up the two sacks. Daniel was right behind him and the two boys made their way out of the motel room by the light of Daniel's torch. The pair walked quietly but with purpose out of the motel and into the scrub. They passed Harry and Sam jogging back to collect more loot. They found the first canvas bank bags placed neatly against a tree. Placing their load in the same manner, they doubled back and once again saw Sam and Harry laden with their final bags. Daniel drew level with Jeremy and whispered, 'This is it. The last four bags and we're out of here.'

'All I want is to be back at the raft.'

The pair wasted no time returning to the room to retrieve the final canvas bank bags. As they stepped into the dusty, dark room, Daniel's heart almost stopped. Just visible through the dirty window beside the front door, he saw the beams of two flashlights sweeping over the paved hardstanding, near the garden. Voices, rough and uneducated, carried over the pool enclosure. Daniel froze. Jeremy heard the voices too and reacted quicker. Keeping his torch pointed at the floor, he tore into the bathroom and wrenched the money sacks out of the bath cavity. Hefting all four, he retraced his steps and hissed at Daniel, 'Come on.'

Daniel recovered and followed Jeremy out of the room. He had the presence of mind to pull the door to the porch closed behind him. Weighed down with four heavy bags, Jeremy made good time across the grassed area behind the room and out into the light scrub, Daniel hot on his heels. Jeremy made it to the fence line and finally dropped the sacks. Daniel picked up two of them and together they joined Sam and Harry in the forest. Jeremy, panting hard, explained their near miss. Sam took charge and said simply, 'Let's get out of here. We'll have to grab the chem lights on the way down. No point leaving a trail of breadcrumbs for them to follow.'

CHAPTER 29

he five men trudged down the last hundred yards in the darkness, shadows created by their torches dancing about the forest. As their boots kicked at the light scrub on the track, a curious wallaby got the message and hopped away. Stan pressed the light button on his watch. Nine-fifteen. The motel came into view, silent and forlorn, as the men stepped out from the forest's canopy into the moonlight. The ground levelled off and torch beams probed the former office block. Emerging from the overgrown garden, their footfall on the paved hardstand seemed loud in the deathly quiet of the forest.

A noise over by the pool caused Bob Pitman to jump and he whipped out his .45 and aimed it around the pool area. A possum, caught in the beam of several powerful torches, scampered along the pool edge. Satisfied that all was well, Pitman pocketed the pistol. The five shadowy figures, led by Stan Reed, moved over the flagstones to the end of the accommodation block. Reed reached into his coat pocket for the key.

The key was slotted into the lock. Reed paused for effect and addressed the group, 'Okay, lads. This is it. This is what we've all been waiting for. We all know what we must do.

Four bags each and straight out the door. We meet up at the lake-end of this building.'

The men muttered various comments as Reed turned the key. It rotated easily and the door squeaked open. Stan Reed knew as soon as he stepped into the motel suite that something was dreadfully wrong. The door into the bathroom was open and moonlight spilled into the narrow hallway. He fought to stay calm, telling himself that he mustn't have shut it after all. The men piled up behind him, eager to see the cash that they had dreamed of for the past six years. Reed almost didn't want to go into the small room, fearful of what he might see. Frank Taylor moved past him and stopped at the threshold of the bathroom.

'So they're under the bath, are they?' Taylor asked. 'You should have lowered the bath when you left, not left it propped up like that.'

Stan fumbled with the key but followed Dennis Hayne, who said simply, 'He did put the bathtub down. I saw him.'

'Well, it ain't down now,' Frank said, unnecessarily, for Reed and Hayne were now beside him.

The night was made ugly; the moonlight, streaming through the window, accused. Stan called for calm, which, under the circumstances, was akin to throwing a pie at a freight train. Frank Taylor looked as if he could tear the head off Godzilla. Dennis Hayne, predictably, punched a hole in a wall. Bob Pitman stormed outside and let fly with a string of obscenities. Les Truscott turned a shade of white and just stood mumbling to himself.

Accusations of double crossing flew back and forth. At this stage, nobody suspected outside interference.

'The money can't be very far away,' Stan said quietly. Only Les seemed to hear. 'We last saw it at four-thirty. It's now nine-twenty. That gives whoever took the cash almost five hours to get it away from here. That's assuming they took it away. They might have it hidden in this old motel, waiting for a better opportunity to get it away.'

'One of us is very rich then,' muttered Frank Taylor.

'Cut it out Frank,' ordered Stan. 'In the short time that it was last checked on, not one of us had the opportunity to get up here, steal twenty bags of cash and hide it somewhere. It is outsiders alright, but whom?'

'Johnny left the site. Said he went down to the kiosk,' Taylor persisted.

'He got me a packet of fags,' Hayne was quick to defend. 'He must have got 'em somewhere.'

'Let's start thinking logically,' Stan went on. 'Who the hell, besides the six of us in the trailer, knew about where the money was hidden. I personally can't think of a single person who would have known the details of this part of the operation. The only other one who did know is in the harp farm. No, it has to be local interference, probably just hikers. In which case, the money is still around here. Somewhere.'

'I'm gonna search every room in this place,' Dennis Hayne growled, heading for the door.

'I'll help, Dennis,' Les said and the two men started a thorough rummage of each room in turn.

'Give them a hand,' Stan told Frank, who didn't need an excuse to leave the tense atmosphere of the room. He had hardly stepped out onto the covered verandah, when Les gave an excited holler.

'Look what I've found,' he exclaimed, emerging from the room he had been searching. He held out his hand to reveal chewing gum wrappers. Two of them.

'They're free of dust and you can still smell the flavour distinctly.'

Stan shot out of the room he was in as if by compressed air. He strode up to Les and examined the plastic wrappers. He cast a glance around the abandoned buildings, willing them to reveal their secrets.

'Kids,' was all he said. 'It must be. What we're looking for is a group of teenagers, big enough to be able to carry those canvas sacks out of here. Johnny made mention of such a group the other day. Give me the radio, Frank.'

Taylor produced the slim walkie talkie and handed it to Reed, who switched it on and spoke in clipped sentences. John Allen's voice came through, loud and clear. Stan gave some instructions and Allen replied with 'Roger, Wilco.'

Stand turned the unit off and handed it to Frank. By this time, all five men were standing on the verandah, waiting for Stan to make the next move.

'Okay, listen up. Johnny is going to scour the lake in the boat. The rest of us are going to make our way down there to the bay next to the one we had planned to use. He mentioned a group of teenagers on some kind of raft. Dennis, you were with him. What did it look like?'

Hayne looked flustered at having to remember, but he did his best.

'They had built a small pier and tied the raft to that. They also set up a small shelter on the shore and had stacked some firewood.'

'Industrious little buggers, aren't they?' Stan muttered. Something tells me those kids might be able to help us.'

Hayne went on, 'There was a houseboat too.'

'Yeah, I remember that one. It cruised past us when we collected you and John.'

'No, this one was in the bay, opposite the raft. Had quite a few people on it, too.'

Stan stared at Dennis. 'That changes things a bit. I'm waiting for a sit rep from Johnny. I think we'd better complete searching this dump first. Just in case. Then we'd better get down to the lake as fast as we can.'

CHAPTER 30

As the boys began organising the heavy canvas bags, they heard the first in a series of hollers from the old motel. If that wasn't the catalyst to move, nothing was. Struggling under the weight of four sacks each, the boys stepped heavily down the slope, Sam leading while Jeremy took up the rear. Holding the bags and a torch at the same time was proving impossible. There was no end of gratitude for the idea to leave the chemical lights to follow. The four teenagers tore through the scrub, eternally grateful that it was all downhill.

Jeremy stopped at each chem light to collect it and shove it in a pocket. Then he hefted his bags and continued after his friends. There was some concern when a marker light wasn't visible; then Harry spied it through the trees, off to the right. As the boys altered direction, the inevitable happened. Harry stumbled on an exposed tree root and went flying. Daniel whispered for the party to stop. 'I need lights over here,' he said as loudly as he dared. Crouching beside the dazed, injured boy, Daniel helped his friend into a sitting position, using one of the bank bags for support.

Sam and Jeremy gathered around, and the extent of Harry's injuries were revealed under the red light of their torches. His hands were scuffed badly, both knees the same, showing through torn jeans. Daniel's biggest concerns were the abrasions to Harry's face, his handsome features marred by scratches and cuts. Jeremy produced his first aid kit out of thin air and began wiping blood away with alcohol swabs. The injured teen winced with pain with each application. Daniel procured his own kit and attended to Harry's scraped knees.

'We'll get him to the raft ASAP,' Daniel decided, 'and come back for the bags later. I'll carry him over my back' Jeremy and Sam hurriedly agreed. Helping the still dazed Harry to his feet, Daniel crouched down and the teens manoeuvred the hapless boy into the fireman's carry position. This time, the entourage set of at a much slower pace. Daniel found the downward slope working against him, with constant braking effort required.

'The minor track is just here,' Sam said helpfully, removing another chem light from its perch in a tree branch. 'Not far to go now. The news acted like a tonic on the small group. They surged out of the brush onto the narrow trail and ploughed with a renewed vigour into the trees on the other side. Down the sloping ground they went, Daniel constantly checking that his passenger was okay. He said, 'I think we'd better take him to that houseboat. There's bound to be someone there who can help him better than us.'

They glimpsed lights from the large houseboat through the trees and made straight for them. Now the slope of the ground was easy, and the last few metres were covered at a trot. They burst out of the light scrub and made for the vessel, floating serenely at its moorings. The sound of chatter and laughter came to the boys. A figure appeared on the front deck, silhouetted against a yellow lantern fixed to the deckhouse. A familiar voice said, 'Is that you, Daniel?'

'Hi Allison. I hope we're not intruding. We've got an injured crewman. Slipped and fell in the darkness. I think he's worse than we believe'.

Allison didn't need a medical report. She deduced Daniel wasn't carrying his friend for fun. Leaping over the grab rail and landing expertly on the twig covered ground, she trotted over to Daniel, checked Harry's vital signs and swung into action. 'Bring him on board.' Calling out to a man who had materialised on the top deck, Allison yelled, 'Dad, get down here. We need help.'

By this time, the small group had made it to the gangway. 'I think I can walk from here,' Harry managed through pained lips. Daniel let him down but supported him with Allison's help. They stepped on board, Allison showing them into the most luxurious cabin the boys had ever seen. Sam and Jeremy followed them inside. Alison indicated a comfortable-looking couch and Harry was helped onto it.

A man, whom Sam judged to be in his late forties, appeared in the room and introduced himself; 'I'm Kevin, Allison's father. Your friend is in good hands. What happened by the way?'

The three boys exchanged guilty looks. Jeremy cleared his throat and said, 'Well, I think I'd better start at the beginning.

The four of us came up here on a rafting holiday. Sam and Daniel knew about an old motel up in the hills.'

Kevin interrupted, 'That must be the Lake View Motel. Abandoned in the late eighties. Known locally as The Bates Motel. Some local guy lived there for a few years.'

'Well, those two set off this afternoon to explore it while Harry and I used an underwater camera to explore Old Rupertsvale. We get a radio message from Sam to say that they'd found something and needed help getting it back to the raft. The plan changed slightly, and they appeared back at the raft with four canvas bags stuffed with cash.'

'Then we all traipsed up there and saw more bags. We were getting the last four out, when I saw torch lights moving across the pool area. To say we got out of there in a hurry is an understatement. And that's how Harry got hurt. Virtually running down a mountain at night, with Liberia's national deficit wasn't a smart thing to do.'

Kevin said, 'Well the thing to do now is to get the missing bags here and call the police and explain to them what's happened. We'd better hurry, too, if what you're saying's correct. Where are the bags, by the way?'

Jeremy rummaged through his pack and produced the map. He pointed to a place near the minor track and said, 'Just about here. We were still north of the track when Harry did his party trick. We just left the bags there and got Harry down here.'

Kevin was touched. 'I'm glad you decided what was more important, your friend or money.'

Allison chimed in, 'They sure made the right choice. He's such a good looker.'

'There's no need to go overboard' Sam muttered, his nose clearly out of joint.

'There'll be a problem with phone signal from here,' Jeremy exclaimed, changing the subject. We've had next to nothing since we came up here.'

'You can use my sat phone. You boys found the money, you make the call. I'll be here.'

'There's a bit more to it than that. When Daniel and Sam were at the old motel initially, some men came from God knows where and went into one of the rooms. Daniel thought he recognised two of them. So he crept up and listened to them. That's how we found out about the money.'

'Recognised from where?'

'They walked past our camp the day before,' Jeremy said.

Allison's father reflected for a moment. 'I wonder what they were doing there. Anyway, we must retrieve the other bags, so I suggest we do that now. The three able bodied boys and myself. We'll bring them back here. Then we'll call the cops and hand the whole thing over to them.'

The boys donned shoes and made sure they had torches with them. Kevin pressed a switch on a wall panel and dowsed the foredeck lights. 'No point in advertising the fact the cash is here when we get it down here and I don't particularly want to run into a gang of pissed-off robbers who may just decide to head down to the lake for a bit of recon'.

CHAPTER 31

As the group made its way down the gangway and over the hard-baked ground towards the tree line, Jeremy asked, 'Have you any idea which bank job it was?'

Kevin reflected. 'We're not from Melbourne. The two parties here are from Sydney, Fairlight to be exact. But I have a friend who was in the armed robbery squad in Melbourne. I remember him talking about a huge robbery in a suburb called Bays Water. Kevin pronounced the word as two. I don't know where that is. But I recall him saying that the cops were keeping mum about the amount involved. And a rumour surfaced that it may have been an inside job.'

As the four traipsed up the slope towards the minor track, Daniel said, 'I vaguely recall that. One thing that struck me is the fact that the story disappeared from the limelight very shortly after.'

'That was because the police didn't have the faintest idea who had pulled the job. They played their cards quietly, hoping the underworld would flush out the perpetrators, to no avail. It seems that the underworld were equally clueless.'

'Was it possible that a bunch of complete unknowns pulled the job?' asked Sam.

'Possible, but they would have to be very well organised.'

The ground levelled off and the narrow track appeared through the scrub. Daniel held up a warning hand. Peering out onto the trail, he saw nobody. But he was listening more than looking. Was that someone yelling in the distance? Did the sound come from the lake or the hills? He beckoned to the others. They approached quietly. Daniel whispered, 'The remaining bags are about fifty yards north of this track. Okay, from now on no talking and no superfluous noise.'

The party stole out onto the track, half expecting to see masked men with daggers drawn. The silent forest stared back at them. Moving off the track and into the trees, the small group made their way silently towards the place where their friend fell and the bags of cash were left on the ground. In the tomb-like silence of the forest, a twig snapping underfoot sounded like a small pistol going off. Jeremy almost had kittens. Sam spotted the first of the familiar white objects and darted ahead before Daniel could say anything.

Grabbing two sacks he whispered, 'Let's get out of here. I thought I heard a noise way off to my left.'

This was all the others needed. The remaining money sacks were picked up and the four started the journey back to the camping area. This time Kevin signalled for quiet. Footsteps on the forest floor could be heard approaching the group. The four stood fast. The footfalls got louder and before anyone could speak, a small grey wallaby bounded into view. The animal twitched its nose and hopped away.

Relieved, the group set off again. Voices ahead caused them to stop again. Kevin stepped forward out onto the minor track in time to see two girls with heavy packs walking along the track in the direction of Rourke's Drift mining area. Luckily they were walking away, so didn't see him. Kevin signalled to the three boys to follow him and soon they were yomping down the slope towards the small bay, breaking out into light chatter.

Allison was standing on the foredeck with an adult male, when the money laden group approached the houseboat. She held a finger to her mouth indicating silence. The boys immediately stopped talking and trod over the deadfall covered ground to the side of the vessel.

Allison said quietly, 'Your friend is dead to the world. I gave him some pain killers and he's out for the count. I think he should stay here overnight.'

The man with Allison walked over to the boys as they ascended the aluminium gangway, their sneakers scuffing on the anti-skid surface.

'Is there any more where this came from? I could use a new Bentley.'

'There's enough in each bag for two Bentleys,' Kevin replied. 'Okay, first things first. I'll get my sat phone and the boys can call the police in Melbourne. These bags must be kept out of sight. It is probable, from what I've heard, that the perpetrators are in the area.'

The last bags were carried into the front room of the deckhouse where a comatose Harry lay on the couch. The boys hefted the bags to one side and piled them up in front of the dinette. Allison's father said: 'I'll just have a look at the bags.' and made his way over to the canvas sacks. Kneeling, he examined one closely.

'Well,' he said with a grin, 'these bags are easily identifiable. The words 'First District Bank' are clearly readable. You'll be pleased to know that the police will be able to directly connect these bags here with that robbery in Melbourne.

After adding his bags to the pile, Jeremy checked on his friend. The sleeping boy's face looked more bruised now and Jeremy said as much to Allison.

'Yeah. He sure won't be a beauty contest winner for a while', she replied. 'Hopefully, by the time school starts again, he'll only have a few duelling scars to boast about.'

Kevin interrupted carrying a mobile phone with a thick antenna. 'I've got the number of the Armed Robbery Squad. Ring them and just tell it like it happened. Use the back deck. You'll get a better signal.'

The boys conferred as to who would make the call. Daniel decided to, because he heard what the men said and saw the money in its hiding place. He took the phone from Kevin and made his way through to the aft deck. Sitting on a banana lounge, he nervously made the call.

While Daniel made the all-important call to the police, Kevin invited the two remaining boys up onto the main deck. Here, they were introduced to the holidaymakers from both parties. Small bottles of beer were produced. Sam and Jeremy settled into a comfortable deck lounge. Soon, Jeremy, the most notorious non-party animal imaginable, was getting into the swing of things. Everyone asked the same predictable questions. What were they going to do with the money? Give it back? Keep it?

During a lull in proceedings, Jeremy took Sam aside to the railing. In the glow of fairy lights attached to the rails and looking over the still water towards the raft, Jeremy said, 'This is what *we* should be doing, partying and enjoying ourselves. I've been taking this whole trip too seriously.'

Sam choked on his beer. 'Finally found out what a good time's all about. Well, we've still got a few days left so that's what I propose we do.'

They returned to the gathering and discovered that Allison wasn't the only attractive girl there. Soon both boys were chatting away to girls their own age. Presently, Daniel joined them, having given the sat phone back to Kevin. He gave a brief summary of what the Armed Robbery Squad detectives had told him but broke off when Allison joined the small group. After giving the latest on Harry, Allison was keen to find out more about Daniel.

Daniel took a sip of his drink. 'I was beginning to think I had to throw myself off a cliff before you'd take any notice of me.'

The girl laughed. 'It's just my nursing instinct kicking in. I was seriously worried about your friend. I'm halfway through a diploma of nursing, luckily for you guys.

'You can say that again. Speaking of our friend, when will he be back on deck, no pun intended?'

Allison was in deep thought. 'Well, he can go back to your boat tomorrow, but he needs more rest. I'm still concerned about his knee and his facial injuries. I probed about as best I could, looking for a depressed fracture, but I think he's just going to have some large bruises. I also had a look everywhere else but found nothing. You'll have to do the cooking yourselves for a while.'

Daniel thought, so she got out of Harry that he's the cook. He took another mouthful of beer. 'That'll be interesting. Sam is the only other one who knows how to cook. His Italian background sees to that. Jeremy couldn't cook to save himself. I can prepare basic food, but nothing like what we've been used to on this holiday.'

The two teenagers chatted some more, and Daniel couldn't help noticing that Allison was now standing a lot closer than before. He had also observed Allison's father wandering about, seemingly ignoring the other adults.

'I think you'd better have a word with your father. He's puzzled about something. I can't wait 'till all that money is out of our hands and you people can get back to normal.'

'Let's go to my stateroom. You can tell me about it there.'

* * *

'As I was saying, Kevin,' one of the adults was saying with increasing annoyance.

Kevin came back to reality. 'I'm sorry, Mike. It's just that one of those kids said something that's been bugging me.

I'm going to call an old friend and tell him. This may be very important.'

Without waiting for a reply, Kevin ducked down the companionway and into his stateroom. He picked up the phone and dialled a number from memory. A voice crackled at the other end. 'Coburn'.

CHAPTER 32

The five men stood under the covered verandah and studied, under torch light, the rough map that Stan Reed produced having called a temporary halt to the room search.

'I'm in two minds,' Stan said, 'as to whether to keep searching this place or forget it and follow instinct. If it was the kids on the raft, where would they hide the bags?'

'If it was them, it's possible that they hid the loot in the forest and plan to get it later,' Frank chipped in.

'Anything's possible, but we'd better make tracks. I suggest we scour the bush in an area between here and the boy's camp site. When we get there, three of us can watch that raft while the others scour the lake in the boat. I'll get Johnny on the blower, and he can collect the ones who want to join him.'

Reed pointed towards the end of the building.

'That's the most direct way. We'll have to keep our eyes on the compass, but it should be okay. When we get to the water, we'll have to be careful. No sound. We have to be sure we know where the money is. I'm hoping it's on that raft. Should be easy to retrieve it.'

The other men realised there was a lot unsaid. They

readied themselves and made tracks. They traipsed through the scrub, each man cursing at the branches and creepers that seemed to deliberately get in their way. Stan spoke into the transceiver, 'Johnny, we're on our way down. Hold the fort 'til we get there. Tell me what the kids on that raft are doing.'

Reed heard Allen's reply as soon as he released the talk button. 'Two teenagers have left the houseboat and walked over to the raft. Boy and a girl. Girl must be *from* the houseboat. Wouldn't need to be Einstein to figure what they're up to. Houseboat still has lights on board. No movement elsewhere.'

Reed acknowledged and pocketed the radio. He walked over to Frank Taylor and said, 'It would seem that our young friends have befriended the people on a big houseboat that's parked nearby. That complicates things a bit. More people to deal with. *Now* I'm not so sure that the money is on the raft.'

'You think it's on the houseboat?' Taylor asked.

'I think it's a possibility. We'll have to neutralise the occupants and stop them communicating. Then Johnny can bring the boat around from wherever he's hidden it, and we'll load it up. But first we'll have to make sure the money's not on the raft.'

The men trudged on down the hill, and soon came to the minor track. Reed stopped them on the narrow trail. 'From here on, I want silence. When we get to the edge of the lake, we spread out. Three of us will keep that houseboat under surveillance. I will take two with me to that raft and we'll check it out. If we find that clear, then four will board the houseboat and grab the cash. John tells me that two teenagers are on the raft. They'll be easy to handle. I'll take Frank and Les. Meanwhile, John, Dennis and Bob can wait in the scrub, ready to assist if need be.'

'Okay, let's move,' Stan growled. His companions didn't need any encouragement. The five men fanned out and made their way off the trail and down the slope. Stan moved to the west end of the group and told Dennis to get up the other end. With the order made up, the men made their way as quietly as they could over the last five hundred yards. Stan whispered to Frank that he couldn't see any lights from either vessel. He produced the radio from his pocket and called John Allen.

Allen's reply was that the raft was dimly lit but the houseboat had multiple lights on board and should be easy to see once they got closer. Allen added that he would flash his torch to signal his whereabouts and advised Reed to be on the lookout for it. Stan acknowledged and pocketed the radio. He told the others what to look for and almost immediately, Bob Pitman saw a bright blinking light through the trees ahead. The five almost ran down the slope towards the light.

Down on the lake, John Allen was making progress of his own. As the other five headed off to the motel ruins earlier that evening, Allen climbed into the tinny and made his way out onto the lake. Something about the boys on the raft had been nagging at him. He decided to take a clandestine look at their campsite and raft. Now upon hearing the news, and his instructions to collect two more gang members, he swung into action. He realise that he was able to do some surveillance of the teenagers campsite. Without further ado, increased speed and headed for Robin Bay.

He was fortunate that it was now dark and that he had remembered to bring the binoculars. Motoring slowly to the approaches to the small inlet, Allen killed the motor and retrieving a paddle, made his way closer to the shore. He hastily thought up a plan which included leaving the tinny at the shore and proceeding on foot to observe the raft. The best place to leave the boat unattended was on the eastern side of the bay. This, however, meant a longer walk to a position where he would be able to keep an eye on the raft.

For his share in twenty million dollars, Allen would have hiked up the side of the Eiger. He scanned the lake in all directions but saw nothing of concern. He worried that the boat's aluminium hull might catch in the moonlight, but that was a risk he would just have to take. The shoreline was near now and he adjusted course to meet it side-on. Bumping against a submerged tree stump, Allen brought the tinny to a stop. He checked the small backpack and stood up. Organising a mooring line, he stepped onto the shore and switched on a torch. A convenient, if long-dead, tree presented itself in the blue light of the torch, and the boat was made fast to it.

Getting his bearings with the aid of a small compass set into the end of his utility knife, John Allen set off into the scrub where the darkness was absolute. The little compass glowed surprisingly brightly and he was able to make good time, his heavy hiking boots crunching the deadfall underfoot. Keeping his eye to the left, Allen trudged along, eventually finding a trail of sorts, which made the going easier. The faint glimmer of lights off to the left side made him stop.

Getting his bearings once more, Allen strode purposefully towards the lights. As he neared them, he stepped more carefully, making less noise. He came out of the trees and crouched in the knee-high sword grass. From here he had a good view of Robin Bay and he observed that the large houseboat, which he and Dennis had seen two days ago, was still moored there. He cursed himself quietly for forgetting the houseboat. Its presence presented a problem. Potential witnesses. Allen was under no illusions that if the boys had the money on their raft, the other members of his gang would use extreme violence to get it back.

He decided it was time to contact Stan and give a sit rep. Fishing the small transceiver out of his jacket pocket, he checked himself. Something about the scene before his eyes didn't seem right. Something was wrong. The raft. It still lay at its mooring, but it was awfully quiet. Allen studied the vessel with the binoculars. These kids sure went to bed early. It was only nine-thirty, yet not a single light showed anywhere on board. He thought. *Are they on the raft? If not, where else could four teenagers be?*

Voices carried over from the houseboat. Allen studied that vessel now. A group occupied the upper deck and lights shone from various windows. As he moved the field glasses about the deckhouse, Allen noticed a teenage couple on the darkened rear deck. They were engrossed in each other and didn't notice him. He suddenly wanted to get a better look at the houseboat. Wasn't it possible that the teenagers from the raft had befriended the people on the houseboat? Could the money be there now? Likely there were adults on board. They would know what to do. More space. More people to guard it.

Moving away from the edge of the trees, Allen spoke to Stan on the transceiver. He gave details of what he saw. While waiting for Reed to respond, it occurred to Allen that Stan hadn't asked about the likelihood of Robin Bay being occupied. He was sure going to get a surprise. The radio crackled and Reed's voice cam over clearly. 'We're on our way. It seems we've got more to deal with than first thought.'

So, he did know about the extra people in the inlet. What tactics would he use to get the money? Allen preferred not to think about it. If he could only get the bags of cash himself that would be something. Pocketing the radio, he switched on the torch and made his way north, parallel to the shore. Keeping the torch pointed down and pushing branches out of his way with his free hand, he rambled past the houseboat and reached a position at the head of the inlet, between the big houseboat and the raft. Clearing a space in the undergrowth to sit, Allen decided it was safe enough to use his tiny alcohol stove and brew a cup of coffee.

He had been there for about twenty minutes when he saw two people step out onto the front deck. Allen was certain it was the same teens that he saw on the rear deck. No matter, he watched them. The pair walked down the gangway and over the debris strewn ground along the shore. As they walked past him, Allen kept still and sipped his coffee. He watched the pair walk into the night. The partial conversation he had heard between them revealed nothing. He finished his drink and was packing up the mini stove when he heard noises coming out of the forest to the north.

The radio crackled and Stan's voice gave him instructions to flash his torch so the rest of the gang could zero in on him. He stowed the radio and unclipped the torch from his belt and began pressing the button randomly. Soon there were crunching footsteps metres away.

'That you, John,' Dennis's voice demanded.

'No, it's Santa Clause.'

'It's him alright,' Hayne said unnecessarily.

Allen emerged out of his hide and the six men gathered in the darkness. Reed's red-filtered torch snapped on and he spoke, 'Okay, listen up. We split here. One group search the raft and the campsite. The other three will take a walk over to the houseboat and introduce us. We may have to use the Mohaska. Here are the teams. Dennis, myself and Johnny. We hit the raft. Bobby, Frank and Les, you guys do the honours on that houseboat. Mr. Allen informs me that two teenagers left the houseboat and walked over to the raft. It may be a case of coitus interruptus, but I want that money and I know these kids have it.'

Reed added, 'Oh, yeah, almost forgot. Frank, here's the radio. I'll use the one Johnny has.'

Taylor accepted the transceiver and pocketed it immediately. With few wasted words, the two groups parted and John Allen and his cohorts trudged off to the west, keeping parallel to the shore. They emerged onto the debris littered, hard-baked mud, just as the moon slipped behind a cloud, and slowed their pace. The raft was difficult to make out in the darkness and the men had to use what little light reflected off the water from the houseboat. Presently, the tarp shelter and jetty came into view. Reed suddenly changed direction slightly and headed back into the tree line.

His companions didn't question the move and soon the party stopped. Reed crouched down and under red light from his torch, produced a pouch of tobacco from his jacket and began rolling a cigarette. Placing it in his mouth, he snapped open a Zippo and lit it. He sat back against a tree and watched the scene before him. Hayne and Allen marked time without making it obvious that they wanted action.

Finally, Reed stood up and flicked his cigarette away. 'Let's go,' he commanded.

No sooner had the three moved off towards the campsite; a lone figure appeared on the deck of the raft. The apparition moved around the edge of the deck and stopped near one corner. Crouching down low, it appeared to be looking at something in the water or on the jetty. Standing suddenly, it retreated into the deckhouse. Stan had just entered the campsite, the tarp shelter momentarily blocking his view of the raft. Allen, approaching from his left had the raft in view the whole time.

He watched, as in slow motion, the raft slid backwards along the jetty. He saw Stan step onto the jetty and take a step towards the raft. Reed was too late to react. It glided out onto the middle of the bay while performing a left turn. All the three men could do for the minute, was watch as the vessel silently slowed, then changed direction. Now it nosed its way over to the houseboat and seemed to stop there.

Keeping his voice as low as he could, Reed spoke into his radio. 'Frank, it's Stan. Change of plan. We are all going to take the houseboat.

CHAPTER 34

'**G**lad you could join us,' scolded Sam, as Daniel and Allison appeared up the companionway. 'I'm just going to show Sally the raft.'

'Check on Harry on the way past,' Jeremy chipped in.

Sam and Sally excused themselves and headed for the stairs. Sally suggested they head out onto the rear deck for some privacy. The remaining teenagers were too engrossed in telling of their close call with death to take much notice.

Later, Sam checked on his friend, finding him fast asleep. Then slipping away from the houseboat unnoticed, Sam, with Sally in tow, made their way over the hard ground, around the top of the inlet, towards the boy's campsite. The two teens chatted, mainly about their respective holidays and how things had turned out. Sam's dry sense of humour made the girl laugh and in no time, they were stumbling into the campsite.

It was eerily quiet. The fire had long gone out and only a few embers remained. The tarpaulin shelter still stood sentinel over the site. Sam proudly led the way over to the jetty, explaining the effort they'd gone to. Sally was suitably impressed. They walked single file along the narrow structure and stepped onto the raft.

Sam was serious now. 'There are still four bags of that cash here. I think we should get them over to your boat. According to Daniel, the cops want all the bags together. Makes sense.'

He led the way into the deckhouse. Stooping, the pair entered, and Sam flipped on a light. Sally wondered how four teenage boys could coexist is such a small area. Sam read her thoughts.

'The only real pain is Jeremy. Everything is so bloody organised. Arguments aren't scheduled in anywhere. I had a word with him on the houseboat. He admitted it. Says he's going to try to relax.'

Sally laughed. She studied the bulging bags that lay on one of the bunks. 'Which is your bunk?'

Sam pointed to the money sacks.

'We'll have to use one of the other ones then, wont we?'

*   *   *

It was Sally who noticed something amiss. At first she thought that Sam had wandered out onto the foredeck and was having a quiet cigarette. But that didn't make any sense. She hadn't smelled tobacco or smoke on Sam, and she'd got close enough. Now she detected a strong, distinct smell of rollie tobacco. A sound from the galley made her look in there. Sam was crouching at the stove, in his underwear, waiting for the kettle to boil. He grinned at her 'Won't be too long.'

Sally whispered, 'Can you smell that?'

Sam sniffed the air as he poured two cups of coffee. 'Maybe someone on the houseboat.'

'Nobody smokes rollies. The few smokers there smoke packet cigarettes. The breeze is blowing toward the houseboat. It's as if the smoke is coming from the forest.'

Sam picked up the two steaming mugs and brought them over to the bunk. 'I'll investigate. It could be those guys wanting their money back,' he whispered. Reaching up to the main control panel, Sam dowsed the light in the galley and turned on a blue nightlight. He went to his bunk and rummaged about until he found his hunting knife. Picking up his coffee mug, he said in a normal tone, 'Just going out onto the deck.' Then in a whisper, 'I'm going to cut the front ropes. I want you to untie the back ones. Then we'll get the raft out of here and over to the houseboat. I only hope there's enough power in the batteries. I don't want to start the generator.'

The teen ducked through the doorway and stepped onto the plywood deck. He sipped his drink and wandered about the foredeck area, crouching down at the ropes that secured the front mooring cleat to the jetty. Appearing is if to study something in the water in front of the raft, Sam silently drew his hunting knife and carefully cut the ropes. Casually standing and taking a gulp from his mug, he tipped the rest over the side and retreated into the deckhouse. Sally was just returning from her task at the stern, wearing a big grin.

'I hope the front ones were easy. That back one would have kept Harry Houdini busy!'

Sam assumed that it was Jeremy's handiwork but said to Sally, 'Now for the real test. I can move it without starting the geni. But that's only if there's enough charge in the batteries.'

'Give it a try,' Sally said, full of confidence in Sam.

Sam sat at the controls and selected the main motor switches. He selected reverse and eased the main controller to the mid-position. The raft gently moved back and away from the jetty. And not a moment too soon. A noise outside caused both teens to look outside. A man was walking across the camp and had stepped onto the jetty. Sam turned the control knob to its stops and the raft lurched back. Sally had to hang on to avoid falling over.

The raft glided backwards out onto the bay. Sam spun the wheel to the right and backed up towards the top of the inlet. Bringing the vessel to a stop, he selected forward and motored more sedately over to the houseboat. The raft gently bumped alongside, Sam bringing it to a controlled halt. He switched everything off and ran outside. Jeremy looked down from the top deck.

'What's up, Sam. You brought the whole thing over.'

'Look over there,' Sam replied, manipulating the main searchlight and turning it on. He pointed it at the boy's jetty, that area now bathed in brilliant white light. Two men, caught in the beam, darted into the scrub. A third, unsure which way to turn, made up his mind quickly and began to walk purposefully around the top of the inlet in the direction of the houseboat. Jeremy left the rail and ran down the stairs to find Kevin, who appeared out of his stateroom, satellite phone in hand. 'I've got the cops,' he interjected. 'The Slipper is sending the local rozzers.'

This bit of news seemed to calm Jeremy down. He said, 'Well, let's hope they've got a boat. There's a bunch of guys out there who want their bags of cash back.' Then he heard Sam's voice from the foredeck: 'Help me with these bags, will you'. Jeremy ran out of the deckhouse to see his friend, still on the raft, throwing one of the bulging money sacks onto the houseboat's deck. It landed with a loud plop. Jeremy grabbed the awkward sack and dragged it through the open sliding glass door, where it joined the others. A second thump indicated that another money transfer had taken place.

'Two to go,' Sam hollered from the raft's cabin. Jeremy was ready this time and lifted the sack over the guardrail He placed it on the deck and was ready to receive the last sack. Sam plonked it into his arms and climbed up onto the houseboat. Taking a sack each, the boys carried the booty into the front room and piled them on top of the eighteen others that had found their way from the floor to the settee. Sam leaned against the glass sliding door and stretched. 'I'm officially out of the money recovery business,' he sighed.

CHAPTER 35

Kevin said, 'The Slipper also advised us to get out onto the lake ASAP. While we're out there, it'll be almost impossible for that trash to get their precious money.' He yelled, 'Get that gangway on board, untie all ropes.'

One of the guests manned the helm while others converged on the foredeck and began retrieving the gangway and cast-off mooring lines. Jeremy scurried out onto the foredeck, relieved to see several guests helping with the awkward gangway. Kevin appeared beside him saying, 'I was also told to tell you to ditch that raft. You boys can collect it some other time. I've got to go back in and supervise getting us out of here.'

Kevin turned and re-entered the cabin, leaving Jeremy on the deck. Caught up between leaving his beloved raft behind and getting his friends out of danger, Jeremy was slow to react. A shout from above brought him back to reality. It was Harry, using the upper railing for support and with a Heineken bottle complete with straw in hand. Even in his injured state, he soothed his friend with comforting words.

'Don't worry, Jeremy, we'll be able to retrieve it soon enough.'

Jeremy, however, had a plan. He looked about. The houseboat had begun to move backwards toward the lake. Kevin had gone inside and could be seen talking to fellow passengers. Looking up at Harry, he gave a signal and picked up a length of mooring line and pretended to roll it up before placing it over the handrail. Quick as lightning, Jeremy was leaping over the rail and landing on the raft's retreating deck. He dived into the deckhouse and set the switches for the electric motors. Selecting 'forward', Jeremy eased the controller to the half position. Now he was effectively following the houseboat, albeit the latter was in reverse.

From his position at the helm of the raft, Jeremy was unable to see Kevin, so he assumed that he was toward the back of the much larger vessel. The houseboat was making good progress when it suddenly veered to the left side. Jeremy slowed down and took evasive action. He understood now what was happening. Kevin was ordering that the cumbersome vessel be turned around so that it faced out onto the lake. It must be like driving a block of flats down George Street, the boy mused. Driven forward, it would attain more speed. Jeremy stuck close to the shore. The second part of his scheme depended on this manoeuvre.

He reasoned that the gang of thugs must have a boat near here. He planned to search for such a craft and either tow it onto the lake or disable it. The houseboat had now stopped, and, heading forward, was turning left. Jeremy slowed briefly and ducked out the back to start the generator. The raft was ahead of the houseboat now. He watched the larger vessel straighten up and glide past him out of the inlet. Jeremy followed, but rather than head for the center of the lake; he veered left and switched on the powerful headlights.

It was now virtually daytime ahead of the raft and in the glare the boy saw the gleam of aluminium among the reeds on the shoreline. He motored along and the shape of a small boat appeared. Switching off the headlights, Jeremy brought the raft to a halt alongside the tinny and stepped out of the deckhouse, fishing knife in hand. Climbing onto the tinny, his mind was made up quickly. The tinny was floating, not resting on the shore. The teen stepped onto the dry clay shore and cut the thin rope securing the boat to a dead tree. The sound of crunching footsteps from beyond the tree line, made him look up. Voices were now audible over the muted growl of the generator. Jeremy worked quickly. He took the remaining mooring line and stepping up onto the raft, worked his way around to the stern, and secured the line to a mooring cleat. The voices became yells. Ducking into the deckhouse, he selected 'forward' and thrust the controller to its limit. The raft lurched ahead. As Jeremy swung the wheel to the right and brought the small convoy out onto the lake, his watch chimed midnight.

CHAPTER 36

Jack Coburn woke from the dream. He raised his head slightly and read the glowing display of the clock radio. Twelve-forty. His hand clumsily fumbled for the bedside lamp and switched it on. In the dim light, he studied the room before his gaze fell to the floor where a yellow pad lay, the top page covered in his well-known scrawl. So, he hadn't been dreaming. The phone had rung. Now it was time to stir himself and make a call from the study, to avoid waking his wife.

Sliding out of bed as quietly as he could, Coburn bent down to retrieve the notepad and put on his slippers. He padded over to the door and opening it silently, stepped out into the hall. A single nightlight glowed halfway along. By its light, he moved along to the stairs and flipped the switch for the stairwell light. Descending to the ground floor, he made his way to the study and closed the door.

Coburn placed the notepad on the mahogany desk and switched on the green-shaded bankers lamp. He re-read his hastily written notes. Grabbing a pen out of the brass shell casing that served as a penholder, a souvenir from a raid, he went through the notes again, underlining phrases as he went. On Lake Eildon, four boys, raft holiday, exploring an abandoned motel, bank bags full of cash. The Slipper leaned back in his chair and idly gazed at the *Clemson* class destroyer model on the sideboard, his mind in a whirl.

Bayswater. It had to be. It was still top of the force's most urgent unsolved armed robbery cases. During his visit to Rupertsvale, he had pressed Ray White for more details on the men in the caravan next door, but Ray had come up with very few details. A bit of circumstantial stuff. Nothing concrete. Now a flurry of information concerning Lake Eildon had come through. And from two completely different sources to boot. One, an old friend from Sydney and then a teenage boy holidaying on the lake.

Jack Coburn could feel the exhilaration building inside him. Whoever these kids were, they had nicked a fortune from right under the noses of some of Melbourne's top crims. The problem was now the crims wanted it back. Coburn wondered if the gang knew the teens had the money or if they just strongly suspected it. Either way, they wouldn't hesitate to use violence to get it back. And if the money really was from the Bayswater robbery, The Slipper didn't want to think about the types of criminals involved.

He picked up the phone and dialled a number from memory. An unfamiliar voice said, 'Armed Robbery Squad.'

'It's DCI Jack Coburn. I'm after DS McKenzie.'

'I'll see if he's available, Sir.' The line went to the hold tone. Presently, a familiar voice came in the line.

'Jack, I've got some good news for you. Your friend Kevin Parsons has sent random pics of the bank bags found at Lake

Eildon. You'll be pleased to know that the bags match the job at Bayswater. They've got First District Bank in letters big enough for Hellen Keller to see and, more importantly, a plethora of serial numbers. The file is open, before you ask, and the numbers are matching up fast.'

'Okay,' Coburn replied, scribbling notes. 'That confirms the money the boys found is the loot we've been looking for. The problem is, now it's on a raft or a houseboat or both. Those vessels aren't built like the Bismarck. They're going to be easy targets for our friends to take the money back. We've got to get that money and fast. Get onto the local police and tell them to get a boat of some kind out onto the lake. I also want two detectives to drive up to Eildon and collect that cash.'

The detective paused jotting notes and replied, 'Got that. Given the circumstances I suggest that we also have a couple of guys with pump shotguns either go up with them or go separately.'

'Good point,' Coburn replied. 'Given the circumstances, a helicopter gunship might not be overkill. As usual, I'll have to speak to top management. Given the size of the haul, you might be surprised what we get. I'll get onto the Eildon rozzers and tell 'em to get out onto the lake and keep an eye out for that raft.'

Coburn broke the connection and dialled another number.

CHAPTER 37

es Truscott, Bob Pitman, and Frank Taylor stole around the inlet at the tree line, ready to hide if they should be observed from the houseboat. As they walked, the men discussed what they would do once they boarded the vessel. As they came to a point about fifty metres from their target, Les decided to call a brief meeting. From their vantage point, the three men could clearly see the vessel and anybody who appeared on deck.

Bob Pitman, however, had noticed something on the other side of the lake. The raft, which twenty minutes earlier had been made fast to the jetty, was now silently moving. Simultaneously, he saw a figure, probably Stan Reed, make a belated dash along the narrow jetty. The raft was now out on the small bay proper and turning sharply. As he watched, the transceiver in Frank's pocket crackled to life. Stan's voice announced a change to the plan. Pitman wasn't surprised. He crouched down and told Les and Frank what he'd just seen out on the water. Les said, 'We wait here for the others. Then all of us raid that houseboat.'

What the men couldn't see was the raft gliding alongside the houseboat and a teenage girl climb onto the larger vessel. What they *did* notice was a shaft of bright light, emanating from the raft, illuminating the opposite side of the bay, briefly exposing two of their fellow gang members. The houseboat seemed to come alive with action. Someone was giving orders. The three men watched helplessly as the gangway was dragged aboard the houseboat and lines securing the vessel to trees were discarded. That vessel too began to slip away.

Frank Taylor produced the radio and shouted into it, 'The houseboat's escaping!'

Stan's reply was short and crisp, 'Head for the tinny. We're on our way there now.'

Taylor was in no doubt as to the meaning of Reed's words. He meant *run* to the tinny. Les and Bob didn't require an explanation either. After checking Frank's compass, the three of them ran as best they could through the scrub in the direction of the boat. Each had a torch and shone them ahead, not bothering to hide the beams. Frank Taylor cursed and swore as he struggled through the flailing vines and light branches. The radio in his hand crackled. 'We're right behind you guys. Can see your torches.'

Les, who also heard the transmission, wasn't sure if Stan was rebuking them for allowing the torch light to be seen, or whether he was just stating fact. Frank couldn't have cared less. He tore at the foliage with increasing annoyance, thinking only of the boat. Bob was having an easier time because he thought to bring a hunting knife, which made the going much easier. Out on the inlet, Truscott heard what sounded like a small engine firing up. Presently, the men heard heavy footsteps behind them. Les looked over his shoulder and saw two beams of light dancing towards him.

Stan's voice was reassuring, 'Leslie, is that you?'

'Yeah,' Truscott half-whispered back. 'It's going to be an interesting ride with all six of us in the tinny.'

The group got going again. Les noticed a third torch beam. 'How are you, Johnny?' he asked.

'Good. But I'll be even better when I've got my hands on that money.'

'And slit the throats of those little bastards who took it,' butted in Frank, between cursing the foliage.

The men trudged on and soon the ramble became easier. Les scouted ahead of the party and held up his hand. Frank stopped complaining and the troupe ground to a halt. What Les saw would have made Satan's blood run cold. The tinny was still on the lake alright, but now it was attached to the raft and both vessels were gliding out onto the lake and rapidly disappearing in the darkness. Frank, upon taking in the scene, found a new target for his anger. He let fly with a stream of obscenities that even startled Les. Dennis Hayne even contemplated jumping into the lake and swimming after the retreating tinny. John Allen read his thoughts and reminded him he wasn't Johnny Weissmuller.

But Hayne *did* come up with a good idea. He suggested they haul their arses back to the Rupertsvale Jetty and acquire a boat there. *And* they were going to have to do it now.

CHAPTER 38

Harry Turner watched from the upper deck of the houseboat with mounting alarm. The raft, which had been behind the houseboat as the latter headed out onto the lake, was nowhere to be seen. Then he saw a blaze of light near the distant shore that could only be their raft. But he also noticed pinpricks of light weaving in and out of the trees and fast approaching the shore. What was Jeremy doing?

Sam wandered over and stood next to him at the handrail and was his usual blunt self. 'What is the Nerd up to?'

Harry didn't get a chance to give him an intelligent answer. Sally and another girl joined them. The boys turned away from the water, assuming Jeremy had everything under control. Sally introduced her friend as Jenny. The four teens chatted for a few minutes and were in turn joined by Daniel and Allison. Daniel stifled a yawn and wondered aloud when Jeremy was going to bring the raft back so the four could get some sleep.

Kevin bounced up the companionway and strode over to the group. 'Lads, we are about to enter the Big River Inlet. The plan is to hide there until the local plod can get here in sufficient force to safely take the money and make sure you four boys are safe. Speaking of four boys, I count only three. Where's Jeremy?'

Sam and Daniel exchanged glances. 'He's denying the robbers transportation,' Daniel offered, 'by towing their boat behind the raft. What he plans to do with it after that is anybody's guess.'

'I told him to lose that raft,' Kevin replied, clearly not impressed.

'That would be like asking the Queen to part with the Britannia,' Sam muttered, avoiding Kevin's angry glare.

Kevin left the group, and the teenagers resumed their banter. Harry and Jenny leaned on the rail and made small talk. Harry's gaze fell on the water being churned up behind the houseboat. He followed the trail of white luminescence away from the vessel until it disappeared in the darkness. Then his eye caught something out on the lake. A flash of bright light. Then another. It was as if someone was signalling. Jeremy!

*   *   *

Jeremy sat at the helm, his face bathed in red light from the controls. He relaxed for the first time since commandeering the aluminium boat. His eyes strained to see through the darkness, watching for the houseboat. The teen ignored the boat tied on behind. He could feel it pull on the raft as the latter made its way across the lake. The plan was to take the tinny to the opposite shore and tie it to a tree.

He had a mind to sink it but realised it would be full of important evidence. He also realised that he had well over an hour's head start on the robbers. They had no choice now but to head back to wherever they came from, probably a local trailer park.

However, he *had* taken a risk to do what he did. He had some explaining to do, not only to his friends but to Allison's dad. He wasn't sure which was worse. Still, he had thought the situation through and come up with the best solution. Now all he had to do was dump the tinny and catch up with the rest of the boys.

Jeremy was having trouble keeping focused. He was dead tired, both physically and emotionally. His brain, which Sam affectionately called his 'neck-top computer' was going to blow a valve. The teen wondered how his friends were fairing, particularly Harry. He wasn't quite so worried about Daniel, whom he had seen in very close company with Allison. He almost felt like he was abandoning the other boys, but he was sure they would understand.

Getting up from his sitting position, Jeremy flipped the switch for the rear floodlight and made his way out to the generator. Unscrewing the fuel cap, he peered into the tank. It could do with some more petrol. Fortunately, everything was within reach. He had the plastic fuel container and the siphon pump set up in seconds and the transfer took half a minute, if that. Satisfied, the boy stowed the pump and fuel container and headed back into the deckhouse. Eyeing the stove, he suddenly felt a cup of coffee calling him. He filled the kettle and placing it on the single gas ring, pressed the igniter.

Resuming his position at the helm, Jeremy ramped up the controller a notch and peered out over the dark water. There in the gloom, the shoreline could just be made out. Ever so faintly silhouetted against it was a familiar shape. As the kettle began to whistle, Jeremy set a course for the darkened houseboat. He made a mug of coffee and strode back to the helm. Sitting there, he had an idea. He switched the raft's headlights on and off a few times and waited. Nothing. Jeremy tried again. This time there was a response.

Fired up, the teen sipped his coffee and focused only on the retreating houseboat. Thinking quickly, he grabbed the laminated map of the lake and studied it under the glow of the instruments. Checking the GPS unit, his findings put the houseboat well into the Big River Inlet. So that's what Kevin was doing. Hiding until morning and giving city police a chance to get here. The GPS put the raft at the entrance to the inlet. Jeremy would hide there as well. He had no choice, the way he saw it. He had to catch up with the other boys.

For the thousandth time, Jeremy cursed the fact that there was no radio communication with the houseboat. When the boys had first been invited onto the houseboat, carrying the injured Harry, Sam took the radio back to the raft. So now both radios were lying next to each other on Sam's bunk. Jeremy knew they would come in handy soon, but for now it was a major inconvenience. His friends would be worried about him, and he couldn't pacify them.

Gulping down the last remnants of his coffee, the boy peered ahead and noticed that the houseboat had stopped. Good! Just a matter of a few minutes now. He glided ahead, suddenly remembering the tinny still attached. Quick change of plan. Jeremy swung the wheel to the right and made for the shore. Quickly switching the headlights on and off, he saw a small re-entrant with heavy scrub on both sides. A perfect place to hide the tinny. Approaching the inlet, Jeremy realised that he would have to push the aluminium boat sideways to hide it properly.

Stopping just outside the inlet, he stopped and rammed a mooring pole into the muddy riverbed to hold position. Unleashing the tinny, Jeremy worked the small craft around to the front of the raft and lashed it on. Now removing the mooring pole, he manoeuvred the raft with tinny attached as deep into the tiny inlet as possible. Sacrificing the mooring pole, at least for the time being, he used it to fix the tinny in its muddy hiding place. Satisfied with his handiwork, the teen reversed the raft slowly out of the small inlet. Selecting 'Forward', he adjusted his heading down the Big River Inlet. Here, houseboats of every size were moored cheek by jowl, a perfect place to hide one. Scanning about, the boy felt it was safe enough to use the headlamps. He flicked them on and saw a familiar vessel. In a matter of minutes, the raft was drawing up level with the houseboat. A familiar face peered over the rail. Sam!

Jeremy switched off everything and stepped out onto the foredeck. His friend, keeping his voice low, said, 'Glad you made it back in one piece. There's a beer up here for you. I think it's only fair to tell you that you're on Kevin's Top Ten Most Wanted List.'

Jeremy rubbed his forefinger and thumb together. 'This is my violin for his list! Thanks to me, the robbers have no means of pursuing us. If we had done things his way, they would have had the tinny and the raft.'

Sam realised his friend was angry. Controlling a pissed-off nerd took a bit of care. 'I'll be down in a sec.' Leaving the handrail he reached into the cooler, grabbed two beers and made his way down the rear stairs, thus avoiding Kevin. Making his way over the lower deck handrail, no mean feat with two beer bottles in his hand, he stepped lightly onto the raft's rear deck, and ducked through the cabin to greet Jeremy. Sam put the bottles down and hugged his friend. Jeremy was trembling with anger, no doubt at the mention of Kevin and his list.

'Maybe it wasn't the best time to bring it up, get this into you,' Sam said, handing Jeremy a bottle. Jeremy took a long pull on his beer. It worked like a tonic; he calmed down at once.

'Get the other two here. I don't want to wear out our welcome, and I've had enough of Mr Know-it-all. Tell me what happened when we separated.'

Sam sipped his beer and related the scene on the houseboat after they left Robin Bay. When he came to the part where Kevin was counting them, Sam could almost see the steam issuing from his friend's ears.

'That reinforces my theory about getting back here. It's

not that I don't appreciate their hospitality. But there's no place like home.'

'You sound like Dorothy. All you need is a pair of ruby slippers!'

Jeremy laughed for the first time in quite a while and it cheered Sam up immensely. 'Okay we'll round up Daniel and Shorty and get them back here.'

A window on the houseboat cracked open and a familiar voice said, 'I'm not short.'

CHAPTER 39

The jetty was bathed in a halo of soft light from the single lamp standard. Several pleasure craft lay fastened to the structure. From his crouching position, Dennis Hayne observed the whole area. His gaze missed nothing. Through hard experience, he learned to read what was there and what wasn't. When he deemed the place to be safe, Dennis led the gang softly over the fine white gravel and onto the jetty. He crept along the plastic lattice decking, silently as a cat. Passing a trim Cruise Craft half-cabin, Hayne saw the keys dangling in the ignition. His search over, he beckoned to the others.

Climbing aboard, Bob Pitman whispered, 'If we hurry, we could have this tub back before anyone notices it's gone.'

With some anticipation, Hayne turned the key. The two-hundred horsepower Suzuki outboard motor roared into life. John Allen, still on the jetty, cast of the lines and climbed aboard. Stan settled into one of the captain's chairs and studied his watch. 'Almost one-thirty. They've had about ninety minute's head start. If I were them, I would head straight for Eildon. Probably try to get the cops to meet me halfway. But that's not considering those kids.'

Hayne eased the boat away from the jetty and turned it to

face the lake. Under Stan's guidance, he kept the speed down until the boat was out of earshot of the shore. Then he gave it the gun. The boat tore through the darkness, churning up the otherwise placid lake. It was fortunate that at this late hour, the lake was devoid of traffic. The boat bore right and soon passed Fry's bay and approached Robin Bay. At this point, Allen spoke.

'It just occurred to me that our friends may hide somewhere until morning. Imagine trying to wake up the dozy local plod and saying you've found umpteen bags full of cash. In which case, they could try to make it to the town and hide among the boats there or stop halfway. I favour option two.'

Reed listened intently and said, 'Okay, it's option two. But where do we start?'

Allen thought. 'There are a couple of probabilities. Big River Inlet and Jerusalem Inlet. Both have camping grounds, and the latter has a launching ramp. It's going to be a process of elimination, I'm afraid.'

'Okay, Big River it is. I'll just get Donald Campbell to take us there.

CHAPTER 40

Taking their leave from the houseboat had gone smoothly, albeit with a mixture of feelings by the passengers. Sam had explained their desire to go back to their own boat to get some much-needed sleep. Luckily, Allison talked to her father for them, and Kevin completely understood the situation, except that he had virtually taken responsibility for the bags of cash the boys found. He and his daughter were still concerned about Harry's injuries but were reassured the teen would be in good hands. Sam joked that Harry would be fit enough to make breakfast, but Allison's stony look told him the joke had fallen very flat.

The boy in question appeared from a stateroom with Jenny in tow.

With mumbled goodbyes, Daniel and Sam Helped Harry over the guardrail and onto the raft's deck. Jeremy, already at the helm eased the raft away from the houseboat. The other three boys found their bunks and crashed out. Jeremy eased the controller to one quarter ahead and the raft glided over the inlet and into a small re-entrant he had seen earlier. He chose this spot because there were other houseboats and smaller pleasure craft moored there. The raft would be much less noticeable here. Shutting down the generator and motors, Jeremy flopped into his own bunk.

The raft bobbed at its new mooring, the great trunk of a long-dead gum tree. The surrounding forest appeared ghostly in the moonlight, which glimmered off the still waters of the lake. The tic-tic-ticking of the slowly cooling generator had long ceased, and the vessel had a tomb-like quiet about it. The occasional baying of a dog was the only sound to be heard.

* * *

The Cruise Craft half-cab, with no lights showing, slunk into the inlet, the shoreline coming under the scrutiny of six pairs of eyes. The roar of the big Suzuki was now a muted growl as Stan Reed studied a map under a red torch and gave clipped directions to Dennis Hayne. The plan was to study any likely vessels as best they could under cover of darkness, and then send one gang member ashore for a closer look. Crude, yes. But what choice was there? Police were bound to be on their way, so they had to do something fast.

The gang passed their first potential target roughly five hundred metres down the inlet. A quick appraisal established that this was not their quarry. But there were plenty more opportunities ahead. Too many. This could take time. Time they didn't have. John Allen was deep in thought. Bob Pitman said, 'What's up, Johnny.'

'I'm just trying to recall the finer details of that houseboat.

Would make things a bit quicker.'

'All I remember for sure is that it was quite large and appeared to be very modern,' Pitman replied.

'That might be all we need,' Allen said. 'Dennis and I were the only ones to see it in daylight. But it was over the far side of that small bay. At the time, we had no reason to take any notice of it. And we were distracted by the raft and that tall nerdy looking kid who was giving us the evil eye.'

'About all Dennis remembered was that there was a pint-sized Asian punk,' Pitman added.

That would be right, thought John Allen. Ever the racist was our Dennis.

The boat chugged on. The potential targets were chosen with the help of Stan's red torch. Several possibilities presented themselves almost immediately, but most were too old or too small. Another fitted the bill, but its rear deck was longer. The gang continued their silent search; all hoping the muted growl of the outboard motor wouldn't waken any potential witnesses. They passed a re-entrant which had several small cabin cruisers moored in it. Nothing there. Back out on the inlet, John and Dennis almost agreed on one craft but Dennis changed his mind, claiming the windows looked different.

And so the search went on. Stan pointed out that the inlet was long and that if it *was* the hiding place, it had been well chosen. He added that they might just have to pull the plug and try the next inlet. John Allen was only half listening. He was going back over the previous vessels they had looked at.

There was something. Something familiar. That houseboat he and Dennis had almost agreed upon. What was it Dennis had said? *The windows looked different.* It just occurred to him that they had viewed it from the opposite side. These vessels were not exactly alike either side. That would also explain the rear deck being too long. It was the front deck.

He made up his mind. Addressing Stan, he said, 'Turn around. It's back there.'

CHAPTER 41

It was Les Truscott who discovered the raft in its hiding place. The Cruise Craft was motoring slowly back along the line of moored houseboats, six pairs of eyes vigilant. When Les saw the raft among the fibreglass pleasure craft-noticeable because of its stark square shape- he informed Stan. At least, that was his intention. No sooner had he opened his mouth, Stan became transfixed on something. He pointed ahead and muttered something that Les didn't catch.

Now Les saw what had distracted Reed. A string of party lights on the top of a moored houseboat blinked twice and went out. While the men studied the boats in vain the lights blinked twice more. Stan said, 'Now what do you make of that?

'Kids, probably,' Truscott muttered. 'I think you should know that I've located our friend's raft.'

The news brought Stan back to Earth. 'Where.'

'At the end of that inlet over there. Hidden among the smaller boats.'

'Okay, listen up.' Reed kept his voice down. 'We split up again. John, Dennis and Bobby. The raft is yours. The rest of us, I think that houseboat with the lights is signalling to someone. We have to move fast. Dennis, drop 'em and yourself at the shore. I'll take this boat to where I suspect the money is.'

Without further ado, Hayne steered over to the opposite bank. Nudging the muddy shore, he handed over to Stan. Bob Pitman and John Allen were already out of the boat and standing on the hard-baked clay. Hayne joined them and the three men crept silently through the scrub toward the dark, silent raft.

*   *   *

Daniel Graham was finding sleep hard to come by, despite the ordeal of the past day. He stirred himself from his bunk and silently made his way to the tiny galley. Figuring the kettle would make too much noise; he placed some water in a saucepan and placed it on the ring. While he waited for the water to boil, the teen looked out the back hatch and studied the peaceful scene before him. He thought he heard a single outboard motor and wondered what anyone would be doing at such an hour.

When the water in the saucepan boiled, Daniel made a cup of coffee and stepped out onto the tiny rear deck. He placed one foot on the generator housing and glanced about. At that moment, the moon came out from behind a cloud. In the pale light, the boy thought he saw several shapes moving among the low scrub between the shore and a clearing that was set aside for camping. He thought his eyes must be playing tricks on him so he shifted his focus to the area beyond the clearing. There was a road up there somewhere that led to some old mining ruins, according to the map.

A twig snapping behind brought him out of his dream. He walked around the cabin to the foredeck and looked about. The moon was gone now, making it impossible to make anything out. He had the impression that somebody stirred on the half-cabin boat next to the raft. To hell with this. Daniel tipped the last of his coffee into the water, ducked into the cabin and climbed back into his bunk. He made a mental note to tell his friends about the ruins over breakfast. Maybe he could entice Jeremy to go off and explore them with him. He dozed off with that thought.

Sam Dillon woke out of a deep sleep not long after Daniel returned to his bunk. His throat was dry so he wearily climbed out of bed and tip toed to the galley. Opening a cooler, he reached in and grabbed a small bottle of chilled water. Closing the cooler, the lid slipped out of his hands and shut with a loud plop. Sam silently cursed and sipped the cool water. He too studied the scene before him. Only this time there was no mistaking the three shapes that materialised out of the darkness. Moreover, one of them had a sheath attached to his belt that doubtless contained a large knife. As the teen gazed out into the night, Harry Turner stirred in his bunk and putting his head up, asked Sam sleepily what he was doing.

'Just wettin' the whistle. I think we got company out there. Saw some shadows movin' near those trees'. Harry climbed awkwardly out of his bunk and stood next to his friend, peering out into the gloom. Sam offered Harry the water bottle. The smaller boy accepted it and drank off the remainder. Sam held a forefinger up to his lips and beckoned toward the front of the raft

The boys watched three figures moving silently around the head of the inlet, over the tiny creek that fed into it and approached the foredeck of the raft. Sam didn't waste any time. Telling Harry to stay put, he ducked out onto the rear deck and found Jeremy's spear gun in the makeshift toilet cubicle. As he fumbled to load the weapon, he felt the raft move. Peering through the deckhouse, Sam saw a thickset figure standing on the deck, the moon glinting evilly off something in his hand.

*   *   *

John Allen was several meters behind Dennis Hayne as they approached the raft. Not content with his machine tool hands, Hayne produced a large knife. He stepped onto the front deck, almost tripping on the light bar that adorned the front of the vessel. Straightening up, he could just make out the interior of the deckhouse through the gloom. And the first thing Hayne saw was a small Asian boy, undoubtedly the same one he and John had seen during their exploration of the lake. Hayne pointed at Harry and snarled 'You little runt, where's our money?

The boy stood rooted to the spot. A voice from deep

within the dark cabin said simply, 'It's here'. The next thing Hayne felt was a sear of pain and saw a flash of brilliant light. And then nothing.

John Allen had watched as Dennis clambered onto the raft, his foot clipping some object on the deck. He stood straight and appeared to point at someone or thing. Then he watched as his friend staggered backwards and this time stumbled over the same object and fall backwards into the shallow water. It was only then that Allen noticed the shaft of a spear protruding from Hayne's left eye. As he looked on stunned, Allen saw an apparition move from the cabin cruiser on the far side of the raft onto the raft's deck.

*   *   *

Sam, another spear in his hand, ducked out through the doorway onto the deck. As the teen fiddled with the spear gun, a firm hand grabbed his shoulder. A deep but rather kind voice said, 'He's dead son. He isn't going to hurt your friend anymore.'

Sam swung around to see a man standing on the edge of the deck. The man was quite tall and broad shouldered. Sam realised the stranger was getting on a bit too. He had a trusting intelligent face that Sam immediately warmed to. The stranger spoke, 'I'm Ray White. I'm a former copper. We've been onto these guys for a while. If it wasn't for you and your friends, we wouldn't have had a thing on them.

CHAPTER 42

Unaware as to how their fellow robbers were fairing over on the raft, Stan Reed and his cohorts eased over to the other side of the inlet. The men conferred. Reed was positive the money was on the houseboat, somewhere, probably stashed in a stateroom. Frank Taylor, on the other hand, couldn't help thinking they were acting on a gigantic assumption and were making majestic fools of themselves. Not once had any of the gang seen the familiar white sacks with the tell-tale black stencilling on or anywhere near the houseboat - or raft for that matter.

He wanted to ask the question that must have been in the back of everyone's mind; what had started this wild goose chase? However, Stan was adamant, and Stan was always right. The way Taylor saw it, albeit with a few hesitations, was that someone had taken a massive amount of money from virtually right under their noses. Those people must have been very close by. He knew Stan was just being methodical, but it *was* possible that the money had been taken from the old motel and had gone in the opposite direction, overland. The question that ate at him was *who*?

Stan had an annoying habit of not listening to anyone

when he thought he was right. Frank had seen how difficult it had been for Les to break the news that he had spotted the raft. To try telling Stan that he might be barking up the wrong tree would be like trying to move the Matterhorn. He was now caught between hoping the money was on the houseboat so they could all get out of here and hoping it wasn't so Stan could be wrong for once.

Stan's voice brought him back to reality. 'We enter the cabin from both ends. With as little noise as possible. For all we know, they may have the bags stacked in the living room. We deal with the occupants as we meet them. Frank, you take the rear door. Les and I will go in the front way.' Reed, knowing Frank's penchant for violence, felt that he could cope on his own. He pointed to the right gunwale and continued. 'This boat has oars. I think we should paddle over to the houseboat and tie up to the front deck.'

Without further ado, Reed reached over and grabbing both oars, he handed them to Frank and Les. Truscott pushed off from the muddy shore and he and Frank paddled as best they could generally in the direction of the houseboat. Reed studied the latter, watching for any signs of life. The Cruise Craft made slow progress toward their target. Now finally bumping along the edge of the darkened vessel, Les and Stan clambered nimbly over the rail and touched down lightly on the deck.

Using the handrails, Frank worked the boat down the side of the houseboat. As he did so, the string of party lights on the upper deck blinked twice. Frank knew it was now or never. Using all his strength, he propelled the half-cabin the last few meters. In his peripheral vision, he saw two things almost simultaneously. A figure appeared at one of the big windows as he passed, and a large cabin cruiser was making its way down the inlet toward the houseboat.

Time to act fast. Taylor clambered onto the foredeck of the Cruise Craft and taking the mooring line in hand, he made the boat fast to the handrail of the houseboat. He climbed over the rail and landed on the rear deck adjacent to the metal stairs leading to the top deck. His weight shook the vessel. He studied the door to the main cabin. He thought it was most unlikely that it would be locked. The party lights blinked again. Taylor stood and strode over to the cabin door.

As he gripped the brass handle, the entire back end of the houseboat and surrounding forest was illuminated in the brilliant glare of a spotlight. Not wasting time, he flung the handle down, opened the door and closed it behind him. As his eyes got accustomed to the darkness, he realised he was now in a short passageway with two doors in each side. The passage ended in a vestibule. Frank thought about briefly checking these rooms which were doubtless staterooms. However, he decided that twenty bulky sacks would be located in a larger room. Probably further forward.

Taylor crept forward, feeling his way in the darkness, to the open area of the vestibule. Here there was a second stairway to the upper deck, behind which a door opened presumably to a galley. On the opposite side of the vessel, a wide entryway lead into what must be a lounge. Frank could see a sideboard and part of a sofa. And on the sofa he could just make out a white bag of some kind with black stencilled lettering on it. Frank stole over to the doorway. The sight before him took his breath away.

Packed haphazardly on the sofa and the floor were the twenty bank bags he and his friends had waited six years to see. So, Stan had been right. As he stood mesmerised, Frank heard metallic noises and cursing from behind a curtain that stretched across one side of the room. He realised then that Stan and Les were still out on the foredeck. Stepping over to the curtain, he pulled the two halves apart to reveal Stan's face glaring in at him through the glass.

Fumbling with the catch, Frank slid the door open, and his friends burst into the room. Reed began to berate him about something. Whatever Reed was saying was drowned out by the thump-thump-thump of an approaching helicopter.

CHAPTER 43

Detective Sergeant Bob Wall looked about the muster room at Mansfield Police Station with mild surprise. Given the early hour, he hadn't expected so many volunteers. The reports that came in from Melbourne indicated that this was going to be a big job. However, those same reports had been lacking in one detail, a detail that every seasoned police officer likes to see. The nitty-gritty of the perpetrators. There had been nothing. Not for the first time, Wall had muttered to himself, 'Bunch of bloody unknowns.'

As he surveyed the officers before him, he sensed the excitement that permeates this room before an operation. This time however, there was a difference. He was getting more questioning looks, even from experienced guys. Wall waited patiently for the last stragglers to enter the room, with Styrofoam cups of coffee in hand. When everyone was seated and the chatter died down to a murmur, Wall cleared his throat and spoke in the quiet monotone that always commanded complete attention.

'We have been tasked, on this beautiful summer night, to go out and retrieve a very large sum of money that our colleagues in Melbourne claim was stolen in a heist about six years ago. I don't know if any of you remember the First District Bank job out at Bayswater.' A few gleams of recognition among the faces. 'Well, it appears that the stolen money has turned up. Found by a bunch of teenagers, believe it or not. Apparently, just as these kids were taking the loot away, the robbers turned up to retrieve it themselves. Hell of a coincidence, if you ask me. Our mission, if we should accept it, [a few sniggers] is to retrieve it. Some detectives from Melbourne will be here later today to take it back to Melbourne. That's the gist if it. Now the not so good bits. We haven't the faintest idea who we're dealing with. Also, we don't know if the robbers know for sure who now has the money.'

At this point Wall was interrupted. 'So, what you're saying is these kids took a king's ransom in cash from right under the noses of seasoned thieves and made off with it. I've got that bit right, haven't I?' The detective, who asked, had been scribbling notes like an IBM Selectric. He saw the coincidence.

Bob Wall continued unruffled. 'I am told, by none other than Jack Coburn by the way, that the boys, all from Dandenong, built a raft and took it up to Eildon. A week earlier, a group of fairly normal looking guys hired a caravan over in Rupertsvale. We know this because the poor sods picked a van right next door to a retired detective by the name of Raymond White. The boys were doing some exploring of the area, found the old motel, and the loot. A group of men entered the grounds of the motel at the same time the boys were helping themselves. We have good reason to believe that the two groups of men are one and the same.'

Wall paused and let his words sink in. The mood under the fluorescent lights was alert, eager for more information. There was a sense of urgency now. A group of innocent teenagers, and a band of violent criminals who would stop at nothing to get their hands on that money.

A hand went up.

'What did the kids do with the money?'

Wall glanced at his notes. 'It appears that they planned to take it back to the raft. However, one of them was hurt on the way down the mountain, so they left the cash where it was and took their injured friend to the raft but some people on a houseboat intervened and all four boys ended up on the houseboat. The cash was retrieved later. Believe it or not, someone on that houseboat knew The Slipper and called him.'

'So now the money is on this houseboat and all we have to do is transfer it to one of our boats?'

'That's correct,' replied Wall. 'However, there is the added complication that we don't know if the robbers are aware of the current location of the loot. We don't know for sure if the robbers are even aware of the existence of the raft or the teenagers for that matter. So, without further ado, we are going to drive down to the lake and board two launches. We are taking shotguns with us, so I expect the usual safety.'

* * *

The throaty roar of the twin Johnsons filled the night and sent the odd water bird scattering. Bob Wall, occupying the front left captain's chair of the trim police launch, studied a chart of the lake while occasionally glancing at his big Citizen Dive watch. He glanced across the water at the other launch, keeping pace but just behind his own.

The launches travelled side by side, blacked out. Even at that early hour, they passed the odd tinny or other small vessel, which rocked in the twin wakes of the passing boats. The lights of Eildon appeared in a cluster off to the right. Bob Wall glanced over his shoulder at the faces of the men huddled in the rear of the launch, each with their own private thoughts. He cast a quick glance at the luminous dial of his watch. Ten minutes to go. He held up both hands, fingers splayed.

The men patted their pockets and made last-minute adjustments to their clothing. Side arms were checked and re-holstered. Over the roar of the Johnsons, Wall yelled, 'When we enter the Big River Inlet, the houseboat in question will energise some coloured fairy lights around the top deck for a few seconds. There will be a code of signals. Two blinks means the money is on board, four, the money is on the raft. So, we have to be vigilant.'

Senior Constable Wright throttled back at a hand signal from Sergeant Wall. In the gloom, the two launches rounded the spit of land that juts out into the lake and made their way into the Big River Inlet. The boats were now in line, Bob Wall's vessel leading. The surrounding hills closed in on the small armada. The growl of the outboards seemed to echo back down the valley. He held up a hand and Wright brought the controller back almost to idle.

Wall pointed to the right, at the same time muttering some instructions into a small microphone on his vest. Their craft broke away from the other and headed towards the shoreline. They were now entering a small cove. Straining his eyes in the darkness, he thought he saw the faint outline of a small boat. He reached for the hand-held spotlight and, pointing it ahead, flicked the switch.

The cove was illuminated like day and in the glare a small tinny bobbed at its moorings. 'This must be the tinny belonging to the Bayswater gang,' Wall said to nobody in particular. 'The Slipper said something about that. Apparently one of the boys towed the bloody thing away from right under their noses. Well, we can check that one off our list. On the way down the inlet, I'll contact Melbourne and tell 'em we've found the tinny.'

The more astute members of the group were developing a sense of admiration for this group of teenagers whom they had yet to meet. As the launch made its way back out onto the main inlet, one member of the team cocked his Mossberg automatic shotgun. So, there was going to be some action after all. The men shifted about, as if expecting something to happen any second.

Resuming formation down the inlet, Bob Wall continued his survey of the lake. As they rounded a bluff, Wall saw a red light way down the inlet, near some moored houseboats.

It appeared to move about, like a torch. Curious, he turned and beckoned to one of the men. Standing now, both men examined the strange light. Wall was silent but his partner simply said, 'I think we'd better hurry up.'

CHAPTER 44

ob Wall surveyed the scene before him through the night vision goggles. He identified the houseboat that he had been briefed about, if only due to the blinking string of party lights. Everything seemed serenely quiet, the silence broken only by the muted growl of the twin Johnsons. He noticed that there was a small cuddy cabin boat moored next to the houseboat. There had been no mention of that in his briefing. The occupants of the houseboat had departed half an hour previously, leaving only one of Kevin's friends aboard, mainly to work the string of lights. There was no movement anywhere, onshore or on the cluster of pleasure craft riding gently at their moorings

Wall returned his gaze to the houseboat and almost at once saw a small pleasure boat alongside the vessel. He simultaneously noticed that somebody was climbing over the railing of the rear deck. He fumbled for the spotlight switch and using the joystick, brought the intense white beam to bear on the rear of the houseboat. A figure dashed for the back door and was lost from sight. Wall barked into the hand-held radio and presently the second launch drew level with his own. Over the sound of the water smacking against the hull, Wall instructed the driver of the second launch to take up his pre-arranged position. That vessel surged ahead and Wall's own craft veered left, cutting across the other's wake. Both craft bore down on the houseboat, black-clad occupants making final adjustments to their gear and bracing in readiness.

* * *

The two robbers burst into the room to escape the glare of the searchlight that was now almost level with the houseboat. Realising that they were in effect cornered, the three men looked around the room they were in for a possible escape route. The helicopter was getting louder and added to the glare outside with its own searchlight.

For the first time in his fifty-five years, Frank Taylor panicked. Torn between the pile of money that lay in a heap on the floor and escape, he was quite unable to function properly. Over the roar of the helicopter, Stan's voice said, 'We've got to leave it. Let's go.' Frank just stood there, rooted to the spot. Stan tugged at his arm saying something that Taylor couldn't make out. Then, two figures, dressed in black, appeared on the foredeck.

Stan's mind was made up. He departed through the companionway and up the steps to the deck, Les Truscott hot on his heels. Truscott appeared to be carrying something. Suddenly shouts came from the foredeck and then two loud shots followed by two even louder reports, which appeared the shake the whole vessel. Stan and Les burst out onto the top deck, making for the handrail. That was as far as they got. The helicopter searchlight, which had been scouring both shores suddenly swept over the inlet and focused squarely on the two men who, quite blinded by the intense beam, stumbled about, falling over deck furniture and fittings, both arriving at the horrible realisation that the game was up.

Frank Taylor never stood a chance. When Stan and Les departed, he drew his .357 and fired twice at a black-clad figure tiptoeing in the still open glass door. The man was thrown back and crumpled to the deck. The response was instantaneous. Two shotgun blasts caught Frank in the chest knocking him clean off his feet and sending the revolver sliding across the floor of the vestibule. His last sight was of black stencilled lettering close to his face and blurring into nothingness.

CHAPTER 45

John Allen saw a tall stranger materialise from the shadows after Hayne fell backwards, undoubtedly lifeless, into the shallow water. The stranger spoke to one of the boys, who dropped what appeared to be a speargun, and stared mesmerised into space. Bob Pitman, hot on his heels, whispered, 'We're going to have to leave Dennis. We've got to get over to the others.'

Allen wasn't wasting any time. He broke into a jog and the two men sprinted along the shore, albeit the wrong one, and began looking for an opportunity to reach the other side of the inlet. The big plan to join Stan, Les and Frank however, was about to come unstuck. A helicopter, which had been getting nearer, now hovered over the inlet, down near the lake, its bright searchlight sweeping the shoreline on both sides. Allen noticed rather than heard the police launch cruising slowly up the inlet. He also saw another boat appear alongside the first.

The two launches parted company and headed straight for the houseboat. Bob Pitman said something which Allen didn't hear because the words were lost in the roar of gunfire echoing across the water from the houseboat. To the two men on the opposite shoreline, as yet undiscovered, that was the catalyst to leave in a hurry if nothing was. John Allen turned to Bob Pitman and said, 'We're going to have to acquire another boat. Hopefully they're as careless with keys here as at the caravan park.'

Pleasure craft were moored haphazardly along the water's edge, tied to flimsy-looking bollards. Pitman produced a pen flashlight and trained the beam on any of the smaller boats that looked like possible contenders. Luckily, most were moored stern-first to the shore, making it easy for the men to see if any had keys. He nudged Allen and was about to climb aboard a trim Savage runabout, the ignition keys of which dangled from the dash, when a light from a nearby campervan suddenly illuminated the area. The men hit the ground but Pitman was determined that this boat was their ticket out of here.

He slithered like a lizard over the transom and crawled up to the front seat. Allen instinctively knew what had to be done. Using his ubiquitous knife, he cut any ropes he found and joined Bob, who was checking the fuel level and motor trim controls. Pitman directed Allen to use the mooring pole the push off into deeper water so he could lower the Evinrude outboard motor. After a few shoves, the boat drifted out a short distance and Pitman pressed the button to lower the motor. Both men were deathly scared that the whine from the hydraulic actuator would arouse campers.

When he deemed they were far enough from shore, Pitman pressed the starter. The motor roared to life and the pair wasted no time heading for the mouth of the inlet. They had to keep speed down to avoid being noticed. This was particularly frustrating for John Allen, who seemed to use will power to propel the boat faster. Rounding a bend in the inlet, Bob took the speed up a notch. Now he spoke freely.

'When we get back to the caravan, we just pack our own stuff and take one of the cars. We've got to get back to Melbourne without being noticed. We're gonna have to be careful of that old bitch next door and her nosey husband. So speed is the key word, Johnny. I don't remember how much fuel is in each car but Stan always kept a spare container in each.'

The boat reached the mouth of the inlet and in total darkness, Pitman eased up the throttle and the boat made a steady pace across the lake and to safety. The two men said next to nothing on their journey, each thinking his own thoughts. Like which of their associates had made it. The meaning of all that gunfire. How were they going to explain to Dennis's partner?

Two pairs of eyes studied the jetty at Rupertsvale Holiday Park closely. Light from the single light stanchion bathed the jetty and glinted off the glass windshields of moored pleasure craft. Pitman eased off the controller and the boat glided to a stop. Using a mooring pole, Allen reached for the timber edge of the jetty and hauled the boat in. Pitman spoke, 'With that light and nowhere to hide we're just going to have to act as normal as possible. Just a couple of guys back from a late fishing trip.'

Quickly looking about the boat, John Allen spied a fishing rod on the back seat. He grabbed it and climbed up onto the jetty. Helping Bob up, the two men strolled away from the boat and made it to the fine gravel without noticing anyone, except for a stray cat, which darted away when they passed. They strode as quickly as they dared along the path, relieved when they reached the tarmacadam road. Eyes scanning everywhere, the pair walked almost noiselessly along the road, passed silent trailers and cabins.

Pitman grabbed Allen's arm and beckoned ahead and to the left. The familiar modern house trailer stood sentinel, darkened now, but Bob wasn't convinced. He moved over to the side of the road, into the shadow of a large bush and from there made his way, with John Allen on his heels, from one shadow to the next. Allen dared not breathe when they passed the neighbouring trailer, silent as a tomb, and eased up to the Mazda van, glad of its protection. They slunk around the bonnet of the Commodore utility and over to the annexe. Pitman lifted the canvass aside and the men almost dived into its dark embrace.

Now Pitman was all business. 'No lights Johnny. Just get your things together and the van keys. I should set fire to this place. I know that's what Charlie would have said. I've got to get the guns from under the caravan.' Without another word, Bob was gone, and Allen went over to his bunk, all the while thanking his lucky stars that he was a neat packer. He grabbed the duffel bag by the cords and shone his torch about his bedspace for any loose items. Satisfied, Allen stepped up into the caravan and picked up the keys to the Mazda.

He thought he heard Bob Pitman outside in the narrow

space between their van and the dividing screen. His immediate thought was to have a look at the neighbours to see if they had noticed the pair's arrival. Allen moved over to the window and parting the Venetian blinds, peered out. Noticing nothing amiss, he was just about to let go of the blind when the penny dropped. The couple's car was missing. He cursed himself for not having noticed it before. Bob would be interested in that bit of news.

Duffel bag and keys in hand, Allen strode out through the annexe and crept over to the van. Fumbling with the keys, he unlocked the front door, figuring it would make less noise than the side door. Hefting the duffel bag into the back, he closed the door and pocketed the keys. Thinking Bob would probably want a hand with the firearms, Allen made for the path that surrounded the annexe. He almost collided with Pitman coming the other way, a shotgun in each hand.

'Take this, Johnny,' Pitman whispered, handing Allen a pump shotgun. Allen accepted and for the first time he noticed that Bob Pitman was wearing latex gloves. 'Let's go,' Pitman whispered. The men made their way over to the van like a pair of ghosts. Allen elected to drive and climbed in the right-side door. Pitman boarded and with the firearms safely out of view, John Allen started the Mazda's engine and reversed away from the utility. Selecting 'D', he eased the van out onto the road.

Driving without headlights, Allen drove cautiously through the park, eyes everywhere. As they approached the log cabin office, silent now in the moonlight, a cat darted across their path and scurried between the phone booths. The van's tyres crunched on the fine gravel and both men were relieved when they reached the latticed gateway and could see the tarmacadam road ahead. Allen thought it was safe enough to switch on the headlights. The area ahead of the van was illuminated like day and Allen remembered that Stan had instructed that high output Halogen bulbs be fitted.

Pitman remarked, 'You sure that's not high beam.' For an answer, Allen flicked the headlight stalk and it seemed that the southern part of the state was momentarily bathed in brilliant white light. Brushing cobwebs from his jacket, John Allen kept his foot on the accelerator, wanting to put as much distance between Lake Eildon and themselves as possible. Pitman remarked, 'You seem to have picked up some foliage. Must have been when you were crashing through the scrub like a D9.'

Allen couldn't have cared less if he had picked up a tarantula. Over and over in his mind was the big question: how did such a meticulously planned job go so horribly wrong?

Over the muted roar of the Mazda's four-cylinder engine, Allen shouted, 'We've got to find a motel. Change clothes. Get cleaned up. Must be one that doesn't ask any questions but gets told a lot of lies.'

'We might have to check in as Salman Rushdie and Elvis,' Pitman said, showing the first traces of humour in quite a while. Allen's face, however remained a mask of fear and frustration as the taillights of the van vanished around a bend in the road.

CHAPTER 46

The first sound that Daniel heard when he woke was the ping of a Bellbird. He opened his eyes and took in his surroundings. From his bunk, he could see out through the doorway, past some clumps of reeds and sword grass to a clearing, where two campervans were parked, annexes attached, pop-tops raised. In the darkness, Daniel hadn't realised that fellow campers were so close. A woman stoked a campfire and placed a kettle on a grate over the flames.

The teen took in the scene, the first time he had seen it in daylight. He was surprised at how many campers were in the immediate area. At least half of them were glaring at the raft, as if the night's shenanigans had been all their fault. His gaze returned to the cabin and his sleeping shipmates.

Finally rousing himself, Daniel crawled out of his sleeping bag and made for the galley. He looked at his friends, still snoozing. The sound of the kettle should wake them up.

It was the metallic click of the igniter that roused Jeremy. One arm flopped out of his bunk, and he slowly raised himself up and stared at Daniel as if not recognising him. When the fog in his brain cleared, Jeremy sat up, yawned and mumbled something about coffee. Daniel got the message.

As soon as the kettle boiled, he made an extra strong mug and added some Haig whisky. Jeremy sat up as best he could under the low roof and accepted his drink.

Both boys chatted about the previous evening's activities. Jeremy finally climbed out of bed and he and Daniel took their drinks out onto the foredeck. Jeremy said, 'This is a nice spot. I'd willingly stay here except that I can see that you all want to get away and see more of the lake. Also, supplies are getting low and we need to stock up.'

Daniel sipped his coffee and replied, 'Yeah, you're not wrong. But poor Sammy wants to get as far away from here as possible. Don't blame him either. It's not every day that you kill someone with a speargun. Even if it was a creep trying to slit your best friend's throat'

A noise within the deckhouse made the boys turn. Harry stood in the doorway, squinting into the bright sunshine. 'I think we've got visitors,' was all he said.

A police launch made its way slowly into the inlet and motored up level with the raft. A policeman whom the boys didn't recognise alighted onto the raft followed by a familiar figure. Ray White walked gingerly around the deckhouse and emerged onto the foredeck, which was now rather crowded. Daniel excused himself and ducked into the cabin to get a round of coffee going. White chatted with the remaining boys until Daniel emerged with drinks. Then he got down to cases.

'Well boys,' he said, 'I suppose you would like to be filled in on the details of what happened on the houseboat?' All four boys nodded. 'It seems that the gang of robbers, not knowing where the loot was hidden, split into two groups. One attacked you four and came off second best. The other group headed for the houseboat, where the money was. They gained entry to the cabin via both ends. We arrived at that time. Two of the gang tried to escape via the upper deck but one decided to shoot it out. Unfortunately, one of our guys was killed.'

This news hit the four teenagers like an express train. Jeremy closed his eyes and put a hand up to his face. 'All our fault,' he mumbled. 'We should have left that stupid money where it was.' Sam stood frozen, thinking of yet more death. Ray White poured oil on troubled waters. 'You boys are not to think like that. You did absolutely the right thing from the beginning. What happened was happenstance. It goes with the territory when dealing with human filth. It may please you to know that the guy who shot the police officer is brown bread too.'

Ray paused to take a sip of his drink. 'The other two are in custody. It appears however, that at least two escaped. We don't know who they were. But I distinctly saw three people approach this raft and one got knocked. You wouldn't have to be Stephen Hawking to figure that leaves two. The helicopter prowled around for a while but had to leave on account of low fuel. We didn't bring dogs with us, so we couldn't mount an effective search.'

Ray White let this information sink in. His uniformed colleague, who had been looking decidedly uncomfortable, spoke into a microphone on his shirt. He then said to Ray, 'They've found a boat over at Rupertsvale jetty matching the one reported missing from here, Ray. Fingerprint crew are over there now. They've been crawling over the caravan next door to you as well. Your wife has been making endless cups of tea and coffee.'

For the first time, Ray White's stern exterior melted. He smiled at the thought of Beatrice getting the all too familiar production line going. He was brought back to earth by Harry, who asked what was on everyone's mind, 'What happened to the passengers on the houseboat? Where did they go?'

'You will no doubt be pleased to know that Kevin and his party were advised of what was going on. They departed the vessel and made for an empty houseboat moored a short distance away. They're on that boat now. After we've cleaned up their own boat, they should be able to return to it later today.'

Fortunately for Sam, Ray didn't mention *what* was to be cleaned up. Instead, he concluded, 'Well I suppose I'd better let you kids get on with your day. I take it that you want to see more of the lake. Let me know when you're heading back to Melbourne. I'd like to say goodbye.'

The boys promised to do just that and the two men left via the front, stepping over the light bar and re-joined their launch further down the inlet. Sam turned to Daniel and said, 'Let's get out of here.' His friend didn't need asking twice. He ducked through to the generator and soon the rhythmic hum filled the morning air. Sam untied the few mooring lines and with Jeremy at the controls, the raft backed slowly out onto the water. Harry collected empty mugs and returned to his galley. As the raft made its way onto the main inlet, he began preparing lunch.

Sam decided that the beer supply was looking a bit ordinary. He procured the last can of Sainte Moritz and poured it into four Styrofoam cups. Jeremy made an imaginary trace on the map with his finger and looked up. 'We could stop over at Eildon on the way. We need to call home as well. Our folks will be worried.'

'That reminds me,' Sam said, rummaging through his pack and producing a small wind-up and solar powered radio. He extended the telescopic antenna and switched the unit on. Studying the controls, the teenager soon found a clear FM station. As it was near the hour, they listened to Shawn Mendes until a news broadcast came on.

'And returning to our breaking news from Lake Eildon. Police have uncovered a huge haul of cash that they say is proceeds from a bank robbery in Melbourne five years ago. In other news, . ..' Sam lowered the volume and the news anchor's voice trailed off.

'Well, what do you make of that?' he asked, placing the radio on the main control panel.

'We're almost famous,' Harry exclaimed. 'I don't like the way the cops get all the credit.'

'The police don't want us getting the wrong kind of attention,' Jeremy remarked. 'I daresay we'll be in line for some kind of reward. But it will have to be done discreetly.'

The raft glided over the water, making its way up the main inlet toward the lake proper. Boat traffic was heavy and Jeremy had to concentrate. He blasted the electric klaxon as some smaller boat crossed his path and it looked as if a collision would be imminent. Sam raised the radio volume again and the boys relaxed. Daniel, lying on a towel on the foredeck, finished the last of his beer and cursed that there was no more. Harry took his empty Styrofoam cup and poured a healthy measure of Haig's whisky and passed it back to him.

Sam, towel in hand, joined Daniel on the deck and was about to reveal his fishing plans for the day, but fell asleep instead. Daniel didn't blame him. He too felt totally lethargic and decided that the day was going to be spent exerting as little energy as possible. The raft made good time along the inlet and presently the lake itself appeared. Jeremy turned the wheel to the left and eased up the controller to ¾ ahead. The morning breeze drifted through the cabin and acted like a tonic on the boys. They were determined to forget the previous two days and just enjoy the beautiful lake.

Rounding the spit of land that jutted out into the lake, Jeremy announced, 'This is the home run into Eildon. When we get there, we'll call home. Reassure our folks. And, before Sam says it, stock up on beer. We can stay moored alongside at the main jetty for as long as we like, according to Inspector Coburn. The local plod will look after us.'

Harry produced a plate of toasted sandwiches and passed them around. Sam woke and all four boys munched hungrily, each thinking their own thoughts. Small pleasure craft passed the raft and Jeremy occasionally had to weave through groups of fishing craft. The sun was high in the sky now and the four friends soaked up its warmth. They motored past the Jerusalem Creek inlet, a plethora of small boats sailing in and out. While eating his sandwich, Harry studied a map of the Eildon area.

'When we get to our destination, it's still quite a hike into the town. Therefore, I suggest two of us wait with the raft and the others see if they can get a lift into town. That shouldn't be difficult. We'll also check mobile coverage at this marina. If good, then we can call home. I think we should just spend the rest of the day there and probably tomorrow as well.'

Sam mumbled in agreement and resumed his sleeping posture. Jeremy and Daniel nodded their approval and swapped places at the wheel. Harry collected the paper plates and suggested a round of Red Bull. He ducked back into the galley, glad of the respite from the white heat of the day and raided the fridge. Intending to let Sam sleep on, he procured only three cans.

*   *   *

Daniel steered the raft into the protected marina and past several jetties packed with pleasure craft of every description. The boys noticed children and adults swimming in the area immediately surrounding the moored vessels. Jeremy pointed them out, unnecessarily, and said, 'That's what we'll spend the remainder of today doing, and the bulk of tomorrow. I don't have the energy to think about doing anything else.' Checking his heavy Doxa dive watch, he continued, 'It's right on five now. I say we tie up and organise the evening. Possibly explore the area. Then tomorrow, hitch a ride into town and stock up. Harry, is your list ready?'

Harry, dozing against the front of the cabin raised a thumb to signal 'yes'. Daniel hit the klaxon button as some small children swam near the raft. Peering ahead through binoculars, he spotted the small jetty that the police had suggested they tie up to. He pointed it out to Jeremy who gave instructions on coming alongside.

Swinging in a wide arc, Daniel brought the port side of the raft up against the flimsy-looking structure and killed power. Harry turned off the generator and tied off the stern cleat to a mooring post. Jeremy and Daniel, standing next to the still-sleeping Sam, studied the jetty with critical eyes. Jeremy stroked his chin thoughtfully and said, 'Okay, now we must make a list of provisions. I've spotted a bin that we can dispose of the rubbish bag. We'll get that out of the way first. Then we had better organise a ride into town.'

Sam joined the land of the living, and the boys spent the next hour making a list of supplies and generally tidying up about the raft. Daniel tested the structural integrity of the jetty when he took the trash bag to a skip. On the way back to the raft, a familiar voice called out, 'Ignoring me now, you snob?' The boy looked about surprised. Allison stood on the foredeck of a sports cruiser in a bikini, a towel around her waist. Daniel stopped as if he had walked into a brick wall.

'Boy, are you a sight for sore eyes,' he gasped. 'How did you get here? Where's the rest of your party?' Without waiting for a reply, he climbed over the stainless steel rail onto the deck. He stepped up to the grinning girl and kissed her. Allison hugged him and Daniel remembered that she had a grip that would put most builders' labourers to shame. The two teens chatted about the events of the previous two days. Presently they were joined by Sally who enquired about Sam. Allison suggested they go into the cabin and have a drink. As they stepped into the cool embrace of the cabin, Allison explained her and Sally's presence on the boat and Jenny's absence.

'This boat belongs to a friend of Dad. He heard what happened and offered this as a sort of getaway. Surprisingly, not many took up the offer. Dad and I did more out of courtesy. Jenny stayed behind. It was only while the police were cleaning and repairing our houseboat. Dad is out on the lake on another boat, fishing. Those total scumbags did enough damage, and all to get their hands on stolen money.'

Daniel soothed her, 'Well, the police have them now. No need to worry. He accepted a glass of chilled water and he and Allison sat at the curved dinette. Sally sensed she wasn't wanted and said, 'I'll just go and see Sam. Where is your raft parked by the way?'

'Turn right as you leave this boat and then take the first right. The jetty we're tied up to looks like the one from the film 'Popeye', but it's quite safe.'

Sally grabbed a small bottle of water from the fridge and departed. When they were alone, Daniel and Allison strolled out onto the rear deck and made plans for the next day. Sally, meanwhile, found her way down to the raft. The first person she saw was Harry, who was on the rear deck, tending to the generator. He waved and climbed onto the jetty to greet her. After inviting Sally on board, Harry called out, 'Hey Sam, you have a guest.'

Sam appeared out of the deckhouse, wiping crumbs from his mouth. 'Sorry, Sally, you just caught me in the middle of a snack. 'Great to see you again. We all feel guilty about the ruckus we caused. Your houseboat got damaged too.'

Sally cut him off. 'The police shot one of the losers with a shotgun, according to Kevin. Another two were arrested. But I didn't come here to talk about them. I came here to see how you were getting on.'

Seeing that his friend wanted some private time, Jeremy beckoned to Harry, who took the hint and both boys climbed onto the jetty. Jeremy suggested that they explore the area around the marina. They strolled along the pier, examining the array of pleasure craft moored about. Harry remarked, 'We've still got to organise a ride into town. Maybe Sally can help.' Jeremy didn't reply and both boys let the subject drop.

When they returned to the raft, Daniel had returned and was with Allison. A trip into Eildon had been organised, much to Jeremy's relief. He was even more relieved when told that the trip to town was happening in the next five minutes. He and Sam elected to go along with Sally and another girl whom the boys didn't recognise. Sam had Harry's list of provisions in his pocket. Harry passed one of the coolers from the galley up to Sam. The new girl, whose name was Emma, drove. Those left on the raft killed time by taking a late dip in the marina.

The car returned an hour later, and the teens victualled both the cabin cruiser and the raft. The boys invited Allison, Sally and Emma for dinner on the raft. The teens spent the remainder of the evening sitting on the raft's foredeck chatting laughing and relaxing, soaking up the dying sun's rays. At one stage, Allison took Sam aside and spoke in low tones, 'I was wrong about you. I got a bit short with you on our houseboat when you brought Harry in. I'm sorry. I should have realised that you love your friend very much and you would do anything to protect him.' She kissed Sam lightly on the cheek. Sam was too surprised to say much, but he did manage to mumble, 'Well he is a pint-sized guy, so we need to look after him.'

CHAPTER 47

The raft bobbed against the jetty as the surface of the water rippled from the passage of a small boat. From a nearby cabin cruiser, Justin Bieber's One Less Lonely Girl rolled out over the water. Two large crows fought for finders rights over some discarded trash. Despite the hour, ten-thirty, only now was the area coming to life. Small children played on the foredecks of moored houseboats, while adults, nursing sore heads reached for the Eno tablets.

On board the raft, Harry Turner wiped the sleep from his eyes and propped himself up on one elbow. Even though his limbs were still a bit stiff and sore, he was quite willing to get breakfast going himself rather the unleash Jeremy in the galley. His friend had clearly had too much done for him over the years. Jeremy couldn't boil an egg, and Harry wasn't going to introduce him to the complexities of making scrambled eggs.

With a sigh, the teen climbed out of his bunk and strode into the galley. Eyes darting everywhere to make sure things were in their place; he filled the kettle and placed it on the burner. Not bothering to study Jeremy's list of who wanted what, Harry pressed the igniter on a second burner of the triple burner stove and soon had a hearty breakfast going. Looking out over the calm water, Harry quite forgot any discomfort he was in and focused on the day ahead.

Daniel was the second crew member to surface and asked Harry if he needed a hand. Harry replied in the negative and handed Daniel a mug of steaming hot coffee, who took his drink out onto the deck. The sun, now appearing over the distant hills, sure had some bite, the boy thought. Yet another scorching hot day in store.

'This is nearly ready. Set up the table will you, Dan,' Harry said. Daniel placed his mug on the deck and ducked into the deckhouse. Reaching under his bunk, he grabbed the green plastic folding table and set it up in the bright sunshine. Harry handed him his breakfast and both boys sat down at the table. As the boys consumed their meal, a houseboat pulled alongside and jockeyed for position along the jetty. Mooring in front of the raft, Harry watched as ropes were tied off and various passengers made their way onto the jetty.

Sam appeared on deck and Harry indicated the galley with his thumb. 'Help yourself.' Presently, Sam joined his friends at the table, balancing a mug of coffee and a plate of poached eggs and thick slices of bacon, glancing at the water which looked ever so inviting.

'So, what's on the cards for today?' Sam enquired, between mouthfuls of bacon. 'Besides getting Jeremy drunk.' His other secret plan was to hitch up Jeremy with Emma.

Harry pointed at the water. 'We're going to be in that all day. It's going to be great. The raft will stay here. Just plain relaxing. The girls said we can get a lift to town when we need it. In fact, I'm going to swim over to their cruiser.'

This sounded too energetic for Sam. 'I'm reserving a space on deck for myself and sunbaking all day,' he managed to say while devouring Harry's superbly cooked poached eggs. 'What's you're agenda, Dan.'

Daniel stretched and gazed out over the water before answering. 'I'm going to join you and just relax. After the last few days, I really need to chill. I think it will be a while yet before any of us are over this. I've still got visions of those flashlights moving across the pool area and heading straight for us.' He stood, collected his breakfast things and was just about to add something when Jeremy appeared in the doorway of the deckhouse.

The fourth member of the group emerged into the sunshine and took his place at the plastic camp table. Jeremy rubbed his eyes and took in the tranquil scene. He echoed everyone's thoughts when he said simply, 'Let's just stay here.' Harry collected the breakfast things from Sam and Daniel and asked Jeremy, 'What'll you have for breakfast?'

'Iced water, coffee and poached eggs will do nicely Harry.'

Harry ducked into the deck house and presently could be heard bustling about in the galley. Jeremy sighed and watched some children splashing in the water adjacent to a moored houseboat. Turning to Sam, he asked, 'What's on the cards for you two today? Nothing too energetic, I hope.'

Daniel answered for Sam, 'We are going to veg out all day. Harry is planning to swim over to the girl's cruiser, but

I'll believe that when it happens. We have gotten your day planned for you though. We are going to get you drunk. It had previously occurred to me that we've never seen you captain legless. Therefore, today's the day. Also, you really need to unwind.'

Jeremy countered, 'We all do. I think Sammy here most of all. I mean, it's not every day that you nail someone with a speargun and just shrug it off. As for Shorty swimming over to the cruiser, it's not exactly the English Channel. He should be able to do it easily.'

Harry appeared with Jeremy's breakfast, scolding him for calling him short. 'Thanks, Harry. I'll wolf this down then we'll plan the day properly. We still must have another look at Old Rupertsvale town, so we can go over the charts again. Plus, we've got to get the camera out and give it the once-over.'

Harry held up his hand and stopped any further conversation from his friend. 'Today is an official rest day. We aren't doing anything more technical than working on our suntans and maybe taking a dip. This was decided while you were still asleep.'

Jeremy took a large gulp from his coffee mug, wiped his mouth and contemplated Harry's words. Finally, he said, 'Okay, I suppose that's not a bad idea. Today and maybe tomorrow we just chill. Now what's this idea of me getting drunk?'

Sam ducked into the deckhouse and stepped out onto the rear deck to brush his teeth. He was soon joined by Daniel.

Harry explained to Jeremy a small amount of amber fluid might cool down the vacuum tubes in his brain. These simple words acted like a tonic. Jeremy immediately warmed to the idea and helped Harry clear up. Soon all four teenagers were on the foredeck, Sam and Daniel spread out on beach towels, soaking up the golden sun.

Harry produced cold cans of Heineken from the big cooler and after distributing them among his friends, sat at the table and viewed the water until Jeremy suggested they pack it away to free up deck space for sunbaking. This accomplished, the boys lay about the deck and sipped their drinks.

Sometime later, and on his third Heineken, Jeremy announced that he was going swimming. Daniel winked at Harry and gave him a knowing look. This had to be seen. Without further ado, their friend dived into the marina and when he surfaced, found that swimming wasn't his strong point. He also realised that consuming three Heinekens wasn't such a good idea before swimming. Daniel joined him, more to act as a potential lifeguard than anything else. Not wanting to end up like lobsters, Sam and Harry dived into the water, enjoying its cool embrace.

As the afternoon wore on, the boys soon forgot their recent scrape and just enjoyed the marina and its attractions. Allison, Emma and Sally had promised to come by later, which in each of the boy's minds was the perfect ending to what was a perfect day.

As the sun set over the mountains, bathing the marina in an orange glow, the four friends sluggishly stirred themselves and contemplated the evening ahead. It was still an hour and a half until the girls were due to come over, so until then a game of cards was planned. Daniel was on dinner duty and soon the four were munching on toasted sandwiches. Orange and lemon soft drinks were being consumed now; the boys didn't want to be too merry when the girls showed up.

The three girls arrived on the jetty at about nine o'clock armed with small deck chairs and bottles of alcohol. Giggling like schoolgirls, they stepped onto the foredeck, now illuminated with one of the raft's floodlights. Cramming seven teenagers into that small space was going to be the main challenge of the evening, but one that the boys were looking forward too.

CHAPTER 48

Jeremy woke with the morning sun streaming through an overhead skylight. He reached up, blocked it out with his hand and studied the unfamiliar surroundings. He certainly wasn't on the raft, that was for sure. The walnut panelling, padded leather and shag pile carpet were not luxuries he had factored into their humble accommodation. Movement next to him also confirmed that he wasn't alone.

A head popped up from under the doona and bade him a sleepy good morning. Emma! Now, everything was beginning to make sense. Jeremy had vivid memories of Emma leading him away from the raft, along the jetty and onto the cabin cruiser. Everything after that was a blur. Now, it was morning, and his mind was clear. He sat up and stretched, realising that he was naked under the doona. Emma crawled out from under the doona and kissed Jeremy. The two teens chatted for a few minutes before Emma announced coffee time.

Emma soon had breakfast going in the well-appointed galley. Allison and Sally appeared from their cabin and, after saying good morning to Jeremy, helped Emma with breakfast. The teens sat at the semicircular dinette table and had breakfast overlooking the marina's glass-calm water.

As breakfast concluded, Emma suddenly asked, 'How would you like a ride into town? Just the two of us.'

Jeremy suddenly felt like taking a trip somewhere and never coming back. Instead, he said to Emma, 'Yeah, I'd like that very much. Hit the town. I suppose I'd better check up with my folks. Friggin' mobiles are still out. It only occurred to me last night that they're probably worried. I don't know how much they've been told.'

After breakfast, Emma and Jeremy strolled along the pier to Emma's car, a sporty Mitsubishi. Emma drove carefully on the short trip to Eildon, much to the relief of Jeremy, who didn't make the best passenger. When they reached town, Emma parked the car adjacent to a small general store. Jeremy spied a pair of phone booths on the opposite side of the road and said to Emma, 'I think I'd better make that call.'

'I'll meet you in the store.'

The first phone was unserviceable, so Jeremy successfully tried the second one. The call was answered on the second ring. A very relieved Peter Williams answered. Jeremy greeted his father, who understandably berated the teenager for messing with criminals. Jeremy eventually got his side of the story across. Then Mr Williams dropped the bombshell: he had organised Steve Graham to drive up to Eildon and bring the boys home that day.

Jeremy just about exploded. He calmed down and, in a controlled voice, explained to his father that they still had things to do on the lake and that they just plain weren't going to be at the launching ramp if Daniel's father happened to drive up that day. Tomorrow would be more logical for all concerned. Father and son finally agreed that midday the next day they would be collected for the journey home.

Jeremy rang off and strolled over to the general store. He caught up with Emma who was adding a few last-minute items to her basket. He gave a brief synopsis of the conversation he had with his father and finished with the good news that they had an extra, albeit busy, day on the lake. Emma was very impressed. The teens strolled back to the car and Jeremy packed the shopping items on the back seat. With windows wound down, the pair enjoyed the warm late morning sun on the drive back to the marina.

Jeremy took his time getting back to the raft. The morning sun was warm on his back as he admired the other pleasure craft lined up to the pier and briefly chatted with some of their owners. He finally turned left onto the rickety jetty and carefully made his way over to the raft. The familiar sound of water slapping against the pontoons reached his ears but otherwise the vessel seemed rather quiet. He soon found out why.

His three shipmates were lying on beach towels on the foredeck, sound asleep, soaking up the pre-midday sun. They didn't even stir when he stepped onto the deck, causing the raft to gently bob up and down. Jeremy snuck past Sam's outstretched feet and into the cabin. Making for the galley, he put the kettle on. As he knew it would, the igniter signalled his presence and Daniel's head popped up.

'Good afternoon. Glad to have you back on board,' Daniel

greeted his friend. 'So, how was your evening?'

Jeremy gave his friend the thumbs up sign and picked two mugs from the drying rack and placed them on the bench. Daniel stepped deftly over a still-sleeping Harry and Sam and ducked into the cabin. After giving Daniel the gory details of the previous night, Jeremy suddenly looked serious and said, 'Dad wants us home today. I stalled him until tomorrow but that was it.'

Now it was Daniel's turn to look serious. 'Oh, that changes things. Tomorrow, huh. Well we'd better get over to the campsite and retrieve our gear.' He looked pained and continued, 'It'll take us until the next Ice Age if we go in this,' he indicated the raft. 'Is there any way you could persuade the girls to use their cruiser?'

'I've already done that. Around eleven this morning, we're to take the raft over to their mooring and swap places with them. Then we all proceed to the campsite. That should give us time to enjoy our last few hours here.'

'We'll need to tell the other two,' Daniel said. 'Then we can get going as early as possible.'

'Wake them up. I'll get coffee going.'

Daniel wakened his dozing friends and informed them that Jeremy had an announcement. A minute later, the four were sitting on the lower bunks, two of the boys nursing mugs of steaming coffee; Harry and Sam opting for lemonade. Jeremy cleared his throat to speak. 'The powers that be have cut our time here short. This is going to mean different things to each of us. I'm fully aware of how worried our parents must be, but from our point of view, we had a limited time here and we've got a very full year ahead, with no time for breaks. We will have to wait at least twelve months before we can go on a really good break again. So what I propose is to have a final blast out on the lake, and I figure that this will involve borrowing the girl's cruiser.'

Pausing to take a long drink from his coffee, Jeremy continued, 'But we stand firm about when we leave here. Daniel's dad wanted to get us this arvo, but I said no. Tomorrow would be better for everyone.'

Sam chipped in, 'Yeah, their boat would run rings around this crate. We left quite a few things behind at the jetty we built, including Dad's folding camping spade, mainly thanks to our hasty departure.'

'I agree that we should have some say as to when we leave,' Harry said, between mouthfuls of orange lemonade. 'But I also think that the ordeal of the last few days would be of great concern to any group of worried parents. So, we do what Jeremy suggests and get Dan's dad to meet us over at the launching ramp tomorrow at around midday. That gives us the rest of today to really enjoy the lake and retrieve our gear from the former campsite.'

'I'm glad you agree. I had a chat with Emma and Allison, and they said without hesitation that we can use their cruiser. I didn't even have to ask. I said that we would take the raft and go over to the old campsite and collect the remaining gear. Allison cut me off and pointed out that the raft would be too slow to get there and back. And right there and then she offered the cruiser.'

'Well, I'm glad we've got that sorted,' said Daniel. 'So now when do we leave?'

'Now. The plan is to take the raft over to their mooring and swap with the cruiser. They're in the general mooring section. They understandably don't want to lose their spot. From there, we all go directly over to the old campsite and pack all the camping equipment. The jetty stays. Then we head back here and swap moorings again. Then it's just a matter of transferring camping gear.'

The boys got up from the table and began packing away any loose items. Sam untied the mooring lines and Harry started the small generator and waited until the unit had settled into an even rhythm. He gave the thumbs up sign to Daniel, who selected ¼ power and deftly manoeuvred the raft away from the jetty. Jeremy was busying himself in the galley, preparing lunch for the next phase of the day, transferring to the girl's cruiser and hopefully recovering their belongings from the first campsite.

With Daniel at the helm, the raft glided over the mirror-like surface of the marina, dodging the odd swimmer and making its way to where Allison and her friends had moored their sports cruiser. As the raft rounded the main pier, Sam could see Sally waving from the deck of the cruiser which had been backed out from its space and was now tied temporarily to another boat. For the first time, Daniel noticed the name on the transom, *Petit-Clamart*. He ducked into the cabin and asked Daniel, 'Do you think you'll make it into that space?'

'I'll need someone to guide me in. You and Harry can do that.'

Sam and his pint-sized friend stood on opposite sides of the raft and yelled instructions as Daniel slowly manoeuvred it into the narrow space. When the raft touched the pier, Daniel killed power while Harry tied off to a mooring bollard. Sam ducked into the cabin and said, 'Good job.'

Daniel remarked, 'Piece of cake.'

With lots of chatter, the seven teenagers swapped equipment between vessels, some items on the cruiser being deemed superfluous for the trip to the camping area. When all was ready, Allison manoeuvred the craft away from the pier and out onto the marina. The area was alive with splashing, yelling children and small pleasure craft criss-crossing the small inlet.

Once out on the lake proper, Allison gave the cruiser the gun. Ignoring any speed limits, she had the cruiser tearing over the glass-like surface, shrugging off any shouts from angry fishermen in their tiny boats, bouncing in her wake. The thick insulation reduced the diesel engine's roar to a muted growl. The boys took in the vista, knowing that this was their last real chance to enjoy the lake.

At close to forty miles per hour, the cruiser soon ate up the distance to the campsite. The boys watched familiar landmarks go by and received the occasional wave from a passing houseboat. Daniel reached over and sounded the electric klaxon in reply. The small peninsula of land that jutted out into the lake came into view ahead. Jeremy couldn't help wondering if the two missing robbers were hiding up there, observing the lake. Emma put his mind at ease, and he chilled out.

Rounding the sharp bend in the lake, the entrance to Big River Inlet appeared ahead. Allison kept the cruiser on the opposite side of the lake and didn't even glance in that direction. Sam couldn't help noticing this and wondered if the girl just wanted to get this part of the day over with. He raised the subject with Sally, while pretending to point out something on the shore. Sally put *his* mind at rest, saying, 'I know Jeremy suggested it, but Allison was the biggest supporter of the idea. She was the one who said the raft would take all day.'

Jeremy, binoculars in hand, suddenly exclaimed, 'There it is. Dead ahead.'

The others stood and peered ahead as the re-entrant that formed Robin Bay loomed closer. For the boys, memories of their first day on the lake came flooding back. Allison reduced power and brought the cruiser onto a level plane. As the boat glided into the inlet, Sam spied some items on the opposite bank and nudged Jeremy, who noticed the same things and suddenly felt very guilty.

Not once had he or his friends considered the fact that the house boaters may have had to leave anything behind in their rush to get out of Robin Bay. As Allison gently manoeuvred the trim sports cruiser against the boy's jetty, Jeremy took charge. He divided the group into two and directed that one clear up the lean-to and supplies and generally tidy up. The other group was to head over to the other side of the inlet and retrieve any gear that the houseboat party left behind.

The teenagers traipsed along the narrow jetty and soon both groups were busy at their tasks. Luckily there wasn't much to clean up on the other bank and that group, which consisted of Harry Turner, Daniel Graham and Sally, soon made their way back around the top of the inlet to join the others. Sam suggested leaving the fireplace in situ and the frame of the lean-to for future campers. It also went without saying that the jetty would be left for boaters to make use of. Jeremy was pleased no end with the thought that his structure would probably still be there for future trips.

'Well, that does it, I think,' Jeremy announced. Only one item remained on the jetty, the now folded tarpaulin. Sam gave Harry a hand to stow it in the cruiser. Sally got behind the wheel and started the twin Volvo Penta diesels, a subtle signal to everyone that it was time the head for home. With a last look about the old campsite, Daniel was the last on board. He gently pushed the boat away from the jetty with his foot while Sally engaged reverse gear and backed out onto the inlet.

Wasting no time about returning to the marina, Sally pushed the throttles almost to their stops. The cruiser left the inlet in the roar of the twin diesels. Sally kept sharp lookout as they passed Big River Inlet and on down the lake. Luckily, there was no other traffic on this part of the lake and all passengers were snug in their seats.

Unlike Allison, Sally reduced speed when the cruiser

approached other boating traffic, even more so when Daniel spied a water police vessel lurking near the launching ramp. The teens discovered that they received more friendly waves if they kept to a moderate pace. This they did until Sally brought the boat to a crawl and weaved her way through the throng of light pleasure craft at the marina entrance. Approaching their mooring, Sally brought the cruiser alongside the stern of the raft and Harry jumped over to the tiny rear deck and tied off. Allison rounded up the troops and organised the transfer of gear to the raft.

With this accomplished and with Harry at the controls, the raft eased away from the pier and headed for familiar territory, the rickety jetty. Tying off to a bollard, Daniel checked his watch; five-thirty. He suggested a round of beers. Jeremy and Sam accepted and flopped into their bunks. Harry announced that if anyone was interested, dinner would consist of toasted jaffles.

Later, after the four friends had consumed their light snack and polished off a beer each, the girls wandered over and stayed for about an hour, until they could see that Jeremy and Sam were scarcely able to keep their eyes open. The seven teenagers promised to catch up the next day for final goodbyes.

As he was about to climb into his bunk, Jeremy reminded everyone about the early start they should make the following day. 'I've set an alarm that'll have us up bright and early.' His shipmates muttered replies most of which weren't too complimentary.

As the four boys went to sleep one by one, each couldn't

help thinking that the next day was going to be busy. There was no doubting it would be a mix of emotions, caught between wanting to continue their holiday in this idyllic place and really wanting to get home to their families.

CHAPTER 49

An annoying, shrill alarm pierced the morning calm and invaded Harry Turner's dream of standing ankle-deep in the warm water on Kuta Beach in Bali. The teenager shook himself awake, but the piercing sound was still there. Still groggy with sleep, his eye scanned the interior of the deckhouse for the source of the infuriating sound. His gaze rested on the sleeping form of Jeremy Williams. Harry remembered that Jeremy had said he would set some alarm to get everyone up early so they could prepare the raft for transport back to Melbourne.

Cursing his nerdy friend, Harry reluctantly slipped out of bed and, ignoring his pain, set about finding the device producing the piercing alarm. He soon discovered a gunmetal grey plastic project box fixed to the upper bunk with a cable tie. The box had several buttons on one side and a round plastic grille. Harry pressed one of the buttons, and the screaming sound ceased immediately. He checked his watch—ten minutes to seven. Annoyed at having been woken earlier then he wanted, the teenager wandered out onto the deck. The marina was quiet; the only sounds were made by birds jostling for position along the jetty.

After about five minutes, Sam joined him on deck, cursing

Jeremy. 'I wonder if anyone would notice if we left him here?' he asked nobody in particular. Harry laughed and said, 'The locals. They'd post him back to Melbourne' Sam was about to reply when a familiar voice called out from the jetty, 'Hope we're not too early, but we wanted to catch up before you guys went back to Melbourne.'

The boys looked over to see Emma and Allison making their way along the decrepit jetty. Sam didn't hold back. 'The nerd had us up bright and early, as expected. Yet to make an appearance himself, though.'

A voice from the cabin said, 'I am up. I was getting coffee.'

'Well, we have guests, so get an extra four cups,' Sam replied. To the girls, who had now stepped across the raft, he asked, 'Would you girls like a cuppa?'

'No, thanks,' Allison replied. 'We've just had one. Sally will be here in a minute.'

Daniel poked his head out the doorway, grinning and bade the guests good morning. Sam re-calculated the coffee order and passed it on to Jeremy. Harry, who would set a D9 loose in the galley rather than Jeremy, moved away from the front rail. Reading his thoughts, Sam stopped him.

'He should be able to get a round of coffee going. I don't think he'll wreck anything.'

Harry wasn't so sure but let it pass. Presently, Jeremy emerged with a tray laden with mugs.

Emma asked, 'So what time will you weigh anchor and head to the launching ramp?'

Jeremy reflected for a moment, and looking around the

raft, he said, 'It's seven-thirty now. I've allowed two hours to get to the ramp. We agreed to meet Daniel's dad at twelve. So that means we leave here around ten. You don't have to be Euclid to figure that gives us two and a half hours.'

'Well, that gives us plenty of time. No need to get up so early,' Harry said, giving Jeremy the evil eye.

Allison intervened, saying, 'Now that you've got some spare time, how about a quick barbeque on our boat? We'll even help you clean up.'

If Jeremy was going to object, he didn't show it. Instead, he said, 'Great idea.'

For the next thirty minutes, the seven teenagers tidied up until there wasn't anything left loose or lying about. Daniel switched off any superfluous lighting and closed the main circuit breakers to the batteries. Harry combined the contents of two three-way fridges into one, and he and Sam carried the empty coolers out onto the deck to drain.

Sally bounced down the rickety jetty, jumped onto the raft, and greeted Sam. With most of the clean-up completed, the teens sat on upturned coolers and talked in low tones until Allison announced it was barbecue time. Harry and Daniel carried the thermoelectric cooler containing the boy's beer supply while Sam and Sally grabbed a folding chair each. The seven teenagers trekked along the jetty onto the pier and soon relaxed on the sports cruiser.

Daniel plugged the cooler into a handy socket while Emma distributed cans of Carlsberg from their fridge. Harry helped Allison and Sally prepare the barbecued meat. Sam and Jeremy kept out of the way, took their beers over to the stainless steel rail, and took in the peaceful scene. The promise of yet another scorching day meant that families were getting out on the water early, avoiding the brass heat of the afternoon.

To the background clatter of children splashing and yelling, the teenagers, who had all been through a life-changing ordeal, unwound and relaxed for the first time. Despite their ordeal being no more than a few days ago, it was only mentioned once or twice. The main topics were life in their various home suburbs and the previous year at school. Allison told a joke, and Jeremy just about wet himself laughing. After only two beers, Sam almost dozed off, so he strolled into the galley and put the kettle on. A caffeine fix was what he needed.

Jeremy had forgotten entirely about the timetable he had prepared for the day. The boys were in their element, talking about the year ahead and the challenges that would bring, challenges that now seemed insignificant. Not wishing to rain on everyone's parade, Sally, standing in the companionway to the cabin, got Daniel's attention and pointed at her watch. Daniel, who had left his watch on the raft, studied the dial of Jeremy's big Doxa: ten minutes past ten. Remembering Jeremy's schedule and not wishing to keep his father waiting any longer than necessary, he whispered to his friend, briefly explaining the situation.

Jeremy looked startled and, rising from his seat looking slightly embarrassed, he announced, 'I hate to have to bring our barby, and I might add, our holiday to an end, but our presence is needed at home. Our families are concerned about our wellbeing. We could all do a few more days here, but it's not to be. We had quite an ordeal and met an amazing group of people, some of whom are not here.'

The teenager opened a can of Carlsberg with a soft hiss and continued. 'We owe Allison's dad and all the house boaters a tremendous amount of thanks. I don't want to think of how it might have been. Now that two groups have had their holiday plans thrown into disarray, it's time to salvage what's left and make plans for next year. We'd better make tracks and get our boat ready, although I hate to leave this one.'

'Finish your beer first,' Emma suggested. Jeremy didn't need telling twice.

* * *

With Sam Dillon at the controls and Daniel Graham allowing the last of the mooring lines to slip into the water, the raft backed slowly away from the jetty, Harry's voice on the small two-way radio announcing that the area behind the raft was clear. The three girls stood on the rickety jetty offering last-minute travel advice and making the boys promise to ring when they reached Dandenong. With a final blast of the electric klaxon, Sam selected 'Forward' and applied power. The raft glided into the marina and weaved between the other pleasure craft ploughing the water.

Sam kept the speed low, observing a water police boat near the entrance to the marina. Harry joined Jeremy and Daniel on the foredeck and helped tidy up superfluous ropes; Jeremy said he wanted the fo'c'sle clear of any obstructions. Harry, who decided it was break time, asked 'Coffee anyone? Sachets only, I'm afraid,' adding that this was the last meal of any kind. The galley was virtually packed away.

The boys took in the scene, now not quite so sure that the decision to leave had been right. Saying their goodbyes after the barbeque had been difficult, and mobile numbers had been exchanged. There was little hint of a breeze, and the lake looked more inviting. As Sam steered the raft around the headland, the dam wall came into view and beyond it, the launching ramp. The latter was crowded with cars and trailers, but Daniel could make out a familiar vehicle with an even more recognisable figure standing beside it.

Harry distributed coffee in paper cups and sat on the deck with his legs dangling over the front. Like his friends, his mind was filled with thoughts of the past week and going home. The boys sipped their coffee and watched as the ramp approached. Sam slowed down; it was clear that they would have to wait while several boats ahead of them were retrieved. Jeremy suggested manoeuvring over to the shore adjacent to where Daniel's dad was parked.

Swinging to the right, Sam brought the vessel gently into the shallows until the boys felt it rub gently on the fine gravel. Harry was ready with a mooring pole when Sam killed the power. Daniel leapt ashore and greeted his father, who embraced him like an anaconda crushing its prey. After briefly scolding his son for messing with the criminal element, Mr Graham greeted the other boys, who had also jumped onto solid ground by this stage.

Sam reboarded the raft and positioned himself in the disordered queue near the ramp. Steve Graham took his turn and backed the trailer down to the water's edge. The other three boys helped manoeuvre the raft until it fitted snugly in the cradle they had made. Once on level ground, the boys climbed aboard and began removing coolers, bedding, packs, and other loose gear. Steve and Daniel Graham began the tie-down process as the other boys organised the car.

The police cruiser crunched down the gravel road toward the concrete launching ramp and stopped near Mr Graham's car. Two familiar faces descended from the front: a man in his mid-forties and an older man. Another man, whom the boys didn't recognise, climbed from the back seat. The three men went over to where the four boys stood beside the tandem trailer with the raft now firmly tied down. Sam Dillon recognised the older man straight away.

'Well, boys, finally getting out of this madhouse. You'll be glad to get back home,' Ray White said with a grin.

'The lake won't be the same without the four of you,' Wall declared

'I never thought I'd live to see the day that I'd be glad to see Dandenong again,' Sam said with a laugh. 'But there's no place like home.'

'Now *you're* sounding like Dorothy,' Jeremy said.

'I hope you've got good security for that money,' Harry chimed in.

'Tighter than a mouse's arsehole son,' the man at the back said, causing the boys to notice him for the first time. Of all three men, he was the only one who looked like a detective. He surveyed the lake and then turned his attention to the raft. He nodded to Steve Graham who was giving the heavy straps a final check. Turning to the boys, he said, 'I'm Jack Coburn. I'm a detective in the Armed Robbery squad in Melbourne. Well that was one interesting phone call I received at midnight. As the information came in, I couldn't believe that the Bayswater job may finally be solved. And how; by a bunch of teenagers.'

Turning to Harry now, Coburn said, 'And you must be the famous Harry. You're the reason the money ended up on Kevin's houseboat in the first place. How are you feeling now, son?'

Harry was somewhat taken back by the moniker of fame. Well, thank you, sir,' he stammered. 'Nearly recovered. So, you know Kevin and the others on the houseboat? We certainly owe them something.'

'Nonsense,' Coburn said gruffly.' Kevin and I went to school together. He got into banking, and I joined the force. He's rich and I'm not,' he added with a laugh. Harry smiled and Coburn said, 'It's Jack by the way, no need to be so formal.' The pair shook hands and Harry couldn't help noticing that the detective had a grip like a vice.

'Well, that's it. I suppose we'd better let you all get on your way,' Bob Wall said. 'But please do come back here. It's really a very nice place.'

Daniel spoke for the group. 'We will, don't worry. But we're going to have to wait a while. We've got a tough year ahead.' The boys murmured in agreement. Wall turned, his shoes scuffing the gravel and the three men walked over to their car. As the cruiser motored slowly out of the carpark, the boys waved and turned their attention to helping Mr Graham tie the raft down. Sam took charge of making sure that all the coolers and packs were accounted for. Jeremy climbed onto the raft itself and checked the interior of the deckhouse. Emerging a few minutes later apparently satisfied, he jumped down and stood with Daniel, admiring their handiwork.

Mr Graham made a final adjustment to a heavy tie-down strap and said to the boys, 'Well lads, that's it. Let's hit the road. One again, I apologise for cutting your holiday short, but there's a group of worried parents back home, Michael Turner and Vince Dillon to name two of them.' The boys took a last look at the glass-calm lake and resignedly climbed into the car. Daniel's father got behind the wheel and started the engine. Shifting into 'D', he eased the car away from the launching ramp and out onto the road that would take them to the outskirts of Eildon and eventually home.

The car rolled through the back roads of Eildon and down onto the flat plains through Taggerty. Steve Graham pointed out some interesting features, but when he got no response, he checked his passengers, finding them asleep. He smiled to himself, knowing at least it wasn't his commentary that was boring.

Unlike Jeremy, Steve Graham didn't have a fit every time the trailer hit a bump in the road. The raft appeared to be behaving, his only concern being wind drag, but this didn't seem to be causing any problems.

Due to the loaded trailer and the generally lower speeds, Steve Graham deliberately stayed off the freeway and meandered through the lesser roads. Coupled with the fact that they weren't in a hurry, he took his time, remembering some of the acid stares he had received from other motorists on the way up to the lake when they had taken the freeway.

The well-known sights and streets flashed by the car window as they approached the outer suburbs, but they seemed somehow strange to Daniel Graham as if he hadn't seen them before. Ever since the boys had left Lake Eildon, he had a burning desire to get home.

Harry was the first to be dropped off. His parents were waiting for the motorcade as it swept into the street. Michael Turner opened the door as the car stopped and practically dragged his son out. Harry's parents hugged him like they hadn't seen him for a decade. Jeremy remarked, 'After all he's been through, it would be ironic if he died from a bear hug from his folks.'

Sam tried unsuccessfully to suppress a smirk, getting out of the car and helping Daniel unstrap various coolers from the car's rear section. Jeremy joined them and carried Harry's pack down the driveway. Sam had his friend's sleeping bag and roll. Daniel and his dad hefted the cooler into the house and made a neat pile in the entry way.

Anxious to keep moving, Steve Graham stepped out the front door and almost collided with Harry and his parents as they entered the house. The adults made small talk briefly, but Harry's parents could see that the rest of the gang wanted to get to their homes. Once on the road again, the next drop-off was the Dillon residence. Jeremy expected half of the Italian community to be there and wasn't disappointed. He said goodbye to Sam, embracing his friend before the latter exited the vehicle and was instantly mobbed by family and friends.

Leaving him to it, the cavalcade hit the road for the short run to Jeremy's home, where the welcome was somewhat more subdued. It consisted of Jeremy's younger brother making inane comments, which Jeremy ignored. He shook hands with Daniel and said goodbye to Mr Graham. Lugging his pack, he traipsed wearily into the house.

Daniel and his father made the short distance to their house in silence. The past week had finally caught up with the teenager; all he wanted to do was sleep. Steve Graham deftly backed the trailer down the driveway and parked outside the garage. 'We'll untie it later,' was all he said. Daniel barely heard him. He mumbled something about bed and slowly entered the house like a zombie. He greeted his mother and sister, who suggested he put his head down for a few hours. Megan and her father unloaded Daniel's belongings from the car, and Megan even assisted in detaching the trailer from the vehicle.

CHAPTER 50

Daniel Graham slept for seventeen hours after his head finally hit the pillow. Some of Megan's school friends dropped around early the morning after the boys returned from Lake Eildon. They made a bit of a ruckus, but Daniel didn't notice. He would have never noticed, even if the USS Enterprise had gone past. When he finally awoke, it took five minutes to realise where he was. The golden morning sun was streaming in through a gap in the curtains. He reached over to the bedside table and checked his G-Shock. Eight-thirty. He had better start making tracks. He and his friends were due in Melbourne at twelve-thirty to meet with the bank president whose money the boys had recovered.

The teenager sat up and refreshed after such a long sleep, dived into some clothes and crept out into the hallway. Hearing voices, he walked quietly towards the kitchen with the television on in the background. He poked his head around the door and saw Megan at the table, buried in a glossy magazine. She looked up, saying, 'The dead has risen.' This brought a stampede from the living room, and Daniel soon found himself seated at the kitchen table with a mug of steaming coffee in hand, answering questions about his ordeal.

Steve Graham gave his son a few pointers about the forthcoming meeting. Daniel only half listened, feeling quite confident about handling a bank president.

* * *

Sometimes, Sam Dillon wished he hadn't been born into an Italian family. He wasn't much bigger than Harry, and after being mobbed by his extended family and whacked on the back by a ham-fisted aunt or two, he finally made it into the house and flopped onto his bed. When he returned to the world of the living, it was three am by the luminous dial of the bedside clock. Even at that early hour, he felt hungry, and now was as good a time as any to fix a quick snack.

The teenager stole barefoot through the darkened house and into the kitchen. The sound of ice clattering in the ice-maker echoed around the room, startling him. Opening the fridge, the boy procured the ingredients he needed and risked using the hot water dispenser to make coffee. Sam carried his sandwich and coffee mug back to his room, relieved that he hadn't wakened anyone else.

Sitting on his bed, he sipped the coffee and munched the sandwich, staring idly at the floor. His mind was on the day ahead. He and his three rafting chums were to travel to the city and attend the head office of the First District Bank, where they were to receive an award for turning over the stolen money. According to the bank's president, the whole thing had to be as low-key as possible to avoid any unwanted attention. The police feared that there were still members of the gang out there somewhere.

$$* \quad * \quad *$$

At the Turner residence, Harry woke about the same time as Sam, but instead of getting up, he dozed on until a more reasonable hour. Once fully awake, however, the teenager was all action. He dressed in a tracksuit and made his way to the kitchen. Only his younger brother was about, and Harry patiently answered a barrage of questions the youngster had. James Turner found it very hard to believe that Harry and his friends handed the money over to the police. Luckily, the interrogation changed to Harry's injuries and the two boys chatted about these until the rest of the household strolled into the kitchen.

Michael Turner asked the odd question about the boys' meeting but mainly let Harry's siblings grill their brother about his ordeal and his injuries, particularly his stiff-legged gait, which Harry had been assured would fade with time. His mother had organised clothes for him to wear for the big occasion, an outfit which he detested. Harry was very much like his father; he hated dressing up. The boy couldn't wait for the presentation to be over. He was looking forward to enjoying a few beers with his friends.

$$* \quad * \quad *$$

In typical fashion, Jeremy Williams was using the internet to research the First District Bank, particularly its President. He was dead tired but felt more comfortable knowing something about someone he would meet and a bank President to boot. Like his three friends, Jeremy realised that this meeting would officially end their ordeal, the rubber stamp to say it was over. And, like the other boys, he couldn't wait for life to return to normal. Having found the information he wanted, the teenager shutdown the laptop and flopped down on his bed.

Jeremy awakened with the golden summer light casting shadow patterns on the wall. Realising he was still clothed, the teen stripped to his underwear and grabbed his dressing gown. He listened for signs of life in the house and, satisfied that there was movement in the kitchen, stole out into the hallway and made for the meal area. Peter Williams looked up from his newspaper and greeted his son with a cheery wave. 'We were just discussing where to put your award.'

'That's assuming he gets something,' his sister put in. Jeremy's younger brother was adamant. 'I told you, you should have kept the money. The bank won't appreciate your efforts.'

Instead of getting annoyed at the comment, Jeremy said patiently, 'Yes, they will. Returning things is always better, especially when you know they're stolen. That hurts the bad guys.'

The younger Williams was not satisfied with this but let it pass. Jeremy started to get his breakfast before he was distracted further. His father offered a ride to the station, and Jeremy accepted, even if it meant sharing the car with his brother.

All four teenagers had agreed to meet at the local railway station and take separate trains into Melbourne. They would arrive at the office building separately and meet outside the president's office. After the meeting and presentation, the boys were to leave separately. However, they had arranged to convene at a nearby pub, where a few pints would be had.

* * *

Standing on Dandenong station platform, Daniel watched the black smoke curl away from the twin exhausts as the city-bound diesel-hydraulic multiple unit pulled away. He had arrived at Dandenong Station before his three friends, so he waited near a group of businessmen chatting idly about the day ahead. The big plan was to meet there and catch successive trains to the city. The idea was to avoid being seen together in town or entering the bank head office in a group. The police weren't sure if the boys were being watched. The teenager also felt very conspicuous dressed as he was, hence the idea of standing near similarly attired people.

Daniel didn't have long to wait. Harry and Sam came bouncing down the ramp and onto the platform. The three boys pummelled each other and made light of the other's attire. Unlike Harry, Sam loved an opportunity to dress up.

Of the four boys, he was the only one to revel in the situation. He'd been told umpteen times that good clothes matched his handsome Italian looks. Daniel brushed some lint off Harry's jacket as the more petite boy studied the destination board. Sam produced some handwritten notes from his pocket and perused them. He said, 'The building we've got to go to is three-sixty Collins Street. Level fifteen.'

Daniel was about to reply when he saw a familiar figure strolling down the ramp, holding a rolled-up magazine in one hand. He waved, and Jeremy replied by waving the magazine. When the four boys were together, Jeremy, from memory, announced the trains they all would catch. Sam repeated, for Jeremy's benefit, the address in the city. Jeremy reflected momentarily before saying, 'That **was** Collins-Wales House. God Knows what it's called now.'

Jeremy studied the slim dress watch on his right wrist. 'Nine-thirty. One of us gets the nine-fifty-one. That gives us a bit of time to do some train spotting.'

A chorus of groans was the reply. Sam announced that he was going to the news stand. Harry followed. Daniel found an unoccupied bench, and the two remaining boys sauntered to it and plopped themselves down. They chatted about the big meeting, and Daniel's main gripe was that they all had to travel separately. Jeremy agreed, but his thoughts on the subject were interrupted by the sound of an approaching freight train. The sad complaint from its triple wind horn echoed around the station, and Daniel knew from experience that he would get no conversation out of Jeremy until it had passed.

As the train thundered past, Jeremy said to nobody, 'We'll be following that one to the city.'

Daniel managed to draw Jeremy out of his reverie and discuss the morning ahead. The two boys talked until Sam and Harry returned. Sam sat next to Jeremy and lost himself in a copy of Street Machine. Harry had managed to procure a copy of a well-known catering magazine. Several trains came and went. Before Harry could read much, Jeremy announced that the nine-fifty-one was approaching.

The boys stood and stretched. Jeremy said, 'I haven't assigned us to particular trains, so who wants to go first?'

Sam was quick with his reply. 'I will. Got a bit of reading to do.'

Daniel smiled and gave his friend a nudge. 'About the latest Commodore, heh?

Sam ignored the remark and said, 'I'll see you guys at Southern Cross.'

The train hissed to a halt, and Sam jumped in, quickly settling into a seat. Harry said as the train pulled away, 'I'll go next.' Jeremy nodded, studied a list, and made a check mark. He remarked. 'Eight minutes to go for you, Harry.'

Harry looked along the tracks, willing the train to arrive sooner to escape Jeremy's constant organising. He and Daniel exchanged knowing looks. The three boys wandered around the station and chatted about the morning ahead. When the next train arrived, Harry said over his shoulder, 'I'll write.'

Jeremy waved and watched the doors hiss shut. When the train had gone, Daniel suggested to his friend that they catch the next train together, saying, 'I want to get this over with. I think we're being a bit melodramatic with all this separate trains business.'

Jeremy gave in, saying, 'Yeah, I suppose you're right. As Dad keeps pointing out, the cops have the money now, so there's no point in anybody going after us. When you think about it, the bad guys don't even know where we live. Okay, so we catch the next train together.'

The train duly arrived, and the two boys found seats opposite each other. With little more to say, they both became engrossed in their magazines. Jeremy eventually leaned against the wall of the carriage and nodded off. He came to sometime later when the train transversed an uneven section of track. He awoke to the view of Federation Square out the window. Daniel tapped him on the knee with his magazine and said: 'Nearly there'. The train hissed and squealed as it transversed the tight confines of the flyover leading into Southern Cross station.

As their train pulled up at the platform, both boys kept a sharp eye out for their two friends. Daniel spotted them on a seat. Harry was pointing out something in his magazine to Sam. 'Harry's found the throwing knife section,' he remarked unkindly. As Jeremy and Daniel stepped out onto the platform, the boys converged, making last-minute comments regarding their own or each other's attire. 'I hope this bloody office is air-conditioned,' Jeremy remarked, sweating.

The tram trundled along Collins Street, surrounded by cars going about their daily business. Jeremy was trying to read the street numbers. He looked up and saw the number five hundred on a skyscraper. 'Few to go yet,' he announced unnecessarily. Harry had trouble removing his eyes from a pretty girl seated along the aisle, and Sam was still engrossed in his magazine. Daniel helped Jeremy spotting building numbers. 'There's four-forty. Not far now.'

'The Black Stump,' Jeremy said with a laugh. 'Almost there boys. Let's go.'

To please their fearless leader, the three other boys stood and grabbed the handrails. Sam pressed the stop button and moved to the door well.

The tram swept into an island stop and ground to a halt. The boys spilled out onto the low platform and stood gaping at the aluminium-clad skyscraper across the road. Daniel had the idea to enter the building at least a few minutes apart to make it look like they were doing things by the book. They agreed and made their way over to the pavement. Meandering around outside the building next door, the boys ducked, one at a time, through the revolving doors of number Three-Sixty Collins Street.

Within the lobby's cool embrace, the boys made their way to the reception desk. Jeremy cleared his throat and spoke to the rather severe-looking receptionist. 'We have a meeting with Mr Hunt at the First District Bank. Our appointment is for twelve-thirty today.'

'Just go to the elevators, boys, and take one to level fifteen.

The main reception for the FDB is just as you step out of the elevator.'

Jeremy thanked the receptionist and the four made their way down a marble-walled corridor studded on either side with stainless steel elevator doors. One door stood open, and Daniel stepped boldly in. An attractive legal secretary looked up briefly from a sheaf of documents and smiled at him before returning her attention to the papers she carried. Sam, Harry and Jeremy filed in and Harry pressed the button for the fifteenth floor, noticing that level fourteen was already illuminated. The doors wafted shut, and the car began its upward journey with scarcely any sensation of movement.

Standing next to Sam, the legal secretary asked him whom they had to meet at the bank. The boy replied rather significantly, 'Gordon Hunt.'

'Gosh, he's the boss,' the girl laughed. 'I must say it seems strange that you're applying directly to him for a job.'

'We're not applying for positions. ' Jeremy said. We've returned some lost property' as if he was tired of explaining it. Of course, he hadn't told a soul.

The elevator slowed to a halt, and the doors glided open. The secretary moved toward the open door but turned and said to the boys, 'It must have been an expensive bit of property you guys returned.'

'Twenty million bucks worth,' Jeremy replied.

The girl nearly dropped the papers she carried but recovered and walked down a carpeted corridor.

The doors closed, and the elevator made the short climb

to level fifteen. When the doors opened again, the four teenagers stood within the confines of the lift and stared at the reception area of the First District Bank. Daniel made the first move and strode boldly over the thick carpet to where a pretty receptionist typed at a terminal, her long nails clattering on the keys. She looked up when he approached, smiled and asked him politely about his business. As the other three boys crowded around, Daniel answered importantly, 'We have an appointment with Gordon Hunt. Twelve-thirty. I'm Daniel Graham; this is Sam Dillon, Harry Turner and Jeremy Williams.'

The girl stopped typing and picked up a telephone. 'Mr Hunt, your twelve-thirty appointment has arrived. Will I get the boys to wait out here?' She listened briefly before hanging up the phone and said to the boys, 'Mr Hunt will see you in a few minutes. Please wait on the couch. He will be with you shortly.'

The girl indicated a comfortable settee, and the boys strolled over to it. They sat nervously while the receptionist resumed her typing. They cast glances about the reception area, noting awards that the bank had achieved over the years. Sam grew restless and wandered over to a window, impressed by the view down Collins Street. The elevator pinged, and several people in business attire entered the lobby area. They ignored the boys and disappeared into various offices. Sam returned and sat with his friends, who were chattering nervously.

The receptionist stood suddenly and glanced at the teens.

Jeremy thought, *Christ, this is it*. The girl said, 'If you would just follow me, I'll take you to Mr. Hunt. You can leave your magazines here if you like'

After depositing their magazines at the reception counter, the four stood and quietly followed the girl down a broad passage. They stopped at a set of heavy doors that would have looked more at home in a medieval castle. Opening one and pushing it aside, the receptionist waved the boys into the room and departed behind them. The four entered cautiously, all aware that they were entering the epicentre of power.

Gordon Hunt was already standing behind his desk and strode around it to greet the boys. He was somewhere between Sam and Daniel in height and Jeremy couldn't help thinking that the man looked much older than the pictures he had seen on the Web. Stress from such an important position, the boy mused. Hunt had an easy manner and greeted the four teenagers warmly. Harry noticed that he had a firm handshake, but not the bone crusher that Jack Coburn had. For the first time, the boys noticed an expensive couch that had been placed in front of the desk, and Hunt beckoned the boys to sit.

When he spoke, it was in a warm resonant voice. 'I am Gordon Hunt; I'm the president of the First District Bank. I've been in that position since just after the Bayswater robbery. So, this is the group of young men that recovered the money from the Bayswater robbery. When I heard about the possibility that the recovered money was from that job,

I nearly expired. News like that isn't necessarily good for a man my age.'

The boys smiled and Hunt continued, 'I was convinced that we'd never see that money again. The job seemed too damn professional. I wasn't president back then, but I was senior enough to stir things up. From the outset, the words 'inside job' were doing the rounds. One teller reported hearing a robber whisper something to one of the other staff. Most of the robbers were speaking in short, clipped phrases. There was no superfluous talk. It occurred to me that the two might have been related or at least known to each other. We presumed the money would be laundered quickly; we really had no concept of it being hidden until the hue and cry was over.'

'However, that's all in the past. We're here to pay tribute to a group of extraordinary young men who battled violent criminals, treacherous mountains, injury and beautiful girls.'

'This is all being done on the sly, so to speak. The police are still worried about the possibility of reprisals, although I don't know about the likelihood myself. We have the money, or should I say the insurance company does, so there isn't much our criminal friends can do now. The money is very secure.' Harry had to stifle a laugh when he remembered the vernacular of the detective at the launching ramp: 'tighter than a mouse's arsehole'.

'I would have liked to have more of a ceremony, with a lot of banking bigwigs here, but that idea got canned. You boys really deserve a treat, so it was decided to up the ante so to speak and give the four of you a more generous reward.'

'And so, to the main part of our ceremony (a few smirks from the boys), I am greatly honoured to present to each of you these plaques which you will be able to keep in a place of pride. Hunt returned to his desk and reaching down in front of the monitor, produced four polished wooden plaques with the bank's logo and each boy's name underneath and an inscription. 'In addition, a cheque for two-hundred thousand dollars each. We felt that this was the least the bank could do.'

Daniel wasn't sure if he'd heard the man right and stood there, his mouth agape. Harry thought he'd faint. Jeremy's brain almost exploded. Sam recovered first and stammered, 'Thank you, sir.'

Hunt laughed. 'It's Gordon.'

'To make things easier for the four of you, we can arrange to have the plaques and cheques taken to your homes by courier, today probably. One other thing, you'll no doubt want to go and have a drink or two, if you go to the Bricklayer's Arms, you won't be asked for ID,' he added with a wink.

The boys burst out into the bright sunshine and joined the throng of pedestrians going about their business. Above the clatter of the street, Jeremy said, 'Now, how about a beer?' His friends did not need asking twice. He continued, 'We'll call our folks and then head down to the pub.' The boys produced mobile phones and dialled their respective homes, keeping mum about specifics, but warning their parents to expect a delivery sometime in the afternoon.

Sam said, 'I think it's that way.' The four turned in unison and headed down Collins Street to where an old English style pub stood on their left. They ambled through the heavy front door into the dark interior. Old-styled light fixtures, attached to enormous oak beams, provided enough light for the boys to see through the haze of cigarette smoke and find their way over to the bar. A barmaid took their orders, Jeremy getting his last because he ordered a pint of Guinness and had to wait for it to settle. Daniel spied a group of diners getting ready to leave and made his way over to the table.

The four friends, ties and jackets removed, shirt buttons undone, settled into the comfortable padded leather chairs, amid the din of the lunchtime crowd, and for a while didn't say anything, each boy thinking of the past few weeks and how friendship, determination and grit they hadn't known they possessed, had landed them here. They felt strangely at home among the other diners, most of whom seemed to be professional people or office workers. Harry Turner broke the silence, mumbling 'Two-hundred thousand dollars. What am I going to do with that?'

Sam Dillon, taking a large gulp from his pint of Tennent's, said, 'You could spend it on dim sims.' Harry, after a large mouthful of Heineken, returned fire, 'You're talking shit, and you haven't finished your first beer. *You* could always splash out on the restored Pierce-Arrow we've heard so much about. And that's without dredging one up from the bottom of a lake. Or you could go on a spending spree at Franco Cozzo.'

Before Sam could think of a silent way of murdering Harry, Jeremy said, reflecting, 'Christ, I'm glad that one's over. It was only sheer luck that we weren't more directly involved with those creeps. Money aside, we really did what our families would have expected. Let's face it, they're the ones that keep us honest.'

Daniel only grunted in reply. He was still trying to figure out how Gordon Hunt knew about the girls the four had met on their trip. He suspected that Allison's dad may have had something to do with it.

A round of drinks later, the four friends had very much relaxed and had no intention of leaving their comfortable surrounds. Time seemed to be forgotten as each teenager recalled particular instances from their adventure, each boy trying to figure how a simple rafting holiday had gone so askew.

CHAPTER 51

Jeremy knew everything was back to normal at the Turner household when he cycled around early one morning after the boys returned from Lake Eildon. The four had arranged to meet at Harry's house before going into Dandenong for the day. They had been advised to get back into a 'normal' routine as quickly as possible as part of helping the boys get over their ordeal.

He left his bike near the front door but, hearing voices from around the house's side, he wheeled the bike down the side path. Harry and his father were in the kitchen in deep discussion about some point of a recipe. Jeremy couldn't help thinking if he spoke to his father the way Harry did, they'd be visiting *him*, probably in hospital.

With a smirk on his face, Jeremy tapped on the kitchen window. A familiar face appeared, minus the light bandages that adorned it for the past week. Harry waved and pointed to the side door. Upon entering the house, the two friends embraced and entered the meal area. Harry offered a seat at the table and soon returned with two glasses of Creaming Soda. While Jeremy drank and made small talk, Harry resumed working on the gastronomic creation with his father. Jeremy had long since stopped being surprised at how quickly the two Turners got over their differences of opinion.

Michael Turner looked up from the stove as if he had just noticed Jeremy. He gave a cheery wave while tasting something on a spoon. 'Good to see you. I'm glad you brought Harry back in one piece. Luckily, his injuries weren't as bad as they looked in the picture sent to my email.'

'I thought I'd be as welcome as a sausage roll at a Bar Mitzvah after our escapade on the lake, getting caught up with stolen money, robbers, your son getting injured, and Sam shooting one of the robbers with a spear gun. I mean it was me who organised the whole thing.'

Michael looked offended. He paused, stirring some ingredients, and said, 'What on earth for? You dumped a fortune in cash to get my son medical help. You valued your friend above money. I can tell you that there are a lot of kids your age out there that wouldn't have done that.'

Jeremy reflected. 'Now that you put it like that. Yeah, I suppose he's worth it. Harry looked out the window at that moment. Seconds later, the sound of the side door opening came, and Sam Dillon's cheerful face appeared in the hallway.

Sam bounced into the kitchen and hugged Harry, which went close to giving the smaller boy curvature of the spine. Then, he gripped him in a half-nelson and knuckled his head. Jeremy watched these shenanigans with some bemusement. When the two teens had finished their horseplay, Sam strode over and sat next to Jeremy. Michael, while taste-testing the dish he and Harry were cooking, said, 'What are you going to do with your knighthoods?'

'You mean, what are we going to do with the reward money?' corrected Sam. 'I'm going to get a Commodore.'

'Just like a Wop,' Jeremy said with a laugh. 'Why don't you buy a vehicle with some class?'

'Well, what are *you* going to get? That silly scope thing?'

'An oscilloscope,' Jeremy corrected patiently. 'Rohde and Schwartz. The best money can buy.'

'Well, I am getting a Wüsthof Professional set of chef's knives. Aren't I, Dad?' Harry chimed in.

'So I believe,' Michael Turner replied without looking up, clearly having heard this before. A voice from the short hallway near the side door said, 'Do you get a set of steak knives with that?' Everyone turned to see Daniel's grinning face.

The last gang member strode into the room and, after giving Harry's dad a cheery wave, pummelled Harry and sat at the table. 'We right to goin' to Randynong?' he asked? Harry joined them at the table and the four got ready.

Do you guys want a lift?' Harry's dad asked.

Sam and Jeremy answered almost together, 'No, we'll take the bus. Thanks all the same.' The boys collected their belongings together, scooped loose change into pockets and headed for the door. As they walked down the side path, Daniel suddenly said, 'Somewhere, two guys are thinking if it wasn't for those meddling kids, we would have got away with this!'

The boys laughed and Harry added, 'Yeah, there's nothing quite like a Scooby Doo ending!